I glanced down at the terrier, who lo
and no worse for wear, though terribly pioud of himself. "You're
no ordinary dog, are you?" A slight understatement.

The terrier's jaw dropped open, for all the world as if he
were laughing at me.

NOT EXACTLY.

What? Who said that? I could swear I heard it in my mind.
But I thought I could only hear vampires' thoughts . . . and only
when they were trying to control me. Was there another one
here? I glanced around.

I'M NOT A VAMPIRE. THINK SMALLER. DOWN HERE.

I stared down at the scruffy mutt in surprise, mentally
reviewing the facts. A dog whose eyes flashed purple like mine,
who wasn't afraid of my demon side, who attacked vampires,
and understood English. Nope, that wasn't normal. "You can
talk?"

SURPRISE.

Oh, great, a smart-ass dog. But he obviously craved
affection, too. He was lonely . . . just like me.

What was I thinking? I was being taken in by a scruffy mutt
who used 'cute' as a weapon. "What *are* you?" I sat down next to
him.

The dog just looked more forlorn. A HELLHOUND, he said
defensively, kind of like he was daring me to laugh.

## DEDICATION

A lot of people helped me get this book in print. Trana Mae Simmons, Sandra Hill, Deb Stover and Yvonne Jocks gave me input up front many moons ago, Joni Hahn helped with questions about San Antonio, and Maureen McKade, Paula Gill, Karen Fox, Laura Hayden, Angel Smits, and Jodi Anderson heroically slogged through it page by page—more than once.

But my biggest thanks go to the Belles who wanted to see Val and Fang in print . . . and especially to Deb Dixon who made it immensely better with her insights and expertise. You are all goddesses!

# BITE ME
By Parker Blue

Smyrna, Georgia

Bell Bridge Books
PO BOX 67
Smyrna, GA 30081

Bell Bridge Books is an Imprint of BelleBooks, Inc.

ISBN:   978-0-9802453-8-7

TITLE Bite Me

Printed and bound in the United States of America.

We at BelleBooks enjoy hearing from readers. You can contact us at the address above or at BelleBooks@BelleBooks.com

Visit our websites,www.BelleBooks.com
and www.BellBridgeBooks.com.

10 9 8 7 6 5 4 3 2 1

Cover art credits:
Cover design: Debra Dixon
Alley - © Secondshot - Dreamstime.com
Girl with Sword - © Alexander Platonov - Fotolia.com
Interior design: Linda Kichline

# CHAPTER ONE

The stench of rotting garbage filled my nostrils as I scoured the dark streets of San Antonio for something to take the edge off. I definitely needed it—this was one of those nights where I felt less than human. No reason, really, except tomorrow was my eighteenth birthday, and tonight, everyone else my age was having a good old time at Homecoming, watching a stupid football game and going to some lame dance.

But not me—no, the home-schooled freak wasn't invited. Not that I cared. They had no idea what went on in the real world, no idea what horrors prowled the night streets. Horrors like me.

A stifled cry came from a dark alley to my right. It sounded promising, so I checked it out. Sure enough, some dude had a young Emo punk pinned against the brick wall, his head buried in the kid's neck. Either they were indulging in some heavy necking, or a vampire was having an evening snack.

Given the wide-eyed fear in the kid's eyes, I was betting on the latter. Either way, he was going to have one serious hickey tomorrow morning.

I stepped up to the vamp and tapped him on the shoulder. "Excuse me?"

He whipped around, looking shocked, fangs gleaming in the meager light. "Looking for trouble, little girl?" he growled.

I grinned. It had been a long time since anyone had made the mistake of calling me a little girl. "As a matter of fact, yeah. You up for it?"

The kid whimpered. The guy let go of him and I stepped back into the small pool of illumination formed by the streetlight. Not only so I could see better, but to give the kid an opportunity to run for it.

Smart guy—he took it, stumbling off into the night as the vamp stepped into the light. Tall and muscular with long blond hair, the vamp wore skin-tight black leather. As a fashion statement, it was a bit too obvious. He must think he was a real bad-ass.

He looked me up and down and his lip curled in a sneer.

At five feet, seven inches tall, I look pretty innocuous, with an average build and average brown hair that goes with my average olive complexion. Wearing jeans, heavy boots, and a down-filled vest over a long-sleeved T-shirt, I could be any girl stupid enough to wander the dangerous part of the city in the wee hours, alone.

I could be, but I wasn't.

The vamp's gaze was feral—hungry, yet wary. I'd obviously caught him off guard, and he hesitated. He raised one eyebrow in contemptuous query when I didn't cringe. "You think you can handle me?"

I shrugged. "I don't see why not."

He seemed taken aback. "Who are you?"

My name wouldn't mean anything to him, but what the heck. "Val Shapiro."

"Val?" he jeered. "As in Valentine?"

Yeah. So what? But all I said was, "Bite me."

"Love to." He snarled, his fangs gleaming briefly in the lamplight, then charged at me with inhuman speed.

Predictable. I side-stepped just as quickly. He flew past, missing me by inches. I cuffed him in the back of the head as he went by, and I grinned.

First round to me.

He stumbled to a halt, and his hand went to the back of his head as if he couldn't believe I'd touched him. He whirled around to glare at me, totally outraged.

Enjoying this more than I should, courtesy of my inner demon, I placed one hand on my hip and used the other to wag a finger at him. "You've been a very bad boy." Munching on kids was so not cool.

"Bad? You haven't seen bad yet," he growled.

I felt a tickling in my head—he was trying to control my mind. Good. Just what I'd hoped for. Now that he'd opened a line between us, I could read *his* mind. His name was Jason Talbert, and he was a truly evil vampire. But he was nowhere near strong enough to control me.

Obviously believing he had me in his thrall, the vamp rushed me again.

The part of myself I kept suppressed broke free with a burst of elation, and lust for the game fizzed through my blood. Time to play.

I braced myself and met his rush with a sharp left jab, snapping his head back. The surprise factor slowed him, but only for a moment. Baring his fangs, he tried to use his huge fists to batter me into submission, but I blocked his flurry of blows before any of them could land. It was easy when the mental connection allowed me to read his intentions so clearly.

He broke off to stare at me in surprise, circling me warily. I've been told my eyes flash a harsh purple, like the color of a black light, when the succubus within me—I call her Lola—comes out to play. From the look on his face, my eyes had done just that. "What are you?" he demanded. "A slayer?"

I rolled my eyes. "The name's Val, not Buffy. Do I *look* like a blond cheerleader with questionable taste in men?"

"Then *what* are you?"

My mouth quirked into a smile. "Just a girl looking to do some community service by cleaning up the city."

He didn't respond, and didn't telegraph his intention mentally, so he caught me off-guard as he slammed into me. I lost my balance and we both went down in a tangle of arms and legs. Annoyed with myself for letting him surprise me, I head-butted him right in the fangs and scrambled upright.

Good—I needed a real fight.

He jumped me again, but this time I was ready for him. We fought furiously, Jason determined to sink his teeth into my neck and rip my throat out, and me just as determined to stop him. Unfortunately, he liked close-in fighting, and I couldn't get enough space to reach the silver stake I had tucked into my back waistband.

I grabbed his throat and squeezed, but he wrapped me in a vise hold and wouldn't let go. He slammed me up against a brick wall, intent on crushing me. *Trapped.* Worse, the power I tried so hard to keep confined was able to reach him through my energy field in these close quarters and I could feel the lust rise within him as he ground his hips against mine. Pervert.

Though I was able to hold off his slavering overbite and incredibly bad breath with one hand, my other hand was caught between our bodies. He couldn't get to my neck, but I couldn't get to my stake either.

Stalemate.

Time to play dirty. Remembering even vampires had a sensitive side, I kneed him in the crotch.

He screeched and let go of me to bend over and clutch the offended part of his anatomy. That took care of the lust. I hit him with an uppercut so hard that he flew backward, landing flat on his back on the sidewalk. Whipping the stake from its hiding place, I dropped down beside him and stabbed him through the heart in one well-practiced motion.

His body arched for a moment, then he sagged and lay motionless—really and truly dead.

Now that my prey had been vanquished and Lola's lust sated, I could feel some of the aches and pains he'd inflicted on my body. It was worth it, though. And I healed quickly, so I wasn't likely to feel them for long.

But adrenaline pumped once more when I heard a car door open down the street. The light was dimmer here between streetlights, but I was still visible—and so was the body I crouched over. "Who's there?" I demanded.

"It . . . it's me."

I recognized that voice. Annoyed, I rose to glare at my younger half-sister. "Jennifer, what are you doing here?"

She got out of the back seat of the beat-up Camry, white-faced. "I told you I wanted to come along."

"And I told you not to."

She shrugged, displaying defiance and indifference as only a sixteen-year-old could. "That's why I hid in the back of the car."

Stupid. I should have checked. I usually drove my motorcycle—a totally sweet Honda Valkyrie—but on nights when I went hunting, my stepfather let me borrow the old beat-up car since it had a convenient trunk. Unfortunately, it was too easy for my little sister to creep into the back seat and stow away there.

Obviously.

Trust Jen to try something like this. I'd made the mistake of telling her about my little excursions, even giving her some training on how to defend herself in case she ever encountered one of the undead. She'd been eager to learn everything she could, but Mom had gone off the deep end when she found out, especially when Jen had come home sporting a few bruises.

Mom had forbidden Jen to talk about it again and had threatened me with bodily harm if I even mentioned vampires around my little sis. Lord knew what Mom would do if she found out about this.

Jen stared down at the dead vamp and grimaced. "I've just never actually seen one of them before."

"A dead vampire?"

"Any dead man."

Was that censure in her voice? "Dead *vampire*. That's what he was," I said defensively. Mom was right—Jen was far too young and innocent for my world. I had to find a way to keep her away from all this. "I don't stake innocents."

"I know. I saw."

"Jen, you idiot, you shouldn't have come. It's dangerous." And if one hair on her pretty little head was harmed, Mom would have *my* head on a platter.

"Yeah, well, we can't all be big, strong vampire slayers," she said. She tried to make it sound sarcastic, but it came out sounding more wistful than anything.

I sighed, recognizing jealousy when I saw it. I knew Jen envied my abilities—my *specialness*—with all the longing of a girl who wanted to be something extraordinary herself, never once thinking of the cost. Of course, it was Lola, the demon inside me, that gave me advantages she didn't have. All of my senses were enhanced far beyond normal, including strength, speed, agility, rapid healing, and the ability to read vamps' minds when they tried to control me. Unfortunately, my little sister had no clue as to the price I paid for those advantages.

And she also had no idea how much I envied *her*. Fully human, with All-American blond good looks and plenty of friends, she had everything I had always wanted and could never have—true normalcy, not just the appearance of it. With my Jewish-Catholic, demon-human background and the melting pot that went into my heritage, I felt like a mongrel next to a show dog. My lucky half-sister had managed to avoid the bulk of my confusing heritage since we shared only a mother.

But I couldn't say any of that—she wouldn't believe it. "Help me get the body in the trunk," I said tersely.

I usually had to do this part by myself, but why not take advantage of Jen's presence? Besides, participating in the whole dirty business might turn her off for good. I unlocked the trunk and opened it.

She hesitated. "I thought—"

When she broke off, I said, "You thought what? That he'd turn into a neat little pile of dust?"

She shrugged. "Yeah, I guess."

"I wish it were that easy." I took pity on her. "And he'll be dust soon enough—when sunlight hits him. Come dawn, I'll make sure his ass is ash."

Jen grimaced, but I wasn't going to let her off that easily. It had been her decision to tag along—she'd have to pay the price. I grabbed the vampire's feet. "Get his head."

She stared down at Jason's fangs and the small amount of blood around the stake in his heart and turned a little green. "Can't you just leave him in the alley?"

I could, but then Jen wouldn't learn her lesson.

Well, crap, I sounded like Mom now. Annoyed at myself, I snapped, "We can't just leave him here for someone to trip over. What's the matter? Too much for you?"

She shrugged, trying to act nonchalant. "No, I just thought Dad might not like it if you got blood in his trunk."

"He's used to it." Besides, the blood would disintegrate along with the rest of the body when sunlight hit it.

Jen gulped, but I have to give her credit—she didn't wimp out on me. I'd expected her to blow chunks at the least, but she picked up his shoulders and we wrestled the body into the trunk.

Jen wiped her hands on her jeans and stared uneasily at him.

"Is he really dead?"

"Mostly," I said, then grinned to myself when Jen took a step back. There was still the remote possibility Jason could heal if the stake was removed from his heart. But for that to happen, his friends would have to rescue him before dawn, tend him carefully for months and feed him lots of blood. Not likely.

I shrugged. "But the morning sun will take care of that." I closed the trunk.

Just as I locked it, the headlights from a car blinded me and a red light from its dashboard strobed the street.

"It's a cop," Jen said in panic.

Not good. But it didn't have to be bad, either. "Relax. Let me handle this."

The plainclothes policeman exited the unmarked car. "Evening, ladies," he said, obviously trying to sound friendly, though he came across as wary and suspicious.

"Evening," I responded.

He might only be in his mid-twenties, but he had the watchful alertness of a seasoned pro. He hooked the thumb of his right hand in his belt, making it easy to draw a weapon from that bulge under his left arm.

As he came closer, I could make out his features. He was about six feet tall with short brown hair, a straight commanding nose, and a solid bod. Totally hot. I might even be interested if he were a little younger and lost the suspicious attitude.

Lola agreed, wondering what it would be like to enthrall him, get him all hot and bothered, feed on all that lovely energy. That was the problem with being part lust demon—ever since I started noticing boys, Lola had been lying in wait, urging me to get up close and personal, wanting to compel their adoration, suck up all their energy.

I'd given in once, and the poor kid had almost died. But not this time. Not again. I beat back the urges, which was pretty easy since I'd just satisfied the lust by taking out the vamp.

"What are you doing here?" he asked.

"I'm sorry, Officer . . . ?"

"Sullivan. Detective Sullivan." He flashed his badge at me.

I smiled, trying to look sheepish. "My little sister snuck out of the house to meet her boyfriend, and I was just trying to get her back home before Mom finds out."

"In this part of town?"

"Yeah, well, she doesn't have the best of judgment. That's why she had to sneak out."

Jen gave me a dirty look, but was just smart enough to keep her mouth shut.

He didn't look convinced. "Got any ID?"

"Sure—in the car." I gestured toward the front of the vehicle to ask permission and he nodded. Shifting position so he could watch both of us, he asked Jen for her ID, too.

I retrieved my backpack and handed my driver's license to the detective along with Rick's registration. He glanced at them. "Your last names are different."

"Yeah—we're half-sisters. Same mother, different father. We have the same address, see?"

He nodded and took both IDs back to the car to speak to someone on the radio.

"Ohmigod," Jen said in a hoarse whisper. "What if he finds out there's a body in the trunk? We'll go to jail. Mom and Dad will be so pissed."

"Just relax. Everything should come up clean, so there's no reason for him to even look."

Sullivan finished talking on the radio then handed our IDs back.

"Can we go now?" I asked with a smile. "I'd like to get Jen home before Mom finds out she's gone."

"Sure," he said with an answering smile. "Just as soon as you tell me what's in the trunk.".

Oh, crap. Busted.

"Nothing," Jen said hastily, the word ending in a squeak as she backed against the trunk and spread her arms as if to protect it. "Just, you know, junk and stuff. Nothing bad."

Oh, great. Like that didn't sound guilty.

Still casual, he asked, "Would you mind opening it for me?"

Yes, I did. Very much. Swiftly, I mentally ran through the

options. I couldn't take him out—I didn't hurt innocents. Besides, he'd just called in our names so they'd know we were the last to see him. Taking off wasn't an option, either—he knew who we were and where we lived.

*You could take control of him, force him to let you go,* a small voice whispered inside me.

Heaven help me, for a moment, I was tempted. But I couldn't do that. I couldn't take advantage of humans like that. I'd promised the parents—and myself—that I'd never do it again.

My only choice was to do as he asked and hope he'd give me time to explain. Crap. This was so not going the way I planned.

Gently, I moved Jen aside, unlocked the trunk, and braced for the worst.

He lifted the lid and stared down inside. He didn't even flinch. Good grief, was the man made of stone? Expressionless, he asked, "Vampire?"

This was so surreal. I relaxed a little, hoping I might even be able to come out of this without getting into major trouble. "Uh, yeah. The bloody fangs are a dead giveaway."

He gave me a look. The kind that said I wasn't out of trouble yet and he didn't appreciate smart-ass comments. "Why did you stake him?"

Why? He was staring down at the dead undead and he wanted to know *why?*

Jen blurted out, "Because he was drinking some guy's blood." She shifted nervously. "I saw it all."

The cop nodded. "So did I."

I gaped at him. "You did?"

"Yeah, I was just calling for backup when you waltzed up and tapped him on the shoulder."

Crap—I'd been so self-involved I hadn't even noticed the unmarked car. Note to self: *pay attention!*

"And you didn't offer to help?"

He shrugged. "Thought about it. Looked like you didn't need it."

True, but his earlier words suddenly registered. "Backup?" I repeated. "Since when do you cops even know vampires exist?"

He gave Jen a wary glance. "Why don't you go sit in the car?"

She looked ticked off, but went to do as he said, and we moved slightly away from the car as he lowered his voice. "The Special Crimes Unit has known for a long time."

"*Special* crimes?"

"Yeah, you know . . . supernatural, paranormal, weird. But the policy of the San Antonio Police Department is that these things don't exist. At least not officially. No sense in panicking the population. That's why we have the SCU."

"You're a member of this Special Crimes Unit?"

He nodded. "But I'm not dumb enough to take one of these guys on by myself." He gave me a penetrating stare. "Yet you didn't seem to have any problem at all. What's up with that?"

I shrugged, not willing to tell him that I was part demon, just in case he might consider me *special* enough to merit the SCU's attention. I had enough troubles as it was. "I keep in shape, eat my Wheaties."

His eyes narrowed. "Cut the crap. How do you do it?"

"Natural ability and lots of training." When he looked skeptical, I sighed. "Does it matter? There's one less bloodsucker out there. One less monster for you to worry about."

"So it wasn't just a fluke, a lucky kill?"

"I get lucky a lot."

"Look, I don't care how you do it, but maybe you could share—"

An ambulance wailed up just then, lights flashing. It stopped in front of the cop's car. I moved to shut the trunk lid, but Sullivan stopped me. "It's okay," he said. "It's the SCU pick-up unit. They'll take care of him."

The pick-up crew gave Jen and me curious looks, but must have been trained to keep their mouths shut, because they didn't say a word—just efficiently took charge of the body and drove off.

Curious, I asked, "Where are they taking him?"

"To a special morgue designed for the purpose."

"Really? I just let the sun take them."

He quirked a smile. "This one has a skylight, but the SCU

likes to document these things first. Plus, it's a bit messy just to leave them lying around on the street." His eyes strayed to my car. "Or in trunks."

"Yeah, well, I didn't want to leave him in an alley, and I don't have some fancy ambulance at my disposal."

"Do this often, do you?"

"No, not really." Only when the succubus part of me threatened to get out of control. When Lola lusted for an outlet, she could be appeased by channeling that energy into a vampire kill. For awhile, anyway.

He stared at me for a moment. "If you ever want to share a few of your secrets, just call me." He handed me a business card.

Not happening. I didn't need anyone else knowing about the demon inside me. But to get rid of him, I stuck the card in my vest pocket and said, "I'll do that."

"All right, you're free to go."

I drove home, annoyed at how late it was. I had to get Jen in her bed before our parents learned she was gone. But just as we got out of the car, Mom and Rick came out of the house.

Crap—just what I needed. I groaned and Jen turned as white as the vamp.

We were in for it now. In resignation, I turned toward them, but Jen backed up, trying to hide in the shadows of the garage.

It didn't work.

"Stop right there, young lady," Mom ordered. Looking part worried, part pissed, she hurried up the sidewalk. Jen looked like a hybrid of her mother and father—all three Andersons were big-boned, blond, and beautiful. It always surprised people when they could see nothing of my pretty mother in my face. Evidently, my father's strong demon genes had overwhelmed all my mother's blond ones.

"Where have you been?" Mom asked Jen. "When we found you missing from your bed, we were so worried."

"I was helping Val," Jen said in a tone that was half sulky, half proud. "We staked a vampire."

We? Yeah, right.

Fury flashed over Mom's face as she turned on me. "How dare

you take her with you!"

Whoa . . . intense much? "I didn't," I said, hating how defensive I sounded. "She hid in the car."

"She wouldn't let me come," Jen muttered peevishly.

"Sharon—" my stepfather began.

But Mom wasn't about to be appeased or soothed. She turned on Jen. "Go to your room, young lady. We'll deal with you later. We need to talk to Val. Alone."

Jen looked stubborn, but her father nodded sternly toward the front door and said, "Go on, now."

Jen went, but expressed her indignation and reluctance in every movement of her body. I knew how she felt, but right now, I wished I could go to my room and skip this whole scene.

Before Mom could repeat her demand, I said calmly, "She pestered me to come along but I said no. I didn't know she'd snuck into the back of the car. You know how she is." She'd always been a willful brat.

"You should have known," Mom said, her eyes still flashing anger. "You put her in danger."

Okay, she had a point. I should have checked. Maybe. But the rest was all wrong. Since when was I responsible for Jen's idiocy? I glanced at my stepfather, Rick, for assistance, but met only an impassive expression. Apparently, he had decided to stay out of the fray. As usual. Though he'd raised me as if I were his own, he let Mom have her way when it came to me. Sometimes he stuck up for me, but it didn't look like today was going to be one of those days.

"I didn't put her in danger," I said in annoyance. "She managed to do that all by herself. Besides, she stayed in the car the whole time."

"That's not good enough," Mom insisted. "I told you before that I don't want her involved in anything like this."

A little ticked now, I asked, "Why? You think I'm a bad influence?"

"No, but—"

"Well, if I am, you helped make me this way."

Mom sighed and visibly calmed herself. I would have

appreciated the effort if I didn't suspect she wanted to pacify me and ensure the big bad demon didn't get loose.

"It's three o'clock in the morning," I said. "Do we really need to do this now?" Night time on the dark streets of San Antonio was my territory. My family belonged in the bright light of day. Mixing the two made me uncomfortable.

"Yes, now," Mom insisted. She paused, as if searching for just the right words. "For you, hunting vampires is necessary. To take care of . . . that part of you."

"The demon?" Mom would never say it, as if thinking if she didn't voice the word, it would disappear somehow. Unfortunately, it was an irrevocable part of me.

"Yes," Rick said. "The succubus."

My stepfather wasn't afraid to say it. And luckily, he understood and respected Lola. He was careful not to let our energy fields overlap, thank heavens. That would be just . . . wrong.

But he was the one who had helped me realize that if I didn't want to end up insane and suicidal like my father, I had to give in to the demon within occasionally, not fight it. Luckily, the lust of the hunt usually satisfied it enough to keep the other kind of lust from breaking out and breaking men's wills.

Unfortunately, though only one-eighth of my ancestry was demon, it took all the other seven-eighths of me to control it. Was that what they were still worried about? Trying to be patient, I said, "You taught me how to keep it in line. Now that I let it out periodically, I can control it. I would never hurt Jen."

"Not physically," Mom said. "Not deliberately." And her face was set in stubborn lines that I knew all too well. Mom had more to say and wasn't going to stop until she had spewed it all.

"What are you saying?" I asked in exasperation. "That my little sister should be afraid of me?"

"Your half-sister," Mom said. "She doesn't have the same . . . curse you do."

As if I needed a reminder. "I know. No one does." Apparently, I was unique. Lucky me.

Mom's eyes shifted away from my accusing gaze. "Unfortunately, she looks up to you, wants to be just like you."

"Yeah, well, she's obviously not very bright."

Mom shook her head. "I knew it was a mistake to let your sister grow up knowing how different you are."

Yeah, right. Like she wouldn't have noticed. "C'mon, Mom. Jen's not *that* stupid—she knows she can't be like me." Though Jen's obsession lately had run to finding out as much about vampires as she could, under the theory that she was helping me by feeding me all the information she picked up.

"Yes, but she's young and rash. At that age, they all think they're invincible."

Not to mention she thought she could help save the world by helping me. It wasn't flattering, it was annoying, especially since I did nothing to encourage it, knowing how much it bothered Mom. "Okay, so I won't let her follow me."

"No, that won't work. You said it yourself—she'll find a way to do it anyway, then she'll get hurt."

Why was Mom being so unreasonable? "I'll protect her." Then ream her butt for following me.

"You can't protect her and do . . . your thing at the same time. We have to make sure she doesn't go with you."

"Fine. I don't want her along anyway, but how am I going to stop her from following me? That's *your* job, isn't it?"

I'd meant that to sting, but was surprised when Mom took a deep breath and said, "Yes, it is. That's why we've come to a decision."

Uh-oh. Why did I suddenly have the feeling I wasn't going to like this? "What decision?"

"For Jen's sake, it's better if you move out."

"How will that help? She'll still see me at the bookstore."

Mom's face set in stubborn lines. "We'd like you to find another job, too."

My face suddenly turned ice-cold, like someone had just doused me in cold water. Then heat flooded in and nausea followed close behind. I glanced at Rick. He was usually my champion, but in this, his expression showed he sided with his wife. "You're firing me?" I asked in disbelief. How could they do that? I had never even conceived the possibility I wouldn't be working in the family's new age bookstore.

No, that wasn't exactly true. Subconsciously, I'd been expecting this all my life, knowing I wasn't like the rest of them, knowing I couldn't pass, knowing they would one day reject me for it. Apparently, that day was today. My eighteenth birthday. *Happy freakin' birthday, Val.*

"Oh, I get it," I said bitterly, my voice sounding thick with the huge lump in my throat. "You're kicking me out of the family."

"Not out of the family," Mom said. "Just out of the business. Only for a while. If Jen doesn't see you around for a while, maybe she'll give up on this unhealthy obsession, or grow out of it."

I shook my head mutely, afraid to let my many emotions emerge, afraid to let the demon out.

"This is important," Mom insisted. "It's the only way to protect her."

"By throwing me out?" I wailed. How could they do this to me?

"We're not throwing you anywhere," Rick said. "We love you."

Yeah, right. They loved me, but only parts of me—the human parts. The small piece of me that was demon they didn't even like. Or understand. Unfortunately, I couldn't rip that bit out . . . or stop it from holding sway over my emotions. I'd tried. Oh, I'd tried.

And I was tired of being made to feel less than human for something I couldn't help. Shaking my head and trying to keep my pain and fear tightly under wraps, I knew there was nothing I could say. I turned away from their judgmental faces and walked off.

"Val, wait," Mom called. "We'll help you—"

*Hell* no. Ignoring her, I half-walked, half-ran to the motorcycle I had left waiting at the curb. Mom said something else, but I didn't catch it. I was too busy putting on my helmet, starting the Honda Valkyrie's engine, and peeling out of there like the fiends of hell were at my heels.

# CHAPTER TWO

Demon rage sizzled in my blood, making me want to blow everything out of my mind in a fast, wild ride. But the human part of me felt heartsick, disappointed . . . bereft. For once, my human emotions overcame the demonic ones, and I slowed down. Just what I needed now was to be stopped by that suspicious cop . . . or any other cop, for that matter. Not knowing where to go, I headed to my favorite place—the River Walk downtown.

At this time of the early morning, before sunrise, the River Walk was free of the tourists that usually crowded its banks. Twenty feet below street level, the quaint charm of the tree-shaded sidewalk cafes, arched stone bridges, and slow-flowing river made it peaceful, serene.

It was the heart of San Antonio, and I loved the whole city. Spanish colonial architecture combined with pockets of nineteenth century German architecture to give the feeling of a city rich in history—a great backdrop for the city's many colorful celebrations. But right now, at this time of night, it was all gray . . . matching my mood.

I parked my Valkyrie far from the tourist area, walked down to the concrete bank of the river, and sat to watch the water flow by.

No doubt about it, I was totally screwed. No place to live, no job, very little money. My lips twisted in a bitter smile. I had some saved up to go to college. Looked like that wasn't going to happen anytime soon.

I scrubbed my damp eyes as a stew of emotions churned inside me. I didn't know which I hated more right now—the demon part of me that had caused this problem, or the human part that made me feel so damned weak at this moment.

It didn't matter—the fact was, I'd just lost my family. It felt like something vital had just been ripped from my chest. God, what would I do without them? They were my lifeline to a normal life, the only ones who kept me sane in my demon-ridden world.

Could I survive without that touchstone?

This wouldn't be a problem if I had friends. But when I was younger, Mom and Rick had been afraid people would notice my freak side. They had no idea then when the lust demon would first manifest. To avoid the inevitable questions, they kept me out of the public school system, home-schooling me and keeping me carefully away from other kids. Then later, it hadn't seemed worth it to make friends. Not close ones, anyway. Explaining the demon side of myself wasn't an option. So now, I was utterly alone.

I fought back a sob. Well, screw them. They didn't have the only bookstore in the city. I could find another job, a place to live, even friends, damn it. I didn't need them.

Movement caught my eye and I glanced aside to see a small dog approaching warily. A terrier mix of some kind, he had short wiry, wavy hair, long skinny legs, a tail that curled up in a "C" over his back, and light-colored fur—the exact color indeterminate in the faint light of the moon.

I froze. This was not normal. Dogs, cats, and other animals normally shied away from the demon they sensed in me. Though I'd always wanted a dog of my own, it was kind of useless to keep a pet who was terrified of me.

He must be desperate if he was brave enough to approach me. Was he hungry?

I wiped away the moisture from my eyes and laid my hand, palm up, on the ground. Speaking softly, I said, "It's okay. I won't hurt you." I could use a little affection about now.

The dog, his head lowered, looked at me as if he wasn't sure but crept closer anyway. I wished I had some food to entice him into my lap. "It's all right," I said soothingly.

A sudden tickling in my mind made me jump. Was there a vampire somewhere near? But when the tickling disappeared, I dismissed it. Must be my imagination—a vamp wouldn't give up that easily.

Realizing the dog had cowered away, I tried once more to coax him to me. The terrier crept closer to sniff my hand and the tickling resumed. It wasn't my imagination. Someone was trying to enthrall me, make me feel safe and secure. Who? The feel in my mind was masculine. Whoever he was, he was very confident. He obviously thought I was a tourist, an easy meal. For the moment, I stayed still, letting the undead creep think his mind control was working.

As the dog licked my hand, my heart melted. Trying not to startle him, I stroked the terrier's head while I wondered how I could deal quickly with the vamp without scaring off the dog. Unfortunately, I'd stupidly left my stakes on the Valkyrie

Why hadn't he rushed me already? Maybe he was being cautious, ensuring no one else was around. I glanced into the darkness of the trees beyond the walk next to the stone wall, looking for potential weapons. With any luck, there would be some fallen branches there. Maybe I could do it fast enough—

The terrier suddenly jerked his head up and sniffed the air. His eyes flashed purple, then he snarled, baring his surprisingly large, sharp teeth, and leapt to meet the form rushing from the darkness.

Shock cascaded through me, leaving me motionless for a moment. The dog unerringly leapt for the vampire's crotch and clamped down on the sensitive tissues there. The vampire screeched, desperately trying to pull the dog off.

Stifling hysterical laughter, I scrambled to the nearest tree and ripped off a small branch, then charged the vamp and stabbed the sharp end through his heart. He gurgled in disbelief, then fell to the ground, lifeless.

Well, that was interesting.

I studied him. Wearing jeans and a Grateful Dead T-shirt, he was unremarkable, except for the acne covering his face. I'd only seen a few dozen vampires up close and personal and hadn't realized they were susceptible to that condition. I wondered idly how many hundreds of years he'd had to put up with it, and why being a vamp hadn't cured him. I shook my head. It didn't matter.

I glanced down at the terrier, who looked utterly harmless and no worse for wear, though terribly proud of himself. "You're no ordinary dog, are you?" A slight understatement.

The terrier's jaw dropped open, for all the world as if he were laughing at me.

NOT EXACTLY.

What? Who said that? I could swear I heard it in my mind. But

I thought I could only hear vamps' thoughts . . . and only when they were trying to control me. Was there another one here? I glanced around.

I'M NOT A VAMPIRE. THINK SMALLER. DOWN HERE.

I stared down at the scruffy mutt in surprise, mentally reviewing the facts. A dog whose eyes flashed purple like mine, who wasn't afraid of my demon side, who attacked vampires, and understood English. Nope, that wasn't normal. "You can talk?"

SURPRISE.

Oh, great, a smart-ass dog. But he obviously craved affection, too. He was lonely . . . just like me.

What was I thinking? I was being taken in by a scruffy mutt who used cute as a weapon. "What *are* you?" I sat down next to him. After all, the vamp wasn't going anywhere.

The dog just looked more forlorn. A HELLHOUND, he said defensively, kind of like he was daring me to laugh.

I snorted. Yeah, right. The terrier no more looked like the drawings of those huge beasts than I looked like the voluptuous women used to portray the succubi. But he wasn't exactly a normal dog, either. Realization dawned, and I asked, "Are you part hellhound? Part-demon, like me?"

The dog wagged his tail. YOU GOT IT, KIDDO.

I sighed in relief. That explained a lot. "Do you belong to anyone?"

He dropped the brash act and moved closer, cautiously, nudging my hand with his cold nose and broadcasting his emotions—he had a strong desire to please me, take away my loneliness, and ease some of his own. I scratched his ears and he radiated pure bliss as he soaked up my attention like a dried-out sponge.

COULD I BELONG TO YOU?

Who could resist? And why not? I could use a pal right now, and this little mutt didn't seem to be any threat. To me, anyway. And we were definitely kindred spirits. I hugged him, letting the action take away a little of the hurt. He licked my face, cementing my decision. "Okay, what's your name?"

He glanced at me with a gleam in his eyes, the scruffy little whiskers on his chin making him look vulnerable and adorable.

Fang.

I stifled a laugh. That was a heck of a big name for a little dog to live up to. "My name's Val."

He sighed. Nice to meet you, Val.

"Want to hang with me?"

Wriggling with excitement, the terrier jumped up and licked my face. Yes!

I wiped off the doggie drool and eyed him warily. He might appear to have human responses, but he was obviously still fully canine. "You hump my leg and you're dead meat."

His jaw dropped open again as he laughed at me. No humping, I promise.

Who knew hellhounds had a sense of humor?

I laughed, feeling a little hope steal into my heart. What a weird day. I'd never forget my eighteenth birthday, that's for sure. I might have lost a home and job, but I'd acquired a dog . . . and maybe a friend. "Okay, Fang, let's go find someplace to live."

Good timing—a rosy glow heralded the dawn and I waited as the first rays reached out and touched the vampire's body. It burst into searing green-tinged flame that incinerated it in moments.

Good. Now for the next problem—how to get Fang onto the motorcycle. I glanced down at him. "Whatcha think? If I zip you up in my vest, you think you'll ride okay?"

Piece of cake.

I straddled the bike and he leapt up in front of me. I zipped my heavy vest over him so only his head poked out, just below my chin. He enjoyed the ride, sniffing all the wind-borne scents. I kind of liked it, too. It was amazing how a little warm body snuggled up to me could make me feel so much better.

But I needed to find a better long-term solution to take him with me. I had a feeling this little dog was going to be a real asset in sniffing out vampires.

It was getting pretty light when I arrived back home. Or what used to be home. I figured they wouldn't begrudge me a nap. I didn't need much sleep, but then again, I hadn't gotten any last night. I definitely needed some shut-eye. Then I'd pack my things and look for a job, a new place . . . a new life.

I unzipped Fang from my vest. In the light of day, I could see his fur was a reddish-blond color. It made him look even more harmless, made it even harder to believe he was part-demon.

I snuck Fang and myself in my bedroom window just in case someone was up—I wasn't up to having a conversation right now.

Curious about the hellhound, I pulled out my special reference books—the three-volume *Encyclopedia Magicka*. These ancient books were the only thing I'd inherited from my father. But I didn't keep them for sentimental reasons—they were the most accurate references on vampires and succubi I'd seen. Stood to reason they'd be accurate on other creatures as well.

"Hmm, hellhounds . . . "

Fang's ears perked up and he came to sit beside me, his head cocked in inquiry.

"Says here that hellhounds are large, fierce dogs, blood-red in color." I glanced at the small dog, whose strawberry-blond fur and slight body bore no resemblance to the drawing, which looked like a greyhound on steroids. "See?"

I showed him the picture and he studied it for a moment. WHOA.

"Yeah—looks a little different from you. What percentage of you is actually hellhound, anyway?" The rest included a big dose of terrier.

He somehow managed to look exasperated. I DON'T DO MATH— OR FAMILY TREES. I'M A DOG, FERGAWDSAKE.

Yeah, right. A dog with an attitude. Not to mention a soft, mushy side he apparently liked to keep hidden. Just like me.

He nudged me impatiently with his nose. GO ON.

"Okay, okay. Hellhounds have very sensitive noses and were bred to sniff out other demons and creatures of the night at the command of their master, then rip out their throats." I glanced at him. "You do understand the difference between a throat and a crotch, don't you?"

HA HA. VERY FUNNY.

"Okay, so you're a little on the short side. I get it. But . . . why didn't you try to rip out my throat?" I was part-demon, after all.

WHAT DOES THE BOOK SAY?

I read on. "Oh, I see. A hellhound who is bound to its master's will has to obey that master, but once the master dies, the hound is free to choose its own prey." Since he didn't have a master, the throat-ripping was optional.

The book went on to advise that a hellhound who lost its master be destroyed lest it wreak indiscriminate havoc, and it provided some gruesome tales to support that recommendation.

I didn't read that part aloud. No need—my new friend was obviously very discriminate and on the side of the good guys. Must be the normal canine part of him.

YOU GOT IT, BABE.

Oh, yeah, and he could read my mind. I closed the book. "Well, now, looks like a hellhound just might be a demon girl's best friend."

His jaw dropped in a doggie grin. YEP, THAT'S WHAT I'M THINKING.

I scratched his ears. He made me feel a little better about the whole crappy evening. But for now, I was beat. I didn't feel like changing, so I crashed in the clothes I was wearing, and Fang curled up next to me. Feeling a little comforted, I drifted off to sleep.

Surprisingly, I didn't dream. Or if I did, I didn't remember it. I woke about noon and the feel of Fang's furry little body against mine was kind of nice. I wanted to stay in this nice warm place forever, but reality hit and I realized I couldn't. I had to start a new life.

Fang poked me with his nose. I NEED TO GO OUTSIDE. AND I'M HUNGRY.

Oh, yeah—dogs required care. At least he was civilized. Realizing the rest of the family should be working at the store about now, I let him out to do his business then showered and raided the kitchen for both of us. As he chowed down on some leftover stew, I had some cereal and contemplated my next move.

I had so much to do . . . it was kind of overwhelming.

Guess I'd better pack first. I glanced around my room. I'd need clothes, bedding, that kind of stuff. Would they let me take the furniture once I found a place? If not, I'd have to buy some. Not to mention other stuff like dishes and towels.

There was so much to think about. The cereal congealed in my stomach. I'd thought I was grown up, but the sheer number of things I had to do made me feel inadequate and so not ready for this. My small savings probably wouldn't go very far. Not for long, anyway.

And I wouldn't be able to come back. I blinked back tears. It wasn't that much, but it was home . . . a home where I wasn't welcome anymore. I rubbed my chest with the heel of my hand, wondering if the pain there would ever go away. Could you die of a broken heart?

Fang poked me. HEY, YOU HAVE LOTS TO LIVE FOR. YOU HAVE ME.

I couldn't help but chuckle. "That I do. What say we pack this stuff up?"

To keep my mind off the decisions I had to make, I moved swiftly and methodically, stuffing clothes, books, and other things I thought I'd need in my duffel bag. It was tougher than I'd expected. Each thing I touched held memories of better times . . . the beaded bracelet Jen had made me, the pentacle Mom had given me for protection, the amusing vampire doll Rick had stuffed in my Christmas stocking . . . .

Damn, I'd forgotten about the holidays. I dropped down onto the bed, hugging the silly doll with a sinking feeling in the pit of my stomach. The upcoming Halloween and the Day of the Dead were always big at the store, but the biggies at home were Thanksgiving and Christmas. Where would I be then? Would I even be invited?

Even if I was, too many harsh things had been said—on both sides—for it to be anything but strained and uncomfortable. It could never be the same again.

Abruptly, I stood and wiped the moisture from my eyes. No time to worry about that now. I had to pack and get out of here.

An hour later, I heard a knock on the door. I felt my stomach clench—it had to be my family. Make that ex-family. I refused to answer it, not wanting to experience another scene, not wanting to cry and let them know how much they'd hurt me. Besides, who knew what they'd accuse me of this time?

When I ignored a second knock, Mom and Rick opened the door and walked in anyway. They must have left Jen minding the store alone.

Fang leapt to his feet on the bed and growled menacingly. They stopped short. "What's that?" Mom asked in surprise.

I gathered the shreds of my composure together and took refuge in sarcasm to avoid letting them see my pain. "It's a dog, Mother."

"I can see that. What's it doing here?"

"His name is Fang and he's my new friend. As to what he's doing, he's reminding you that it's not polite to barge in to someone else's room."

You know these people? Fang asked.

I glanced at my parents, but they didn't seem to have heard him. It must be just me. To Fang, I said, "It's okay. These are my landlords, though not for much longer. We're moving."

Mom looked hurt. Good. I wanted her to feel the pain she'd given me. "We're more than your landlords," she protested.

"Not anymore. You kicked me out, remember?" Suddenly uncertain if I could face another huge scene, I asked, "What do you want? I'm busy." I turned to the duffel and fiddled with the stuff inside, wishing they'd just go away. They obviously weren't going to apologize, weren't going to tell me all was forgiven, and I didn't want to hear any more rationalizations, didn't want to break down and bawl like a baby.

"We thought you might need some help finding a place, moving . . . "

Continuing to stuff things in the duffel, I said, "No, thanks. Got it covered. Though I might come back later to get my bed and dresser, if that's okay."

"Of course." Mom seemed at a loss. "Maybe we could talk."

"You said enough last night." Lashing out felt good, fed a little of the lust for revenge Lola was stirring up inside me.

"No, we want you to understand—"

"I understand perfectly. Let's not rehash this, okay? I heard enough the first time."

"But—"

"No, I get it," I said, interrupting her and facing them fully for the first time, letting the hurt come out in harsh words. "You good guys, me bad guy. I'm leaving."

Fang moved closer, silently offering support.

"It's not as black and white as that," Mom protested.

How could she say that after she'd so clearly chosen her other daughter—her normal daughter—over me? What a hypocrite. "It is from this side of the fence."

Rick watched silently from the doorway, looking disturbed and somewhat regretful. But that's all he did—stand there. Guess he wasn't going to come to my aid . . . again.

"Val, I know you use this smart-ass façade to keep your true self hidden from the world, but you don't have to use it with us," Mom said.

"This is the real me. Like it or lump it." I paused, then said sarcastically, "Oh, wait. You've already done that, haven't you? Only, I'm the one who took the lumps."

Looking exasperated, Mom said, "You're determined to be difficult, aren't you?"

"Me?" I glared at the both of them. "What if I told you that you had to leave your family, that you weren't wanted anymore, that you were less than human? How would *you* feel?"

"That's not what I said."

"The hell it isn't." No matter how much Mom tried to sugarcoat it, that's the way it played out. That's the way it felt, deep inside. And for once, Lola didn't try to break free. All this turmoil inside me must be feeding her lust somehow.

"Don't you talk to me that way. I'm still your mother."

I'd had enough. Whirling on her, I said, "No, you're not. You disowned me. I don't have to listen to you anymore. Get out."

"What?" Mom appeared truly shocked. I'd never talked back to them.

"You heard me," I choked out past the tears in my throat. "Just . . . leave."

Fang added a low growl for good measure. WANT ME TO MAKE HER LEAVE?

I shook my head at him. *No—she is still my mother.* Though it was nice to have someone on my side for a change.

Looking hurt, Mom left in a huff. Good—maybe she'd get a small taste of what she'd put me through last night. But Rick was still in the doorway.

"What do you want?" I asked tiredly. I hoped he wasn't going to bitch at me, too. I couldn't handle it right now.

With compassion in his expression, Rick said, "She still loves you, you know."

She had a funny way of showing it. "She loves her other daughter—your daughter—more."

"You're my daughter, too, sweetheart, you know that. In every way that counts."

I blinked back the moisture in my eyes and shook my head. I very much wished it were so, but though he had always tried to treat us the same, the fact was, he couldn't—Jen and I were too different. Mom didn't even try.

He added quietly, "And your mom doesn't love Jen more. It's just that you remind her so much of your father . . . ."

Yeah, and I knew how much Mom hated the way my father's lust demon had seduced her, had forced her to feel desire. Would I be forced to pay the price for what my father had done for the rest of my life? "I'm not like my father," I snapped.

"I know that. Just give it time, Val. This'll blow over eventually."

I shrugged, unwilling to let him know how much it hurt. "Who cares? I'm eighteen now. I don't need any of you anymore." And I couldn't take the heartache.

"Oh, yeah. Happy—"

I glared at him, and he was wise enough not to finish that particular sentence.

Sheepishly, he pulled something from his pocket and held it out to me. "Here, we got you this."

I glanced down. It was a cell phone . . . with a little red bow stuck on it. They hadn't forgotten my birthday. Tears pricked against my eyelids again. I turned away. "No thanks. I don't need anything from you."

"Don't be stupid, Val. You'll need it, to find a job, a place to live, keep in touch . . . ."

He was right. With no friends and living at home, I hadn't really needed a cell. But now I would. And it wasn't like it was

charity or anything. Reluctantly, I reached out to take it. "Okay."
Realizing that sounded a little churlish, I added, "Thanks." After
all, I knew he meant well.

"It's pre-paid so you won't have to worry about the bills for
awhile. And here." He pulled an envelope out of another pocket.
"Here are your wages from the store . . . along with a little bonus."

Now that, I'd earned. I stuffed the envelope and the phone in
my duffel. "So, you'll give me a good reference?" I asked around
the lump in my throat.

"Of course we will." He paused. "Do you know what you'd
like to do? I have some friends—"

"No." That *would* be charity. "I mean, I'll find a job on my
own. I found out last night that the cops aren't as clueless as I
thought when it comes to the vampires. Maybe they could use
some help."

"Is that wise?"

"Why wouldn't it be?"

"The reason you hunt vampires is to give the succubus an
acceptable outlet for the lust—"

"I know that," I snapped. Lust for the hunt wasn't nearly as
satisfying for Lola, but it kept her pacified. Even more important,
it helped me live with myself the next morning.

Ignoring my interruption, Rick continued, "But if you let the
demon free that often, you'll give the succubus a lot more
dominance."

"So?"

"So will you be able to handle that?"

Damn him, he actually looked concerned. And it was a good
question. Could I handle it and stay human? Or would the demon's
constant freedom give it more control? "I'll have to handle it, won't
I?"

Rick froze for a moment, looking as if he were struggling with
himself, then said softly, "If you need any help with sparring—"

"What? You'll piss off your wife and help me out? Yeah, right.
I've got a life-sized picture of that happening."

I wasn't being fair, and I knew it. When I'd almost drained that
poor boy of all his energy, Rick had been very patient with my

rampant hormones and raging succubus. For awhile there, I'd been like a cat in heat, and the neighborhood boys had sniffed around me like rutting tomcats.

That's when Mom had changed, had started treating me like something less than human. Rick, however, had helped me to channel the demon through martial arts courses. He'd even let me take out my frustrations by trying out my fighting skills on him— once he was sufficiently padded, of course.

I'd gone looking for trouble, too, sneaking out at night to search for scumbags and rapists to take out my frustrations on. But pounding on full humans didn't quite do the trick, so when I ran into a vampire the first time a year ago, I'd been elated. Finally, there was something I could really sink my teeth into . . . so to speak.

And Rick had helped me research the undead, learn how to deal with them. I owed him. "I'm sorry. I know you helped me. A lot." Especially since Mom had been in complete denial and unable to deal with her daughter's awakening sexuality—no help at all.

He raised an eyebrow. "Didn't you ever wonder how I knew what to do?"

"Uh . . . no." I'd just always assumed my stepfather was the smartest man in the world, especially when it came to the woo-woo stuff. After all, he owned a new age bookstore. "How?"

"When you were twelve, a man visited your mother and me. Said he knew what you were and gave us some advice on how to help you handle your powers when they manifested."

Really? "How did he know?"

"He wouldn't say, but it was obvious he knew what he was talking about—he was part lust demon, too."

"Whoa." My head reeled from a total major shift in world view. "There are others like me?" Then again, why wouldn't there be?

"Apparently."

"And you never *told* me?" It might have helped me live with my oddness if I'd known there were other energy-sucking demons in the world.

"You were doing well, so the three of us decided it would just confuse you if you did know. He stopped by from time to time after that to give me more pointers on how to train you to fight the vampires."

Though my head was spinning with hundreds of unanswered questions, only one emerged. "Why are you telling me this now?"

"Because you're going to be giving the succubus a lot more control. If you have trouble handling it, maybe he can help."

Even talking to someone with the same type of demon might help. With excitement rising within me, I asked, "What's his name? Where can I find him?"

"His name is Lucas Blackburn. But I don't know how to contact him—he always found us. And I haven't seen him at all since you started fighting vampires."

I nodded slowly. "No problem. I'll find him." I didn't know how or where, but I had to know how he knew about me, why he'd helped me.

Now that Rick had dropped that bomb, he left, closing the door gently behind him.

I dropped into a chair, stunned, and Fang nudged me with his nose, looking concerned. ARE YOU OKAY?

"Yeah, I'm okay." I hugged him, grateful for his consolation as my mind tried to make sense of this new information.

Mom had always discouraged questions about my father, and I'd never really wanted to know about the demon who'd spawned me, especially after what happened the day he killed himself. I figured I knew all I needed to. But now, I wasn't so sure. If there were others like me, maybe I wasn't as alone as I thought.

Who was Lucas Blackburn, and what other secrets might he reveal?

# CHAPTER THREE

Now that I was all packed, I stood next to my bed and stared at my duffel bag. I wasn't quite sure what to do first. Find a job, an apartment, or Lucas Blackburn? They all seemed equally important.

Fang pawed at me. FOOD AND SHELTER FIRST.

I jumped, not quite used to him reading my thoughts yet. But he had a point. It would probably be a good idea to find a place near where I ended up working, so I'd just find a hotel or something for the night, then something more permanent once I got a job. I glanced down at Fang. One that took dogs.

GOOD PLAN.

I grinned. He was gonna be a lot of fun to have around. I pulled out the Yellow Pages and called around. Holy crap—I never realized before how expensive hotels could be. At this rate, I'd go through my savings way too quickly. No five star hotels for us—I could only afford one or two. I found a relatively inexpensive one that took dogs and we headed that way, with my duffel on the back of the Valkyrie and Fang in the front.

After a brief hassle at the front desk over my lack of a credit card, I paid cash and got the key to the room.

The place looked like it hadn't been redecorated since way before I was born—with an orange and green color scheme, tired bedspread, threadbare carpet, and a chipped bathtub.

I dumped my duffel on the dresser and Fang sniffed disdainfully. I had to agree. I didn't have his nose, but I could still smell stale smoke and the acrid stench of urine where previous animal occupants had staked their territory. I wouldn't be going barefoot on this carpet.

DON'T USE THE BEDSPREAD EITHER, Fang advised, curling his lip at it.

*Ew.* I didn't want to know why. Unfortunately, I could imagine all too clearly. I scooched the slick bedspread off the bed with my foot and kicked it into the corner. The sheets appeared clean. As I looked doubtfully at them, Fang gave them the sniff test.

ALL CLEAR.

I sat down on the bed and looked around, my heart sinking. Is this what I had to look forward to, being on my own?

My chest grew tight. I just wanted to go home. Unfortunately, that wasn't possible. Now what? I had so much to do . . . and so little experience in doing any of this. What was I going to do? Give me a vampire to kill and I was totally there. But ask me to fit in somehow in the real world as an adult? I wasn't sure I was ready.

Fang jumped up next to me and nudged me. THIS IS TEMPORARY. BESIDES, YOU'RE NOT YOUR OWN. YOU HAVE ME.

That I did, along with an even greater incentive to find a job, with two mouths to feed. I pulled out the Yellow Pages and tore out the section that listed bookstores. Fang declined to stay in the room by himself, so I bundled him up in my vest. It was too warm during the day, even in October, for the vest, but it was the only way I was sure Fang would be safe.

We headed out and I drove to the closest bookstore—an independent like Mom and Rick's—and parked. Unzipping my vest, I glanced down at my black shirt, suddenly sprouting dozens of light reddish blond hairs. "You shed." *Note to self: get a lint roller.*

SORRY, Fang said, sounding kind of embarrassed. NOTHING I CAN DO ABOUT IT.

"No biggie—I'll just try to remember to wear Fang-colored clothes."

Brushing the dog hair off as much as I could, I said, "Do you mind staying out here? I don't think dogs are allowed inside."

He gave a mental sniff. DISCRIMINATION. But he stretched out next to the Valkyrie and laid his head down with a sigh.

Unfortunately, they didn't have any openings. And three bookstores later, I was beginning to get discouraged. I straddled my motorcycle in front of the Rolling Oaks Mall on the outskirts of the city, trying to figure out what to do next. It was nearing closing time and no one was hiring, though they'd had me fill out applications in case there was an opening later.

Heck, even if I did find a job, bookstore clerks didn't get much better than minimum wage. If apartments cost as much as hotels,

I was in big trouble. Not to mention everything that went with them, like utilities and food and stuff. Could I file for unemployment?

FIRST THINGS FIRST. I'M HUNGRY.

So was I. I glanced down at Fang. "What do you eat?"

WHATEVER. MICE, GOPHERS, WHAT I CAN FIND IN THE TRASH. I'M AN EQUAL OPPORTUNITY EATER.

Ick. TMI . . . though I *had* asked. "You want dog food?"

He shuddered. ICK, he repeated back at me.

What *did* you feed a hellhound? "So, if you had your druthers, what would you eat?"

PIZZA. I'M A PIZZA-LOVING FOOL.

I couldn't help it—I grinned. He was practically salivating at the thought. "Any particular toppings?"

LOTS OF MEAT AND CHEESE, NO ONIONS OR PEPPERS.

The thought of a hellhound putting in such a specific order for pizza amused me. "Okay, you got it." I went back into the mall and got a couple of slices for us at the food court, plus a Coke for me and water for Fang.

We ate dinner under a nearby tree and I wondered what to do next. I really didn't want to go back to that hotel room just yet, and it wasn't dark enough yet for the vampires to come out to play. Maybe I should get a paper, check out the help wanted ads. But what else was I qualified for? It's not like I had a lot of experience . . . or education.

YOU CAN KILL VAMPIRES.

"Thanks, Fang. I know you're trying to be helpful, but I don't think there are any paying jobs out there for that."

TOO BAD. I LIKE KILLING VAMPIRES.

I grinned, then suddenly realized I was wrong—there *was* a job out there for that kind of thing, as I'd mentioned to Rick. That detective last night had one . . . and he'd asked me for tips. Maybe I could get a few bucks for passing on what I knew to the cops, help them with training or something.

Fang raised one eyebrow without lifting his head off his front feet. SO CALL HIM ALREADY.

Why not? His card was still in my vest pocket, so I pulled it out and used my new cell phone to dial his number.

"Sullivan."

Now that I had him on the line, I wasn't quite sure what to say. "Hey, there, detective, it's Val Shapiro."

"Who?"

"You know, Val Shapiro. From last night?"

"Oh, yeah," he said in recognition. "You're the kid."

I grimaced at the "kid"—he wasn't that much older than me. "Uh, yeah. That's me." Geez, could I sound any lamer?

"Whatcha need?"

"Uh, well, I wondered if you might want to hire me. You know, to give you some pointers or something."

He hesitated. "That wasn't exactly what I had in mind."

Oh, crap, I'd forgotten about the male ego. He probably wouldn't want to take advice from a girl—not about something as macho as fighting the undead. I was gonna have to play on his sympathies. "Well, you see, I didn't get my sister back home on time last night, and my parents got pissed and kicked me out of the house."

"Whoa, that's cold."

"Yeah, they fired me from my job, too." Before he could say anything else, I added, "So, you know, I kind of need a job and you seemed interested in what I could do . . . ." I trailed off, realizing how pathetic that sounded. "Hey, never mind. I'm sorry I bothered you. I'll just—"

"Hold on just a minute. I might be able to do something for you. How old are you again?"

"Eighteen." My stomach lurched again as I realized it was still my birthday. It sure didn't feel like it.

"Good. Can I call you right back?"

"Sure." I gave him the number and hung up. "So, Fang, you think he'll call back?"

He'd be a fool not to.

Yeah, but would he call?

Chill. He'll call.

I sighed. "I wish I had your optimism."

I didn't move from under the tree, afraid I'd miss hearing the call on the Valkyrie. Fang and I waited for what seemed like forever, but was only about an hour, before the phone rang again.

I wasn't used to it, so it startled me. It wasn't from any phone number I knew, so hopefully it was the cop. I fumbled a bit before I figured out how to answer it. "Hello?"

"Sullivan here. Hey, have you got time to meet some people now? I may have something for you."

Really? Cool! Ignoring Fang's TOLD YOU SO, I said, "Sure. Where?"

He gave me directions to a building near one of the cop shops and I headed over there with Fang, wondering what the detective had in mind. I was feeling pretty optimistic, but I reminded myself he didn't actually say the "something" was in law enforcement. It might be something unrelated, though I hoped he didn't expect me to clean toilets or run a register where I had to ask, "You want fries with that?"

The address he gave me had a sign designating it as the Special Crimes Unit. Things were looking up. At Fang's insistence, I brought him in with me. "Try to look inconspicuous," I suggested.

He just dropped his jaw in a doggie grin and followed me inside. "I'm here to see Dan Sullivan," I told the lady at the desk.

She gave me a disinterested look and paged him. I don't think she even noticed the hellhound at my feet.

The detective did, though. He came through the door, glanced down, and said, "What's with the dog?"

"He's uh, you know, one of those special assistance dogs."

Fang didn't seem happy with my explanation. WELL, THE SPECIAL PART IS RIGHT, ANYWAY.

The detective raised an eyebrow. He wasn't buying it. "And what does he assist you with?"

I glanced warily at the desk lady, not sure how much I should say. "The same thing you caught me doing last night."

"Oh? I didn't see him then."

That's because I hadn't found Fang until later. "Look, it's a bit too cold to leave him outside. Fang is very well-behaved, I swear."

Dan looked down at the dog. "Fang?"

Fang concentrated on looking cute and obedient, though privately he said, MAKE FUN OF ME AND I'LL POOP ON YOUR NICE CLEAN

FLOOR.

*Don't you dare make a liar out of me,* I warned him.

DON'T WORRY—I'LL PLAY THE NICE LITTLE PET.

Sullivan shrugged. "Why not? We're training other dogs to sniff out these targets. Follow me."

I followed him into a large room that looked like a high school gym—must be some kind of training area. Three other guys were there, just talking, and they looked up as we came in.

To keep from having to go through the whole dog-challenging thing again, I told Fang mentally, *Play along with me here, okay?* Out loud, I said, "Sit. Stay."

Fang planted his butt immediately and stayed put as I walked toward the men. YES, MASTER, came the exaggerated response.

*Very funny. But just remember who provides the pizza. If you don't want to continue dining on vermin, work with me.*

One of the guys—a beefy blond with his hair shaved close to his head—took a look at me and barked out a laugh. "This is your super slayer?"

Sullivan just smiled. "This is Detective Horowitz, and the other *scuzzy* is Fenton." He nodded toward a lean Hispanic man who was a little older, a little grayer, and seemed to carry the weight of the world—or at least San Antonio—on his shoulders. "And this is our fearless leader, Lt. Ramirez."

"*Scuzzy?*" I repeated. Was this one of those weird male bonding things where they called each other rude names and beat each other up?

"Comes from SCU," Sullivan said. "It's what the others call us. There are more of us, but they're not on duty yet. Gentlemen—and I use the term very loosely—this is Val Shapiro."

The two detectives folded their arms and gave me short nods of recognition. Curt ones, like they wanted to make sure I didn't think they were nods of acceptance. Ramirez, on the other hand, smiled and shook my hand. "Nice to meet you, Ms. Shapiro. Would you like to show us what you can do?"

I liked this guy, and it appeared he was the one I needed to impress. I shrugged. "Sure. Got a vampire handy?"

The other two laughed and exchanged amused looks. My face

went hot for a moment, then reminded myself not to let them get to me. They had no idea what I could do. But Sullivan did, and he wasn't laughing.

Ramirez smiled, though it wasn't a mean one. "I thought perhaps we'd start with some sparring."

That explained the mats on the floor. "Okay. Who'd you like me to spar with?"

Ramirez made a sweeping gesture that encompassed the three other men. "Take your pick."

They obviously expected me to go for the smallest guy, Fenton, but I had something to prove. Horowitz was easily the biggest—and the most annoying. "I'll take him."

Horowitz stripped off his jacket. "This won't take long."

I didn't say anything—I just peeled off my bulky down vest and laid it next to Fang.

I'LL GUARD IT WITH MY LIFE, the terrier assured me gravely.

Smart-ass. Horowitz rolled his shoulders, looking über confident. Well, he was about to be über surprised.

"Any rules?" I asked.

Ramirez nodded. "This is practice. No maiming. No shots to the genitals . . . " he glanced at Horowitz " . . . or the breasts. You'll go on my mark."

I sized up Horowitz. He had muscles, but not the bulges of a bodybuilder as I'd expected. He didn't rely on brute strength, then. He must practice some form of martial arts. Which one?

They moved to the center of the room and the detective stretched his arm and leg muscles. Good—he was taking this seriously. I did the same.

I tried to stay loose and ready for whatever he threw at me. I wouldn't be able to read his mind like a vamp's, but then again, he would be a lot slower.

He crouched in a fighter's stance and I suddenly realized he must have a hundred pounds on me. What was I thinking?

YOU CAN TAKE HIM, Fang said.

Guess I'd have to.

"Go," Ramirez said.

Horowitz moved faster than I expected, spinning around in an elegant move to land a solid kick to my stomach. Crap, I hadn't expected that. I'd figured him for some oriental martial arts move, not the French *savate*.

But as he danced away, he seemed surprised that I wasn't writhing on the ground. That was one definite advantage of being part demon—I could take a lot more punishment than most people.

"Give up?" he taunted.

"No, just waiting for you to wear yourself out," I gasped. The other men chuckled and I pretended to be more hurt than I was, watching to see what he would do next. Would he stay with the *savate* kicks or try something else?

He stuck with what worked and whirled to try the same move again. This time, however, I was ready for him, and grabbed his ankle and threw him to the floor. Just as quickly, he tried to whip my legs out from under me, but I'd anticipated that and jumped out of the way. He surged to his feet, but before he could get positioned to lash out at me again with his feet, I rushed him, hurling punches that he had to block.

He didn't expect that. I kept it up, chasing him around the mat, throwing my fists as fast as I could while the men hooted and hollered on the sidelines. Horowitz blocked some blows, but not all, and I landed a few solid hits on his face and to his stomach while he was primarily occupied with defending himself. If I could just keep him off balance, he wouldn't be able to get enough distance from me to use those deadly feet of his.

He got a few licks in past my guard, and one really good one, a beautiful right cross. Ouch, that stung. Lola raged to life, and since this time it was a lust for blood, I let her loose, reveling in the power that filled my body.

Fueled by my secret weapon, I slugged him with a powerhouse that had him staggering away, then used his own technique to batter him with a series of lightning *savate* kicks in the shin, stomach, and chin.

He went down.

Instantly, I was on top of him, gripping his throat as I pinned him to the mat. "Yield."

He struggled for a moment, but I had him completely

immobilized.

A sudden weight landed on my back and an arm came across my throat, choking me, cutting off my air. Oof.

"Too bad for you he has a friend," Fenton muttered in my ear. "This is what it's really like on the streets."

All of a sudden, he let go with a curse and I spun around to see Fang clamped to his backside.

"Too bad for you I have a friend, too," I said with a grin. "Good dog."

Fenton tried to beat Fang off his butt, though he was having a hard time reaching him. Ramirez commanded, "Stand down."

When both men went still, I took pity on Fenton. "Let go, Fang."

Fang obediently let go and trotted over to my side. *Good work,* I told him privately. *Thanks for the backup.*

No problem. He wasn't playing fair.

No, he wasn't. Ramirez must have thought so, too—he glared at Fenton. "What the hell did you think you were doing?"

"Helping out my partner." He sounded defensive. But he couldn't meet Ramirez's glare. He looked away, rubbing his rear. "Sorry, I just got carried away."

"Don't do it again." Ramirez turned to Horowitz. "You concede the match?"

He didn't really have to, but he nodded.

Horowitz was good—*very* good. The full humans I'd fought in various martial arts classes had never lasted this long against me. Even better, he hadn't pulled his punches, hadn't treated me like a girl.

At Horowitz's sign of capitulation, the demon lust subsided within me, and I took a shaky breath. It was silly, but I envisioned Lola as kind of a sexy genie—a Marilyn Monroe type—who stayed corked up in her bottle until lust blew the cork out. I mentally stuffed Lola back in and corked the bottle. It wasn't easy, but I could do it. Good. I could handle this. If they'd have me.

Horowitz held out his hand and smiled. "Hell, anyone who can beat the crap out of me like that is all right in my book. Call me Hank."

Shocked, I shook his hand. Fenton offered his, too. "I'm Mike."
Sullivan added, "Call me Dan."

I grinned. It felt good to be accepted. "You can call me Val—
and my partner here is Fang."

They all gave Fang a dubious glance.

Fang grinned back up at them. NO MONSTER HERE. NO SIREE.
JUST A FAITHFUL CANINE COMPANION DEFENDING HIS BELOVED MASTER.

I resisted the urge to snort, but it must have worked, because
Hank asked, "How do you do that, Val?"

I shrugged. "Trade secret."

Ramirez looked at Dan. "So, you checked her out, I take it?"
He nodded.

"Tell us about her."

I thought about protesting, but didn't want to jeopardize my
shot at maybe working with these guys.

Dan Sullivan slanted a glance at me. "Her parents divorced
when she was only a few months old, and a year later, her mother
married Rick Anderson, the owner of the Astral Reflections New
Age Bookstore where she works. Her father died when she was
five."

Damn—I hadn't known he could be so thorough in such a
short time.

He continued. "She was home-schooled until she got her
GED—early. She has a younger half-sister, Jennifer, though *she*
attends public school. Val has taken every martial arts and self-
defense course offered in the city—including *savate*—but never
stuck with any of them long enough to compete or earn belts." He
slanted a glance at me. "The classes bore you?"

Good guess. "Pretty much." Once I'd learned the forms and
how to combat them, I'd moved on. I didn't have to actually practice
them to understand them. Lola's influence made me a natural
fighter, but I learned a lot from watching the matches of the
masters.

He nodded as if he'd expected that answer. "She's a gifted
fighter, but I can't figure out where she gets her speed and strength.
There's no indication of steroids or other drugs. She keeps her
nose clean. It must come naturally."

YEAH—AS NATURAL AS IT WOULD BE FOR ANY PART-DEMON GIRL.

Ignoring Fang, I asked, "That it?" But I had to admit I was a tad impressed. He'd been busy.

"Not all. You have no close girlfriends, no boyfriends, and your only extravagance is a motorcycle, a Honda Valkyrie. Today's your eighteenth birthday, and your parents celebrated by kicking you out of the house."

Well, that last part I'd told him. But the rest—I don't know how he found that out so fast. No wonder he was a detective. "You're good," I admitted.

Ramirez grinned. "How'd you like a job, Val?"

Wow—was it that easy? Getting paid for something I already did for free? "I'm in."

"Good. With your brawn and his brains, you'd make a great team."

Whoa—team? That wouldn't work. Being around the cop all the time . . . what if he found out what I really was? I backtracked quickly. "I already have a partner—Fang."

THAT'S RIGHT. YOU DON'T NEED ANYONE ELSE.

It didn't look like Dan was too crazy about the idea either. But Ramirez didn't agree. "It's unit policy—you have to have backup before you engage one of the targets. And Dan doesn't have a partner right now—he lost his last week . . . to one of *them*."

It was too risky. I'd been hiding my true nature for far too long. Working alongside a hot cop, letting him get close—Lola was bound to make her presence known. What would happen when he found out what I truly was? I'd probably be classed as a monster along with the vamps. Then what would I do?

I took a deep breath. *Hell, I can't believe I'm about to say this.* "Thank you, but I'm sorry. I can't take the job."

# CHAPTER FOUR

Dan looked annoyed. "*What?*"

Okay, he had a right to be pissed after he went to all the trouble of setting this up for me. "I don't think I could do this with a partner," I said apologetically. Not a human one, anyway.

"Mike just showed you why you need one," Dan said, sounding exasperated.

Yes, and it was a good lesson. I needed to pay more attention to my surroundings. Well, Fang would help with that. "I know, but—"

The lieutenant interrupted, looking thoughtful. "Val, could I have a moment alone with you?"

Why not? The guy had been nice enough to offer me a job. Least I could do was hear him out. "Sure."

"Good. Hank, Mike, you can head on out. Dan, you might want to come back a little later."

The guys all nodded and the lieutenant gestured me to follow him. He closed the door to his office and waved me toward a seat. He didn't even carp when Fang flopped down at my feet. I wasn't sure what was going to happen, but this must be what Jen felt like when she was sent to the principal's office.

I glanced around. Heck, the principal's office had to be nicer than this. Cheap wall paneling, scarred linoleum, battered metal desk and ancient chairs . . . the department obviously wasn't spending a whole lot of money on its Special Crimes Unit.

Lieutenant Ramirez rubbed his forehead wearily. "Now, suppose you tell me the real reason you turned the job down."

I glanced at Fang. *I don't suppose you can read his mind?*

No. It only works with demons, vampires, that sort of thing.

Implying he'd met *other* sorts of things? But I let that slide for now and tried to figure out how to answer Ramirez.

When I hesitated, he added, "And why you seem to have a hellhound as a partner."

Fang and I exchanged surprised glances. "What do you mean?" I asked cautiously. Was he using "hellhound" as a figure of speech, or . . . ?

He glanced again at Fang. "Well, part-hellhound, anyway. The purple eye-flash when he took on Mike Fenton was a dead giveaway."

"Oh." *Not* a figure of speech.

"And so was yours when you fought Hank."

I squirmed in my seat. "So, you know what I am?"

"I know you're part demon, which is why you're able to do what you do."

"Uh, doesn't the *special* crimes unit hunt demons?"

He gave me a wry half smile. "Not the law-abiding ones. We're here to serve and protect, not make judgments."

Well that was a relief, but he sounded pretty calm about the whole existence of demons thing. "Do the others know, too?"

"No. The guys have a hard enough time dealing with the thought of vampires. Demons haven't become a threat, so until they do, I'm keeping my unit on a need-to-know basis."

"Then you understand why I don't want a partner. He's gonna have a lot of questions about how I can do what I do."

Ramirez nodded. "I'll handle that, let him know that I know why you're so talented without revealing your background." He cocked his head. "Let me guess . . . succubus, right?"

I gaped at him. "How did you know?"

He smiled. "Need-to-know basis again."

"Then you know why I don't want a male partner."

"In theory," Ramirez conceded. "But you seem to have it under control, and if I understand right, the hunt satisfies the lust cravings."

"Yes, but—"

"Just hear me out, okay?"

When I nodded, he went on to explain how the vampires were a small minority whose population had grown significantly larger in the area about a year ago—large enough to come to the attention of the San Antonio Police Department. Gaining incredible power, speed, immortality, and the ability to control mortal minds seemed to strip them of all moral judgment, so they were fast becoming the city's biggest crime problem. The SCU's job was to stop them, by whatever means possible.

Wow, I hadn't realized all this. I'd just been in my own little world, killing vamps and trying to keep Lola under control. No wonder he looked so strained. "How can you stop them at all?"

"We often don't," Ramirez said baldly. "That's how Dan lost his last partner, and why I've attended so many funerals lately. It's also why you don't see them going through the court system . . . or the hospital. They resist arrest—violently. The only way we've found to stop them is to kill them before they kill us."

Fang approved. THAT'S THE BEST WAY TO DEAL WITH A VAMPIRE.

Ramirez continued. "The key is not to let them take over your mind. And there appear to be three types of people who are able to resist."

Curious, I asked, "What kind?"

"First, those who are very devout. Regardless of your religion, having a deep, personal relationship with a deity seems to make you immune to having your mind taken over."

Surprised, I asked, "How many of those do you have?"

"Not very many. They don't usually gravitate toward law enforcement as a career. The majority fall in the second bracket—those with very strong emotions. Anger, rage, or just plain bullheaded stubbornness seems to make them unable to control your mind."

I nodded. "Like the guys I just met."

"Right. And the third are part-demons—people like you."

Surprised, I asked, "You have others like me in your unit?"

"Not yet, but I'd like to. Three men—*good* men—died over the last six months, just doing their job. If more of them had the advantages you do, I wouldn't have to tell their families they died in the line of duty. I wouldn't have to watch more of them being buried." He speared me with a glance. "I really don't want to attend any more funerals."

Crap. Taking vamps on *mano a mano* was one thing, but having responsibility for other people's lives . . . was I ready for that? I was still only eighteen.

Ramirez grimaced. "The number of vampire kills has tripled in the last few months and we're short-handed. Plus, members of the unit have been hearing about a vein of vampires forming together to plan something."

A *vein* of vampires? I hadn't heard them called that. *Ew.* "Vampires cooperating? That's new." They were usually so self-involved and tripping on their own power that they didn't play well with others.

"Yeah," Ramirez said. "But it can't be good. The sudden rise in vampire kills could be related to this new group. I'm hoping you can work with Dan to locate them, find out if they're behind this sudden rash of murders and if they are, stop them."

Like it was that easy. "Uh, it's not like I chat up the undead before I stake them."

"You don't have to. Just continue doing what you have been doing. The only difference is that you may run into small groups of them instead of individuals, which is why you need a partner. I wouldn't normally hire someone your age, but with your experience and advantages, we could really use you."

I frowned. I'd only gone after them one-on-one before, so this would be a bit more complicated. Sure, I could kill vampires for them, but did I want to? It would let Lola have more control. Could I handle it without revealing my secret to the world? "I'm not sure . . . "

"We need you," Ramirez said baldly. "And I have special hiring authority for this unit. You won't have to go through the normal hiring and training process, though of course, you'll work night shift. If you work with us, your pay won't be great, but it won't be minimum wage either. Plus, we offer medical, dental, vacation time, retirement—a complete benefits package."

I hadn't even thought about that stuff, but I guessed it was important in the grown-up world. I glanced at Fang. *What do you think?*

He looked thoughtful. Do they hire dogs?

I grinned. "Fang and I come as a package deal. He wants to know if you can put him on the payroll."

The lieutenant looked surprised, but took the question

seriously. "I don't think I can justify that, but I can provide you with identification that gives you special dispensation to take him anywhere you want, like a service dog or working police dog."

TAKE IT. YOU NEED THE MONEY TO FIND US DECENT DIGS . . . AND KEEP ME IN PIZZA.

He was right. I needed a job of some kind, and my bout with Horowitz made me more confident I could keep Lola under wraps when necessary. Plus the fact that Ramirez knew what I was—and was okay with it—made me feel a lot better about the whole thing. "Okay, I'll do it."

He beamed at me. "Great. Want to start work tonight?"

Now? He sure didn't waste any time. He must really be desperate.

OOH. FUN AND GAMES.

Well, if Fang was up for it, why not? Otherwise, we'd just have to return to that pit of a hotel room. "Sure."

He came around and opened the door. Dan was sitting outside, a pink bakery box in his hands. "Good—you're here. You ready to show your new partner the ropes?" he asked Dan.

"Yes, sir." Dan looked surprised but pleased, like he liked the idea of working with me. It made me feel kind of warm inside.

"Excellent," Ramirez said. "We need as many people as we can get and her skills will make her an excellent partner for you. Her dog will be a good asset, too. Make sure you take him with you."

I thanked the lieutenant and joined Dan in the hall. Ramirez wished us luck and sent us on our way.

"Here," Dan said awkwardly as we walked down the hall. "This is for you." He handed me the pink box.

"For me?" What was it? I opened it cautiously, not sure if this was some rookie razzing ceremony or what.

Nope—it was a cake, with the words, "Happy birthday, Val" scrawled in pink across the chocolate frosting. It even had pink and yellow flowers on it. Geez—he must have run right out after the sparring and bought it.

I stopped short. I hadn't expected to get a birthday cake from anyone on this lousy day, let alone a total stranger. The words on the cake blurred as I went all misty-eyed.

Crap. Why had he gone and done that? Now I was gonna cry in front of my new partner and he'd think I was a total *girl*.

AWWWW, HOW SWEET. HE LIKES YOU—HE REALLY LIKES YOU.

Fang's sarcasm yanked me out of my pity party. I shot him a glare but was privately glad he'd helped me find a way to buck up. "Thank you, Dan. That's very nice of you," I said, careful not to gush or blubber all over him. Maybe he wouldn't notice that my voice cracked, just a little.

Dan shrugged. "I figure everyone deserves a cake on their birthday. Consider it a welcome to the unit." We started walking again and he added, "Besides, the guys will love you forever if you share."

I grinned. "You got it."

Dan showed me to the break room and introduced me around to the guys who were just going on shift. They seemed surprised by my age and appearance, but when Dan told them how I'd kicked Hank's butt and taken down a vamp on my own, they obviously decided to take a wait and see attitude. That was okay—I knew I'd have to earn their respect and I didn't have a problem with that. At least Dan made sure I had the opportunity.

It helped that I'd brought the cake and Fang—they were both big hits. As I left the break room, I felt suddenly a whole lot more optimistic about my future. I might have even found a place I could belong.

Dan had me fill out some paperwork and got me a locker, then said, "Ready?"

"Sure."

He led us outside to a huge, silver Dodge Ram with an extended cab and covered storage bed.

"Whoa," I said. "This is a step up from the unmarked car you had last night."

"Yeah, well, teams get them—they're specially built. The doors and windows are lined with vampire-repelling silver and the bed cover comes in handy in case we stake any vamps."

Cool. That was a lot better than the trunk of Rick's old car. And this must be where the department's money went—into the fancy ambulances and other stuff necessary to keep the cops safe. I approved.

I hopped in and Fang seemed to have springs in his legs as he easily made the jump to the running board then the seat.

Dan got in the driver's seat and glanced at Fang. "So why are you bringing the pooch along?"

POOCH? Fang repeated incredulously. DID HE JUST CALL ME A POOCH?

"This *pooch* helped me take down a vamp last night."

YEAH. TAKE THAT, DOUGHNUT BREATH.

Dan smirked. "Oh, yeah? How? By holding the stake for you?"

"No, by holding onto the vamp's 'nads—with his teeth."

Dan winced.

"Don't worry. Fang knows you're a friend. Don't you?"

YEAH, SURE. WHATEVER.

But he wagged his tail at Dan just to reassure the guy.

"So we're doing on-the-job training then?"

"Yeah, but first, let me make sure we're on the same page. You probably know all this already, but just to make sure, let's take a refresher."

As they sat in the truck, he lectured me about vampire speed, their ability to cloud minds, how to kill them, yadda, yadda, yadda.

Finally, he broke off and said, "Are you even listening to me?"

Bored, I said, "Yeah, I get it. You shove something pointy in their hearts, drag them into the sunlight, or cut off their heads . . . if you just happen to have a sword handy. I know this already."

SMALL CHILDREN KNOW THIS, Fang thought contemptuously.

"Okay, fine. You don't want to listen, let's go."

As he started the truck, I asked, "How do you decide where to go?"

He shrugged. "We sometimes get details about names, appearance, favorite hang-outs, that sort of thing. If there are no details, we go looking for them in the areas where they tend to congregate. If they're law-abiding, we leave them alone. If they attack us or someone else, they're fair game."

"How do you get this information?"

"From Ramirez."

"Where does he get it?"

Dan gave me a surprised look. "Good question. I don't know, though I've wondered, too. I figure he has an informant—someone inside this vein of vampires we're supposed to find."

Made sense. "Do you have a target in mind?"

"Yeah." He pulled out his notebook and flipped through it. "I've been keeping track of the hot spots, places where the SCU has found victims but no perp yet."

"Where's that?"

"There's a place on the west side that's seen some activity . . . ."

As he drove, he resumed the vampire quiz. "So, how do vampires feel about silver?"

Remembering how nice he'd been to get me a cake, I played along. "It burns like hell when it touches their skin."

"How about garlic?"

"A tasty food seasoning, if you don't mind the odor."

He grinned. "Crosses?"

"If you believe, they can help."

"Holy water?"

"Like acid." Providing the priest believed, of course.

"Mirrors?"

"Reflect vampires just like everyone else. Though it's painful for them to look into the old ones with silver backing."

"How about the invitation thing?"

"That's true—they can't enter a place unless they've been invited. Of course, they can enter public places, which are an open invitation to anyone."

"Can they make themselves invisible? Change into bats? Fly?"

I shook my head. "All myths. But what they can do is cloud your mind, make you *think* they can do all that. That's where most people get caught. They can make you freeze in place until they drain you dry."

He made a noncommittal noise. "So, how many have you staked?"

I didn't know—I never counted. "Uh, maybe thirty or so." Probably more, but that would sound like bragging. "How about you?"

"Two," he admitted.

All of two? Oh, great. Who was the real rookie here? And he'd lost his partner recently, too. Whose fault was that? Sourly, I asked, "So, do I pass?"

"You pass."

*Gee, don't do me any favors.*

He pulled over, parking the truck in the shadows of a seedy area on the west side. The outskirts of San Antonio, consisting primarily of military bases and newer housing developments, weren't nearly as picturesque as the older, historic center. And here, on the crime-ridden west side, the area was mostly industrial with a few office buildings establishing a tentative toehold on the blight. It didn't look as bad in the daytime, but with several street lights burned out or shot out, it looked sinister on this dark night. And it wasn't safe for normal folks at any time of the day.

"This the place?" I asked.

"Yeah. Someone's been killing people in this five-block area.

"Okay, what's the plan?"

"How would you feel about serving as bait?"

Fang's mouth dropped open in a grin. Here, fishie, fishie.

It made sense—especially since I seemed to have more experience here. And of the two of us, I looked more harmless. "Sure, I'll play bait."

"Are you armed?"

"Why do think I wear vests? They hide the stakes I keep in a special holster in my back waistband." I took one out and showed it to him. "Just in case."

He hefted it. "Nice. But maybe I should—"

Exasperated, I interrupted him. "Look, you know I can handle myself. If I get in trouble, then you can ride to the rescue. For now, just stay here and . . . watch the dog."

Watch the dog? Hey, I'm your partner.

*Yeah, but a vampire is less likely to think I'm helpless if I have you with me. Then I wouldn't be good bait, would I?*

Fang conceded the point, but Dan just gave me a long, level look. "That kind of attitude could get you killed."

My face warmed. My mouth always got me into trouble. "Sorry. I'm just not used to working with a partner."

He nodded. "Don't worry. I have your back."

Feeling a little chastised, I got out of the truck and walked off, leaving Dan and Fang alone together.

As I walked swiftly away from the truck, I tried to change my demeanor. No more confident kick-butt vampire hunter. Instead, I hunched my shoulders, let my eyes dart about with wary glances, and checked my watch every couple of minutes as if waiting for someone who was very late. The perfect victim.

I lingered for about half an hour, but nothing happened. As I checked my watch for the hundredth time, I heard Fang yell VAL! from the truck, then he barked for good measure.

I whirled around to see Dan standing outside the truck and an overweight middle-aged blonde regarding him like a midnight snack. Despite the chilly weather, she wore nothing but black leather pants and a tight, laced leather vest that made the pale flesh of her breasts bulge out the sides and top and emphasized the muffin top on her stomach. Gross. Was the smashed cleavage, overstuffed sausage look in these days?

But I didn't want to overreact, in case she wasn't a vamp. She hadn't tried to enthrall me, so I wasn't sure yet. She might just be a skank on the prowl.

She leered at him, showing long pointed incisors. "Hello, handsome." Beckoning with one pudgy finger, she said, "Come to Charlene."

With the speed of a rattlesnake, she darted forward and sank her fangs into his neck. Then, grabbing his butt with both hands, she ground her hips against him and sucked.

*Not* just a skank. The demon lust surged within me and I rushed toward them, but Fang leapt out of the cab and got there first. He clamped on to her heel, evidently trying to hamstring her.

She released Dan to shriek and bat at Fang. "Pick on someone your own size," I said and punched Charlene in the face. Not that I was anywhere near her size, thank heavens.

That got her attention.

"You stupid bitch." Charlene rushed me, her claws extended

to scratch my face or gouge out my eyes, I wasn't sure which.

I'd never fought a vamp who fought like a girl before—she kicked and screamed and pulled my hair. I held my own, but I couldn't quite reach my stakes—I was too busy holding her claws away from my face.

Fang darted in and out, doing damage where he could. Dan was no help—he seemed too dazed to comprehend what was going on. Holding Charlene's wrists away from my face, I yelled, "Stake her!"

That woke him up. He yanked a stake out of his jacket and buried it in Charlene's back, aiming for the heart.

Unfortunately, the stake went in at an angle and didn't reach its destination through all the fat. Where was a sledgehammer when you needed one?

Charlene screeched and tried to reach around to her back to pull it out. That gave me the perfect opening. I whipped out my weapon and stabbed the vamp right in her black heart. Charlene dropped and lay motionless. As I rose slowly to my feet, I concentrated on putting Lola back in her prison. With Charlene vanquished, it was fairly easy.

Dan stood over the vamp, holding his hand to his neck and looking a little stunned.

"What's the matter?"

"I—I've never been bitten before. I don't know anyone who did and survived." He lifted his hand away from his neck to reveal two neat punctures on his neck and blood on his hand. He was clearly wondering if he was going to turn into a vampire now.

"Don't worry, you won't turn out like her." I paused to consider. "Well, not unless you shrink six inches, gain fifty pounds, have a sex change operation, and lose all fashion sense."

A spark flickered in his eyes—annoyance. I shrugged. "But you won't become a vampire unless you drink her blood, too." I glanced down at the corpse in black leather. "You could try it if you want, but I don't know if it'll work now that she's dead."

"I'll pass."

Good—he was handling it just fine. I saw him fidget with the crotch of his pants, looking uncomfortable. Guessing the source of his discomfort, I said, "Now you know why so many people find the vampire embrace so irresistible." Some of them enthralled their victims so they felt nothing but unbridled lust. Apparently, Charlene was one of them.

"That was mind control? She *made* me feel that way?"

It was obvious he already knew the answer and just wanted reassurance. "Yeah. I take it she wasn't exactly your type?"

"Not hardly. My God, that . . . that's rape."

If he felt that way about the vampire, imagine how he would feel about a succubus . . . . I made a noncommittal noise.

He looked thoughtful. "They don't do that to all their victims, though."

"Not all. Actually, you were lucky that she wanted you to feel desire. Some like to feed on the fear as well as the blood. Some . . . just like to kill."

He glanced down at the dead vamp, as if trying to figure out if he felt lucky or not. His mouth hardened. "We need to make sure the rest of the unit knows about this."

GO AHEAD, KICK HER, Fang thought at an oblivious Dan. YOU KNOW YOU WANT TO.

My partner still seemed a little out of it, probably some lingering effect from Charlene's mind control. To goad him back to normal, I said, "You wouldn't have had to go through it at all if you'd stayed in the truck."

His head came up and I saw anger in his eyes. Good—he'd snapped back.

"We wouldn't have caught her otherwise," he said. "You weren't exactly her type. Besides, Fang and I were bored." He glanced down at the dog. "Thanks, pal."

The dog deserved thanks—without Fang's warning, I might not have known Dan was in trouble until it was too late.

Fang stared up at Dan with his tongue lolling out, looking like a normal dog. YOU OWE ME BIG TIME, PAL.

I stifled an urge to laugh. Fang and I had a lot in common—both part demon, both trying to pass as something else. We were doing a good job of it, too, but it was a hell of a way to live. "So, what's next? Pack her in the back of the truck or call the ambulance pick-up unit?"

"The pick-up unit is for when we're on our own . . . or have to rush off somewhere else. Normally, we toss them in the back."

He drove the truck up next to the vamp, and we both wrestled her into the back, then joined Fang in the front. Dan pulled out a baby wipe and cleaned his neck, staring at the blood on it for a moment.

"Vampires are disease-resistant," I said casually. "You shouldn't need a disinfectant but you might like a bandage. Do you have a first aid kit handy?"

"Yeah, there's one in the back, but I'll take care of it later," Dan said.

He went silent, so I tried to divert his attention from what he'd just been through. "Hey, do you know someplace I can rent, cheap? Fang isn't crazy about the roach motel I picked out for tonight."

I was just trying to distract Dan, but he took the question seriously. "Well, as a matter of fact, my sister Gwen is looking for a roommate."

His sister? That sounded just a bit too cozy. "Uh, I hadn't planned on rooming with anyone—what with the crazy night hours I keep and uh, Fang . . . he . . . he sheds all over everything."

WELL, EXCUUUUSE ME, Fang said indignantly. I TOLD YOU I COULDN'T HELP THAT,

*Relax—I'm just using you as an excuse.*

"No biggie," Dan said. "Gwen's a nurse at the hospital so she has crazy night hours, too. And she loves dogs. She won't mind a little hair."

HA. THAT'S WHAT YOU GET FOR USING INNOCENT LITTLE HELLHOUNDS TO FURTHER YOUR NEFARIOUS PLANS.

Sheesh—what made me think it'd be fun to have this dog around? His snarky nature was coming out now. And how could I refuse Dan's generous offer without looking like an ingrate?

I couldn't. "Okay, thanks."

"Great—I'll call her."

Yeah, wonderful. But with any luck, she'd hate me on sight, or take an aversion to Fang.

FAT CHANCE. LOOKS LIKE YOU AND I ARE GONNA HAVE A ROOMIE.

# CHAPTER FIVE

It was hard to sleep the next morning, what with all the noise of people checking out. About noon, someone slammed a door in the next room over and I gave up. I'd only had a few hours of actual shuteye, but I didn't need much.

The only problem was, I didn't want to move. Fang had crawled under the sheet and was curled up next to me, as close as he could get without actually being on top of me. It was kind of adorable. His snarky attitude must be a façade.

YEAH, JUST KEEP TELLING YOURSELF THAT, SISTER.

But he licked my hand and snuggled even closer.

A short knock came at the door and it opened suddenly, surprising me.

Fang was out from under the sheet in a flash and growling at the Latina who stood in the doorway, holding towels.

She shrieked and slammed the door shut, letting loose with a stream of rapid-fire Spanish.

As my heartbeat tried to get back to normal, I said, "Geez, Fang, overreact much? It was just the maid."

Since it was daylight—time for all good little vampires to be in bed—I hadn't been worried. Anyone else I could handle.

WHY DIDN'T YOU PUT OUT THE "DO NOT DISTURB" SIGN?

Because I hadn't thought of it. I didn't spend much time in hotel rooms. "Why didn't you?" I countered.

FLASH—NO HANDS, GENIUS.

Okay, he had a point, but he could have reminded me.

Oh well, no biggie—we were moving anyway, just as soon as I settled where we'd be living. I showered and dressed and let Fang out to do his thing. It was almost time to meet Dan's sister and I'd already paid for one night in this flea trap—I wasn't paying for any more. So, I tied my duffel on the back of the motorcycle, put Fang on the front, and left to meet Dan, grabbing burgers on the way for both of us. Fang liked burgers, too—go figure.

I'd just have to find a way to put Dan off until I could find a suitable place on my own. I wasn't really against having a roommate, but it would be hard enough keeping my demon nature from my partner. The thought of also having to keep it hidden where I lived sounded like a real pain.

But when I pulled up to the place, my heart sank. It was about as far away from the hotel we'd stayed in last night as you could get. Centrally located, it looked fairly new, with rounded adobe architecture, well-kept grounds, a pool, gym, walking paths under big shady oak trees . . . just the kind of place I'd love to live.

FACE IT—YOU'RE TOAST.

Not yet. After all, this wasn't the only place to live in San Antonio.

Dan waved me down and I parked where he indicated. He looked amused when I unzipped Fang from my vest. "Does he always ride there?"

"Yeah, but I'm thinking of getting a sidecar for him." Just as soon as I could afford it.

GOOD PLAN. THERE IS SUCH A THING AS TOO MUCH TOGETHERNESS.

"Are these apartments or condos?" I asked.

"Townhouses—she's renting one from the owner who had to move to another state. But the advantage is that most people own theirs so you get a more stable population here."

"Oh."

IT JUST SOUNDS BETTER AND BETTER.

"Well, come on and meet Gwen."

Gwen opened the door. She didn't look a lot like her brother. A couple of years younger than Dan, she had red hair cut short in a tousled 'do. She immediately dropped to a crouch to beam at Fang. "How cute. Can I pet him? Is he friendly?"

I looked down at the hellhound. *Are you?* I really didn't know how he'd react to others.

In answer, he nudged Gwen's hand with his nose, as if asking to be petted.

*Shameless beggar. Why couldn't you help me out here and growl at her?*

As Gwen oohed and ahed over the dog, even saying his name

was cute, Fang said, I LIKE TO BE PETTED. AND I LIKE HER.

Unfortunately, I liked her, too. She was outgoing and bubbly as she showed me around the place. The unit had two bedrooms, separated for privacy, two baths, and a kitchen that was way nicer than Mom's. She had it decorated with a lot of bright colors and cool funky accessories. Plus it had a door that let out onto a nice patio and beyond to an open area where Fang could roam free if he wanted.

It was perfect. Damn. Trying to find a reason to turn it down, I said, "Great kitchen, but I don't cook."

"No biggie," Gwen said cheerfully. "I do—and I'd love to cook for more than one. Plus I bake whenever I can. You'd just need to help clean up and pay for half the groceries. Oh, and provide your own furniture for your bedroom. I have everything else."

That sounded reasonable, but I wasn't looking for reasonable. I was looking for a reason to turn it down. "I work nights."

"So do I," Gwen said with a smile. "And this place is quiet in the daytime."

"I don't know if I can afford it." It was way nicer than I'd expected.

"Your motorcycle is paid for and you're too young to have any real debt," Dan said. "I know what Ramirez will be paying you. Trust me, you can handle it—and still afford to buy the sidecar for Fang."

Oh, great, there went that excuse. "Fang sheds a lot," I said apologetically.

She waved that away as if it were inconsequential. "Oh, I'm used to dog hair. We always had it around the house growing up. I've just been so busy with school then my job that I haven't had a chance to get a dog yet." She glanced at Fang. "He seems very well-behaved. You can even get one of those dog doors to put in the patio door so he can go out when he wants."

NOW WE'RE TALKING.

She smiled at me. "Please take it. We'll have fun."

How could I get out of this gracefully, without hurting anyone's feelings? "I don't know . . . ."

"Excuse us," Dan said to his sister and pulled me outside onto the patio. He shut the door while Fang stayed inside with Gwen. "What's your problem?" He sounded irritated.

I shrugged. "This is the first place I've seen. I just want to keep my options open."

"Come on—you and I both know you won't get a better deal. What's your real beef? You got something against my sister?"

"Of course not." To tell the truth, I envied the easy, loving relationship the two obviously had together.

"Then why? This place is perfect for you and you know it."

Annoyed, I gave him part of the reason. "Yeah, it would be, if I didn't suspect you were doing it to keep an eye on me. I don't need a big brother, you know."

He snorted. "Obviously. That's not why I want you here."

"Then why?"

"So you can keep an eye on Gwen for me. I worry about *her*. She works nights at the ER, and sees a lot of things she shouldn't."

"Like what?"

"Like fang marks on victims. She's too damned stubborn to find another job, and doesn't want to ask her big brother for help. I'd feel a whole lot better if she had someone living with her she could count on in case of trouble. Someone like you."

Oh. He was asking me for a favor. Shoot, that put a whole new spin on things. After all, the guy had gotten me a job, not to mention a birthday cake. I owed him. And I did like the place . . . and Gwen. But could I live here and still keep my secret safe?

Fang scratched at the patio door and glared at me through the glass. The glass didn't stop his thoughts, though. TAKE IT.

Well, shoot, I was outnumbered. And the thought of searching for another place—or living anywhere else—was depressing. Heck, why not? It would be nice to be able to tell Mom that I didn't need her and that I'd found a job and a really nice place to live all on my own. Maybe even something resembling a family.

*No—don't go there.* Accepting human-Val didn't mean they'd accept demon-Val.

I opened the patio door so both Dan and Gwen could hear. "Okay, you got a deal."

"Good," Gwen said with a happy bounce. "It'll be fun—and

Dan lives close by so you can share a ride to work together."

Close by? Had I just been conned? But when I raised an eyebrow at Dan, he muttered for my ears only, "Not close enough. My place is on the other side of the complex. It's not like I can watch her place all night or anything."

Okay, I could see that. Especially since he knew exactly what kind of things roamed the night streets of San Antonio.

I nodded and Gwen said, "Let's go shopping!"

I grinned. I'd never had girlfriends to shop with, just Mom and Jen. It sounded like fun—another new adventure.

I left my duffel at Gwen's, but Fang didn't want to have anything to do with shopping, so he elected to stay and check out his new digs. Mom, Rick, and Jen were all working at the store, so Gwen and Dan helped me pick up my bedroom furniture, then Gwen— a serious shopper—insisted on helping me buy sheets, towels, and the dog door for Fang.

Even better, I found something cooler than a sidecar at the motorcycle shop. When I got back to the townhouse, I called Fang to try it out. They had a sheepskin-lined leather bucket seat sort of thing with a harness, and they'd attached it to the back of my Valkyrie for me. Fang jumped up into it and turned around a few times, scratching at the sheepskin, then settled in.

This'll work, he said approvingly. But I won't need the straps.

"Here, I got you these, too."

I slid a pair of brown leather goggles on his head. "These'll keep the wind and grit out of your eyes."

How do I look?

Cool. Very cool.

Dan laughed. "All he needs is a hood and a long scarf trailing behind him to look like Snoopy chasing the Red Baron."

Fang pawed at the goggles. I don't want to look like some stupid cartoon beagle.

You don't, I assured him. Besides, they're practical. Out loud, I said, "Well, I think he looks cute. All the other dogs will be jealous and want one. Don't you think so, Gwen?"

Gwen nodded. "Totally."

Now that Gwen had agreed with me, Fang said, Okay, I can

LIVE WITH CUTE.

But it was now time to go to work and it made sense for the three of us to ride to work together in Dan's SUV—a Toyota Highlander. It wasn't as large as the SCU truck, but very roomy. At some point, I'd have to look at buying a car of my own. A motorcycle wasn't always practical.

At the station, we got into the SCU truck after the shift briefing. It felt kind of weird to have a job other than at the bookstore, but I was more than ready for it. "So where do we start looking for this vein of vampires?"

Dan thought a minute and flipped through his notebook to check his notes. He was extremely thorough—I learned he had notes from all the previous shift briefings and worked after hours to cross-reference them and keep track of trends all over the city. "Let's head south."

As he put the vehicle in gear and headed in that direction, I asked, "What do you expect to find?"

"I don't have any notes on multiple perps, except maybe in one area. Let's check it out."

He drove to a neighborhood most people would steer clear of this time of night. With all the graffiti on the buildings, it looked like gang territory. In defiance of the chilly weather, some guys, mostly Hispanic dudes wearing gang colors, were playing basketball in a schoolyard court.

Dan nodded toward them. "If anyone knows about a gang of vamps working the area, it'll be another gang."

"And what makes you think they'll tell you anything?"

"I know a couple of these kids. Why don't you stay here while I ask them a few questions?"

"Yeah, like you stayed when I asked you to. Not a chance." I got out, but figured it was safer for Fang to stay in the truck. Though vampires were evil, they were a known quantity. Gangbangers could be psychotic, unpredictable.

NO CHALLENGE, Fang said, sounding bored, so I left him in the truck and followed Dan to the chain link fence.

"Heads up," one of them said.

They all stopped playing and turned to give Dan stone-faced

glares. It didn't seem to faze him. "Hey, Julio," he called through the fence.

One of the guys, a short wiry dark-skinned kid with a do-rag tied around his head, swaggered over. Julio looked me up and down, obviously liking what he saw. He rubbed his crotch and leered at me. "Nice piece—"

"I don't think you want to finish that sentence," Dan interrupted. "Val kicked the crap out of a guy twice her size the other day and all he did was look at her wrong. You don't want to piss her off."

Not strictly accurate, but I gave him points for trying. And Lola wasn't even tempted.

Julio glanced at me and I tried to look like a gangsta from the 'hood, but when Fang gave a mental snort I could hear even from here, I realized I just couldn't pull it off. I settled for giving him a predator's smile and letting the demon flash in my eyes.

Good—that unsettled him. It always disturbed them when I showed no fear.

"Whatcha want?" Julio asked, swiftly covering his unease. "We ain't done nothin'."

I really doubted that, but Dan said, "All we want to do is ask you some questions."

Julio glanced back at his friends as if for support and said, "We don't know nothin' neither."

"Not even about a new gang moving in to your territory?" Dan asked.

"Don't know nothin' 'bout no new gang. And iffen they come here, they won't stay for long. We'll take care of 'em."

There was a chorus of agreement from behind him—idiot boys posturing for each other, parading their machismo.

"These are different. They kill people for no reason—three in this area last month. They leave marks like these." Dan peeled back the collar of his shirt and showed them where the vamp had bitten him.

Julio was impassive, but one guy behind him said softly, "Them's the same marks they found on Hector's body."

"You know who done that?" Julio asked Dan.

"Not yet. But we intend to find out. You know of any groups around here who might do something like that?"

Most of the boys shook their heads, but Julio looked thoughtful then nodded toward a notice taped to a pole. "How 'bout them? That just went up an hour ago."

The poster advertised a rally for the New Blood Movement. They invited all humans to come take part and meet real vampires, help them enter the mainstream. It was scheduled for the first day of *Los Dias de los Muertes*—the Days of the Dead— on the first of November, four days from now.

How . . . cute. During the Days of the Dead, it was supposed to be easier for the dead to visit the living, and the living used the time to honor their deceased loved ones. Having vampires co-opt the holiday for their own purpose just seemed wrong, even if it wasn't *my* holiday. Then again, the way the poster was worded, it was unclear if they were for real . . . or just playacting.

"It's worth a look-see," I said.

Dan nodded and tore the poster off. "Thanks," he said to Julio.

As we headed back to the truck, someone called out, "Take 'em down, man."

Dan glanced back over his shoulder and gave them a casual wave. "Count on it."

As we got back in the truck, he said, "So, are you going to tell me how you can, as they put it, take the vamps down so easily, or are you going to continue keeping me in the dark?"

"I'm not keeping you in the dark. We've talked about this," I said warily, playing dumb.

"You know what I'm asking. Why are you unafraid to confront gangbangers . . . or fangbangers? Able to take down a guy twice your size? Having thirty vampire kills to your credit at only eighteen?" He raised an eyebrow at me. "Not exactly your normal teenaged girl."

DOESN'T TAKE A GENIUS TO FIGURE THAT OUT.

I knew he'd be suspicious. "Just a fluke of nature, I guess." When he snorted, I decided to give him something a little more plausible. "You know my parents run a new age bookstore?"

"Yeah?"

"Well, we found this book on vampires that must have been written about real ones 'cause it explained a lot about their strengths and weaknesses. Plus, I've had a lot of practice—done a lot of training." To keep him off balance, I said, "You could use some yourself."

I expected that to piss him off, but instead, he said, "Yeah, I could."

I glanced at him in surprise. "You think?" It seemed too easy.

"Yeah, well, Charlene was a wake-up call. I thought I could handle anything, but she showed me I can't."

Charlene? Oh yeah, the vamp who'd played tonsil-hockey with him.

He shifted uneasily, and I wondered if he was uncomfortable remembering the lust she'd brought to life in him.

Curious, I asked, "How long have you been doing this?"

"I've only been in the SCU for a few months. My former partner was training me, but he got . . . " He trailed off, staring into the distance, his expression bleak.

FANGED TO DEATH? SUCKED DRY? BUTCHERED?

"Dead?" I asked, which sounded better than Fang's alternatives.

"Yeah, he got dead—killed by one of those monsters." The expression on his face was murderous. "No one should die like that. These things shouldn't be allowed to exist, and I want to kill every last one of them." He turned to me. "Can you help me do that, give me some pointers?"

Impressed by his willingness to be taught by a girl, I said, "Sure." Then felt immediately uncertain. Could I do it okay? After all, I'd never taught anyone before. I'd always been taught, by martial arts teachers and Rick. That was it—I'd teach him the way Rick taught me.

"Good."

The next few days fell into a kind of routine as I settled in to my new life. Fang and I slept until about noon, hung out with Gwen—who turned out to be a great cook—during the early afternoon, then trained with Dan during the late afternoon and hunted down other leads at night.

I taught Dan how to counter their superhuman speed with everything I could think of. Most martial arts took too long to master, so I didn't try to teach him any, though I recommended he find a class in the relatively unknown swords form of Tai Chi for the future. Not only were the long pointy things great to keep your distance from the undead, but they came in quite handy for lopping heads off. That was, if you could find a way to carry them around without alarming the rest of the population.

Luckily, he took to the crossbow like a natural. Unfortunately they weren't a great option since they were only good if he was able to catch the vamps at a distance, plus the weapons were just a tad conspicuous to carry on the street. So, for close-in fighting, Dan carried silver and small vials of holy water besides the stakes.

He started wearing heavy silver around his neck, wrists, and waist. Though he wore most of his metal under a turtleneck, he took some teasing about his new look from the other scuzzies. But Dan was smart—he didn't see it as jewelry, just weaponry that would help keep him alive.

On the fourth afternoon of our training at the station gym, I pretended to be a vampire and rushed Dan, catching him in a clinch. The last time I'd done that, he'd been unable to reach any of the weapons inside his jacket and had "died."

But this time he was ready. He flipped a stake out of the special harness he'd rigged in one sleeve and a vial out of the other. He popped the cork off the vial with his thumb in a swift motion and dumped it in my face. When I blinked in surprise, he brought the stake down to within millimeters from my heart.

Grinning, Dan said, "Your face is eaten up by holy water and there's a stake in your heart. You're dead, Madame Vampire."

GOTCHA!

Excellent. Even Fang sounded like he was coming to approve of Dan. But lingering with the guy on top of me after the "kill" was a bad idea. Our energy fields merged seamlessly and I had a mental vision of Lola popping her cork, oozing out of her bottle to let me know she was a whole lot interested in the very nice male body plastered against mine. Unfortunately, that part was in the physical realm.

And, from the odd expression on Dan's face, he was feeling it, too.

I DON'T THINK THAT'S SUCH A GOOD IDEA . . . .

Me either. I was so not ready for this. Guys, dating, making out . . . the thought of it made me feel all mixed up inside. I wasn't sure I even wanted to deal with these human feelings, let alone with what Lola wanted. Especially with Dan. Yeah, he was a total hottie, but he was way more experienced than me, not to mention the fact that he was my partner.

I scooted out from under him immediately, wiping the water from my face. "Good job," I babbled. "I think you're ready to take on a few vampires now." Mentally, I shoved Lola back in the bottle. It took some doing, but I managed it. Dan gave me a knowing look, but I averted my gaze and rolled to my feet. "How's your mental block coming?"

I hadn't been able to help him with that, since I didn't really need or use one, so some of the other SCU operatives had worked with him, giving him some tips and tricks they'd learned the hard way. I had, however, cautiously revealed that I was able to feel it if a vampire tried to enthrall me. Dan just seemed to take it as part of my general weirdness.

"The block is good," Dan said. "It takes a conscious effort to maintain it, but I think it's working. I won't know for sure until a vamp actually tries to use it on me." He rose to his feet. "I'm ready for the rally tonight. How about you?"

Relieved that he hadn't mentioned what had just passed between us, I said, "Sure. Let's do it."

Lola stirred again, eager to get on with it. But was the lust in anticipation of the rally . . . or in reaction to what had just happened with Dan? I wasn't sure, so I'd just have to make sure the rally took care of those pesky needs of my inner demon so she'd keep her greedy hands off my partner.

# CHAPTER SIX

By the time we reached the large meeting hall near downtown, the rally had already started, so Dan parked near the back exit. Fang sniffed the air and the hair on his neck ruffled as he let out a low growl.

VAMPIRE.

"What's he doing?" Dan asked.

"He smells vampire."

Dan glanced at him in surprise. "I didn't know he could do that."

WHAT YOU DON'T KNOW COULD FILL AN ENCYCLOPEDIA.

*Give him a break, Fang—he's only human.* "He's been training, too."

"Good to know. Can you tell how close they are?"

I listened. "Nothing nearby. Must be the vamps inside."

Dan glanced at Fang. "But this time, you should leave him here. I know the organizers promised complete safety on their flyer, but a small dog in an excited crowd—not good."

I frowned. "You're probably right. But you can never be too careful. Tell you what, Fang. You stay here, and run for help if we need it, okay?"

Dan rolled his eyes. "Geez, I know your dog is smart, but who do you think he is—Lassie?"

I hadn't realized I'd said that out loud. "He's better than Lassie—he can take down a vampire."

DAMN STRAIGHT.

Just not dozens of them. Of course, he was willing to try, but I wasn't willing to lose him in the attempt. And he was smart enough to know he couldn't handle it.

I'LL STAY HERE, BE YOUR BACK-UP.

*Good—do that.*

Shrugging, Dan led the way into the hall where the rally was in full swing.

The hall had once seen better days as a dinner theater, but now the wooden floor was scuffed and badly in need of polishing. In the harsh lighting, I could see the blood-red velvet curtains framing the stage were worn and shiny in spots. The crowd didn't seem to care, though. Most of those attending were near my age, and the dress of the day seemed to be the Goth or Emo look, with others wearing skeleton or vampire costumes in honor of the occasion.

But the real scary ones were those who wore no costume or make-up at all—the vampires in the crowd. They gave the gathering an edge of danger, the feeling that one wrong word was the only spark it needed to explode.

"This place is a train wreck waiting to happen," Dan muttered.

"Yeah." But with all the security and the public nature of the rally, I hoped it would be all right.

"Any idea how many vamps are here?"

I shook my head. "Can't tell for sure. I can only sense them if they're using their powers. Some of them are, to cloud people's minds about their true appearance. Probably most of them. Not more than twenty or so, I'd say."

"Not as bad as I thought. Can you point one out to me?"

"That one. He's projecting a Goth image. But he's more like a geek caught in the Fifties."

I felt Dan relax beside me. "Good—I see him as he really is— my block must be working."

We watched for a few minutes as a man on a raised stage at the back of the hall spoke to the audience. The vamp, who introduced himself simply as Alejandro, had golden brown skin, long dark brown hair, patrician good looks, and a dramatic black cape that he flourished when he gestured. His seductive voice and charismatic manner were kinda hokey and theatrical, but the crowd ate it up. Though his English was excellent, he had the slight accent and phrasing of a person whose native language was Spanish.

"Yes, vampires are real. But there is no reason to fear, my friends. We in the New Blood Movement wish only to live in harmony with humans. There is no need for fear or strife."

Oh yeah? Tell that to the people they'd sucked dry.

He continued. "We have established blood banks throughout the city where it is easy for humans to make deposits and for vampires to withdraw it as needed." He paused, raising his finger dramatically. "But why should you donate, you ask? It is simple. We will happily reimburse you for this fluid that is so vital to our existence. And it is your choice whether you are reimbursed in cash . . . or in pleasure."

He went on to explain that there was no need for the messy process of sinking fangs into necks and other regions of the body. Unless the human wanted to, of course, then they would arrange discreet rooms to donate blood.

And the suckers—or rather, potential suckees—seemed to be buying it. At least some of them were. Some seemed to think it was a big joke, others scoffed, but the vast majority seemed to be so mesmerized by Alejandro that they didn't even question the fact that he claimed vampires were real.

Dan leaned down. "Can you tell if he's coercing them, using his mind to control their thoughts?"

"It would be impossible to control this many people at once. But I do feel him sending out waves of goodwill, urging trust, cooperation, and acceptance."

He grimaced. "And the susceptible are soaking it up. Let's get closer."

We pushed our way down to the front and a surge in the crowd shoved me up against a vamp standing near the stage. He gave me a lewd look, baring his fangs. Between them and his dreadlocks, he was kind of disgusting.

"Sorry," I said, backing away. Didn't want to start anything. And here, it was too easy for guys to get too close, for our fields to overlap. I edged closer to a knot of girls.

The vamp leered at me. "Don't I know you, sweet thing?"

"Don't think so," I said and turned to face the stage.

Alejandro continued to address the audience, calling upon the unaffiliated vampires in the crowd to join the Movement, to live in harmony with humans and enjoy the perks of having a steady source of sustenance. As for humans, he spouted the benefits and joys of donating blood, hinting at carnal delights for those humans who personally offered up their necks to feed the Movement.

"But enough words," Alejandro finally said. "Let us provide a little demonstration. If my lieutenants would please come to the stage?" He gestured toward the wings.

"Austin . . . " A tall, lean cowboy—complete with the requisite hat, boots, and jeans—joined him, tipping his hat to the crowd. He grinned and the women went nuts. It worked for Marlboro cigarettes, why not the Movement?

"Luis . . . " A handsome Latino joined the cowboy. Wearing a well-trimmed goatee with his long hair clubbed back in a ponytail at the base of his neck, Luis bowed, looking like some sort of historical Spanish aristocrat. He elicited oohs and ahs from the women in the crowd.

"Rosa . . . " A sexy Latina with long flowing hair and a Marilyn Monroe body gave the crowd a come-hither look. The men cheered.

Going by these specimens, you'd think all vampires were totally hot. Talk about false advertising . . . .

Alejandro continued, "And, last but not least . . . Lily!"

As the men in the crowd yelled their appreciation, Dan stiffened beside me. The tall, thin blonde, wearing a slinky hot pink cocktail dress and a short, edgy hairstyle, joined the others on the stage, and Dan muttered something I didn't catch.

"What's wrong?" I asked.

"Nothing," Dan said in a clipped tone.

Yeah, right. But I didn't call him on it, because I wanted to hear the rest of what Alejandro had to say.

"Giving blood can be painless, even pleasurable," the vamp said with a knowing smile. "Who would like to try it with one of my lovely assistants?"

On cue, the assistants all smiled, baring fangs.

A feeling like desire surged out of him over the audience. The sudden surge in lust, thrill, and anticipation throughout the hall made Lola perk up and pay attention. Uh-oh. A hot-cold sensation washed through me, leaving me tingling and hyperaware of Dan and all the vamps in the place.

I had a mental flash of Lola's bottle rocking and the cork threatening to pop off. I couldn't let her loose now when things were so unstable. Would she go berserker with so many targets around? I stomped her down, quick, but could still feel her awareness simmering just underneath my skin.

Dan looked at me oddly. "You okay?"

"Fine," I muttered. Just peachy.

The vamp I'd bumped into earlier shot me a snarky look, apparently annoyed that we were interrupting the show. He did a double-take and said accusingly, "Wait. I *do* know you. You're the Slayer."

What? How did he know that?

Behind me, someone said, "The Slayer? Are you sure?"

Bewildered, I turned toward the second voice, and the male vamp's eyes narrowed. "It *is* her. Hey," he yelled up to the stage, his voice carrying clearly in the expectant silence of the hall, "I thought you guaranteed safe passage for everyone attending tonight."

As Alejandro waited for volunteers to make their way on to the stage, he smiled at the heckler. "Yes, I did."

"Then what is the Slayer doing here? She slaughters vampires for fun."

Appalled, I could do nothing but gape. I'd better defuse this quick, or they'd go all Vin Diesel on my ass.

Angry mutterings arose from the vamps in the crowd, and the hair on my arms rose, prickling with the awareness of rising danger.

"I'm not here for that," I protested to Alejandro. I smoothed the hair on my arms, trying to calm them, calm Lola.

"You see," Alejandro said with an engaging smile. "She isn't here to hurt anyone."

"Yeah, right," someone yelled.

"She's killed a lot of us," came another shouted accusation.

How many innocents have *you* killed? I wanted to ask, but this was so not the time for it.

The tension rose even more palpably in the room, making my skin crawl and testing my control of Lola. The vampires milled around, muttering to each other, glaring at the stage and me. They were obviously working themselves up to something. If someone didn't do something real quick, people might get hurt.

Alejandro must have noticed it, too, for I could feel him sending out calming waves to the humans in the audience, urging them to leave, quietly, safely. They streamed out, hurrying, but not dangerously so. All but Dan, whose block was solid.

The vampire security guards appeared on stage, leveling crossbows at the vamps in the crowd. *Time to leave.* Unfortunately, our way was blocked by the vamps who were closing in behind us, muttering. They were still kept at bay by the threat of the crossbows, but were beginning to gain confidence the more they surrounded us.

I couldn't take them all on—demon or no demon. There must be at least twenty-five or thirty. The only safe way out was through the back of the hall.

Dan muttered in my ear, "Go out through the stage."

My thoughts exactly. I vaulted up onto the stage, followed closely by Dan. Alejandro's lieutenants moved to shield him, but I held my hands up to show I was innocent of any intention to harm him. They let me pass and I backed slowly toward the rear of the stage.

I'd never seen so many vamps in one place. Pulling out a stake would be a bad idea. They'd probably take it as an invitation to rush me.

But, Dan wasn't backing up with me. In fact, the cop was headed toward Alejandro and his lieutenants. "Dan," I called.

He ignored me as he made a beeline for the tall blonde. What was wrong with him?

The mutterings grew louder as the vamps clustered around the stage and the last of the humans hurried out the exits. Soon, the vamps were shouting toward the stage and each other.

"You brought her here on purpose—to identify us."

"Naw, he's using her as a threat to force us to join his pathetic Movement."

"Yeah, they're working together."

"No, no," Alejandro said. "The only way you'll get hurt is if you initiate violence." But his charisma didn't seem to work as well on the vamps as it did on the humans.

If only I could grab Dan and get him out of here. But he was whispering urgently to the blonde who was trying to shake him off.

Alejandro made an imperious gesture and the undead security guards lined up at the edge of the stage, menacing the angry vampires below. Vampires fighting vampires? Heck, they'd do my job for me.

But Alejandro *had* made a point of ensuring all the humans were safe. I hated to admit it, but his heart seemed to be in the right place . . . even if it wasn't beating. Could it be he was really trying to improve relations between vamps and humans like he claimed? Maybe this group wasn't responsible for the increased attacks.

The vampires below were working themselves into a frenzy. I sighed. My appearance had started this, though they seemed to be blaming Alejandro. Maybe if I removed myself—and him—the incipient riot would fizzle out. Besides, he was our best bet for learning what was going on with this group.

I made sure his personal guard saw my hands were miles away from any weapon as I moved closer to Alejandro and muttered, "Shouldn't we get out of here. Like now?" Before Lola broke free and I did something everyone would regret.

He frowned. "My car won't be here for another hour."

"We can't wait that long. Come on, we'll get you out of here."

Austin grinned at him and said, "Go. We can take care of these varmints without you." The others nodded agreement and formed a line behind the guards, still shielding Alejandro.

I pulled Alejandro toward the rear of the stage, yelling, "Dan, come on!"

Dan hesitated, then grabbed the arm of the tall blonde and said something to her that I couldn't hear.

"Tell her to come, too," I urged Alejandro. Anything to get Dan out of there.

The vamp leader gestured, and the woman followed.

Finally. With relief, I hurried Dan and the two vampires out the back, and heard a roar of anger as the vamps realized their quarry was leaving. Sounds of fighting soon followed. How long could Alejandro's people hold them off?

We raced toward the truck and Fang heard us coming. He bristled with his teeth bared. "It's all right," I called to him. "Friends."

I jerked open the door and dove into the cramped back seat beside him. "Don't touch the metal," I warned the vamps. "Silver." They piled a little more cautiously into the front and, wasting no time, Dan started the truck and peeled out of there just as the vamps came boiling out of the hall.

"Go," Alejandro shouted, his head hanging out the passenger side window to check on our pursuers.

Dan went. The howling undead chased us on foot, apparently thinking they could outrun the truck. They were fast, but not that fast. But when Dan slowed down to turn a corner, one actually caught hold of the door frame at the open driver's window. His hand sizzled at contact with the silver, but he wouldn't let go.

DINNER!

Fang darted forward and chomped down on his fingers as Dan elbowed the undead creep in the face. The vamp screeched and let go, and none of his friends were fast enough to catch us. Soon, we left the other vamps in our dust. With the threat gone, Lola subsided and I could relax.

*Good job,* I thought at Fang.

He gave me a doggie grin. GOTTA GET MY KICKS WHERE I CAN, SINCE YOU SAID THESE OTHER TWO ARE OFF LIMITS. WHAT'S UP WITH THAT?

I filled him in as Dan concentrated on his driving. "Where to?" he asked.

Alejandro hesitated, evidently unwilling to let us know the location of his lair. "Anywhere—it doesn't matter. Away from downtown."

Finally, the woman spoke. "The blood bank on the south side. It's closed tonight because of the rally."

Alejandro nodded. "Good idea." He gave Dan directions then flipped open his cell phone and gave instructions to his driver to meet him there.

A vampire using a cell phone . . . . That just seemed wrong, somehow.

He made another call, this time to Austin, asking how things were going at the hall. Alejandro hung up and said, "Now that we're gone, things have calmed down there. No one was hurt . . . much."

Meaning the vamps could heal whatever damage they'd taken.

I nodded, but Dan said nothing, and the woman between Dan and Alejandro was stiff as a board. The tension between them was almost tangible. Weird. What was going on? Alejandro slanted a questioning glance toward me in the back seat. I shrugged, not knowing any more than he did.

Apparently, the vamp didn't believe me, because I soon felt a tickling in my mind. Fang growled, sensing the vamp's attempt by my reaction. "That won't work," I said flatly, soothing the dog's fur.

The tickling vanished. "What won't work?" Alejandro asked.

"You, trying to control my mind. It won't work."

"Why not?" Alejandro laid his arm on the back of the seat and smiled at me, oozing charm and sex appeal with seeming effortlessness. He didn't even need mind control to do it—it came naturally for him.

I bet a lot of women fell for that Latin charm, but I couldn't forget he was one of the undead. Nor, apparently, could the succubus inside me. Lola wasn't even tempted. I just gave him a you-gotta-be-kidding-me look.

He laughed, his voice caressing and full of sexual promises. "I see. I cannot control your mind because you are . . . special."

"Damn straight."

Still grinning, the vamp leader said, "I would expect nothing less of the Slayer."

I scowled at him. "How did you and everyone else learn about me, anyway? And who is calling me the Slayer?"

Alejandro managed to make a shrug look elegant. "A young girl has been showing your picture around, calling you the Slayer, trying to find you."

Oh, crap—not Jen, surely. "Was she about sixteen? Blond? Look like a cheerleader?"

Seeming amused, Alejandro nodded.

It had to be Jennifer. Who else was that moronic?

That got Dan's attention. He shot a glance at Alejandro. "Did she say why she was looking for Val?"

Naw, she probably just had a death wish.

Alejandro's eyes twinkled. "Shall we exchange information, then?"

"Okay," Dan said. "Tit for tat." He pulled up in front of the blood bank, which looked like a renovated hotel, and Alejandro invited us in.

*Are you coming?* I asked Fang.

He sniffed disdainfully. IF YOU'RE JUST GONNA *TALK*, YOU DON'T NEED ME. I'LL STAY HERE. YELL IF YOU'RE ACTUALLY GONNA, YOU KNOW, KILL SOMETHING.

He sounded miffed that I wasn't automatically going into slayer mode, but I was curious about this supposed kinder, gentler vein of vampires—not to mention Dan's odd fascination with the woman beside him and what the heck Jen was doing hanging around a bunch of vamps.

Alejandro and the woman led the way inside a darkened lobby, and Dan and I followed. "What's up with you?" I whispered, but Dan ignored me. If he hadn't had such a set expression on his face, I might have thought he was enthralled. But, nope, he was just being Dan—stubborn as all get out.

Alejandro took us up the elevator to the fourth floor and showed us to a state-of-the-art conference room with all kinds of electronic gadgets. I couldn't begin to guess what most of them were for.

"So," the charismatic man said, smiling at me, "I am Alejandro. I cannot continue calling such a lovely young woman the Slayer. You are . . . ?"

Lovely. Uh-huh. "No one. Just call me Buffy," I said. It was a stupid name, but convenient.

He grimaced. "And your charming friend?"

"Dan Sullivan," the woman answered, her face expressionless. "He's a cop."

So they did know each other. But Dan wasn't happy about it, if his expression was any indication.

"And this is Lily Armstrong," Dan said, his voice tight.

"How do you know her?" I asked.

"Former fiancée," he said curtly.

I couldn't tell whether Lily's new dental work was a surprise to Dan or an old wound. I felt for him, I really did, but I hoped it wouldn't distract him from what was going on.

Alejandro raised one elegant eyebrow as if inviting them to explain more, but neither seemed inclined to fill us in. Dan remained standing next to me, glaring at Lily. The woman didn't respond, doing her best to ignore him as she stood by Alejandro's side like a good little flunky.

She ignored me, too, like I wasn't even good enough to notice— no threat in any department. How annoying.

Alejandro shrugged and quirked an eyebrow at Dan. "So. An answer for an answer?" At Dan's nod, the vampire leader asked, "What did you hope to gain by causing a riot at my rally?"

Dan scowled. "It wasn't intentional. We just wanted to learn more about your group."

"Yeah," I added. "I had no idea anyone would know who I was."

"Why did you wish to know more of us?"

"No, you first," I said. "What did the young girl with my picture want?"

Alejandro shrugged. "She wanted to learn more about our organization, find you, and apparently threaten us with your reputation. Her name I do not know."

Good. My jaw tightened anyway. Obviously, Mom hadn't given Jen my new number. But if my sister continued on this stupid course, she might find more than she bargained for.

"And your reason for being at the rally?" Alejandro probed.

Dan paused, then said, "The San Antonio Police Department heard about your group and wanted us to find out more, see if you're dangerous."

"And are we?"

Alejandro talked a good game, but was he telling the truth? I didn't know.

"You tell me," Dan said.

"I assure you I am sincere," Alejandro said with a hand to his heart. In that cape, the gesture made him look like something out of *The Three Musketeers,* and I wondered just how old he was.

Dan snorted. "Then why are there so many vampire kills in the city?"

"That is something I am trying to stop," Alejandro said with a frown.

"How? By bringing them into the fold?"

The vamp inclined his head. "Just so. If I can convince them to join the New Blood Movement, use our blood banks, they will have no reason to feed on humans without their consent."

Dan let out a short bark of laughter. "No reason except for being evil."

"Ah, but that is a common misunderstanding," Alejandro exclaimed. "Becoming a vampire does not make one evil."

"Then what does?"

"You do not understand. One of the side effects of becoming a vampire is that a person becomes much more of what they already were."

I didn't get it.

Apparently, Dan didn't either. "Explain."

"Their . . . primary characteristics are enhanced. For example, if someone is bad to begin with, they will become even more evil after the change. However, if someone lives by honor and justice, such as my *vaquero,* Austin, he will now espouse those attributes even more."

It made a kind of weird sense, but I wasn't sure I bought it. "And you?" I asked. "Don't tell me—you were a Don Juan wannabe."

Alejandro surprised me by laughing. "No, I was a leader of men . . . and women. A good one."

A Spanish aristocrat, I bet. Home-schooled or not, I knew there weren't a lot of good, noble aristocrats who cared more for their fellow man than power and wealth.

Dan's gaze shifted to Lily, as if wondering what characteristics of hers had been enhanced. Annoyed, I wondered what Dan had seen in the Ice Queen.

Who was I kidding? What guy wouldn't be attracted to someone who was tall, blond, and sophisticated? A real woman, not a scruffy kid like me. I asked the question for him. "What about Lily?"

"She has amazing managerial abilities, and a knowledge of modern technology that has become invaluable to the organization."

"Why?" Dan asked, the sound almost exploding from him.

Okay, surprise then. He hadn't known.

That was all he said, but it was enough. The agonized confusion in his tone asked the rest for him. Why had she abandoned her future for a life as one of the undead?

Lily shook her head, not meeting his eyes. "My reasons are my own."

Dan's eyes narrowed. "Who did this to you?" His gaze flicked to Alejandro. "Him?"

Lily shrugged. "No, and it doesn't matter who did. It was my choice. My . . . necessity."

"Necessity?" Dan repeated, grabbing on to the word as if it were a clue. "What does that mean?"

"Mr. Sullivan, please," Alejandro interjected. "It is considered bad manners amongst my people to ask why and how they made the change." He paused. "But perhaps it will comfort you to know that many choose this life for . . . medical reasons. The healing powers of the *vampiro* are quite remarkable, healing any disease or wound short of death."

Dan faced Lily. "Were you ill?" Like me, Dan had evidently noticed that Alejandro hadn't actually claimed Lily was ill—he had just pointed out the possibility.

Lily turned her head, refusing to answer, refusing to let any expression show on her face. Dan's fists clenched and I felt a twinge of sympathy, though I wondered why he cared so much. She was his ex, wasn't she? Or maybe he hadn't quite gotten over her.

"So," Alejandro said into the silence, making the single word into a full sentence. "Now that you know what we are and what we plan, will your police department believe we mean no harm?"

"I'm not sure I do know or believe that," Dan said.

Alejandro gave him a reproachful look. "If you doubt it, you are welcome to come back here tomorrow night, visit our operation, and see that all is as we say it is."

Okay, I had to admit it looked like he was one of the good guys. But I'd never met a vampire with a white hat before—could we trust him?

Of course, this was Dan's call. Senior officer and all that. I'd feel a lot better if we could talk this over. I wasn't sure his head was in the game since his gaze kept straying to Lily.

In his favor, Alejandro *had* protected the humans at the rally by sending them away, and had even seemed concerned about the fate of those left behind. Could there really be such a thing as a *good* vampire?

Well, if there was, it sure played hell with my world view. But I couldn't condemn him for trying to make things better. Dan evidently came to the same conclusion.

"All right," he said. "I'll give you the benefit of the doubt. But if you make any mistake, if any one in your organization hurts any human, your ass is ash. Got it?"

He smiled. "Yes I have it."

"Good. Val, let's go." He hesitated for a moment, still glaring at Lily as if he would force her to give up her secrets.

"Dan," I said a little louder, "we have no more business here."

Dan grimaced, but followed me out the door. Once in the truck, he clenched the steering wheel so hard that his knuckles turned white, his expression full of frustration.

Fang and I shared a glance.

WHAT'S HIS PROBLEM?

*Later.* "Are you all right?" I asked Dan.

"Fine," he bit out.

Uh-huh. "I—I'm sorry about Lily," I said. Not sorry that Dan was no longer with the hot-shot hottie, but no one should have to learn a loved one—even a former loved one—had become a creature of the night.

He struggled with himself for a moment, but only one word emerged. "Yeah."

Guess he needed more time to take it in. "Hey, if you—"

"Change the subject," he grated, interrupting my offer of a shoulder to cry on.

Okay, sure. "Uh, how 'bout them Spurs?" I ventured.

He just gave me an incredulous stare.

Okay, what did I know about sports, anyway? I searched my mind for a new topic, hoping Dan wouldn't try to operate this vehicle until he calmed down. I had to give him something else to think about besides himself. And, frankly, any talk about our job would lead back to the one topic I was trying to avoid—Lily. I had to get his mind on something else.

*Okay, he can think about me.* "Maybe you could help me with something."

"Like what?" He definitely sounded interested, hopeful even.

How could I ask for his help in finding the other lust demon without telling him why? I'd just have to lie. "Right before I moved out, my stepfather hinted that I might have . . . other family in the area. On my father's side."

"So you're trying to find them?"

"Yes, but he didn't have a phone number or address or anything. Just a name—Lucas Blackburn."

"I assumed you tried the obvious first—the phone book."

"Yes. But none of the Blackburns listed knew a Lucas."

"He's unlisted, then," Dan mused. "That shouldn't be a problem. If he lives in San Antonio, I'll find him." He wrote down the name in his notebook.

"Thanks," I said, feeling genuinely grateful. Wow, I'd just been trying to distract the guy, but this was a huge bonus.

Sudden elation filled me as I realized what this meant. I'd finally find someone who seemed to know a heck of a lot more about my curse than I did. Maybe he could tell me more about how to handle it. And maybe . . . maybe he'd even know how to get rid of it forever.

# CHAPTER SEVEN

Dan couldn't follow up on Lucas Blackburn for me until we went off duty. As we looked for more vampires, I tried not to wonder if I was doing the right thing in attempting to find others like me.

Instead, I kept my mind firmly on the task at hand as we cruised for hours around the areas Dan had identified as most likely to show activity. While we drove, we speculated on whether the New Blood Movement could possibly be a good thing.

I was beginning to think they might be legit, but though Dan had given them the benefit of the doubt earlier, he was still convinced they were all bad. The Movement really changed the way we looked at things. SCU policy was that we couldn't stake the vamps unless we had proof they were really bad guys. Before tonight, it had been easy. See vamp attack, see vamp die. Now, it wasn't so black and white.

But the vamps were either celebrating the Day of the Dead in their own special ways, or were lying low for some reason 'cause we couldn't find any more. At least the constant vigilance seemed to keep Dan's mind occupied and off of Lily.

Finally, a couple of hours before dawn, it was time to quit. And since most vampires were probably heading toward a dark, safe place about now, we called it a night.

After we checked out, Dan drove me back to the townhouse. "What are you going to do now?" I asked.

"I don't know—have a drink or two, maybe listen to some music. Why?"

I shrugged. I wasn't sure Dan should be alone right now. Drinking alone was never a good sign. "I don't have anything else to do and I'm not sleepy yet. Want to hang out? Gwen won't be home for another couple of hours yet."

You just want to know more about Lily.

*Okay, I admit it. I'm curious. What's wrong with that?*

Fang snorted as Dan shrugged and said, "Whatever."

He followed me into the townhouse and Fang said, WELL, I'M BEAT. YOU TWO CHAT AMONGST YOURSELVES. I'M CATCHING SOME Z'S.

I hugged him, then cupped his fuzzy little chin and turned his face up to mine. He might be snarky, but he was still incredibly cute. I kissed him on the top of his head and scratched his ears. *Goodnight, Fang. Sleep tight. Love you.*

He licked my nose. BACK ATCHA, KIDDO. Before things could turn too warm and fuzzy, he turned and trotted toward the bed. DON'T THINK TOO LOUD, OKAY?

How did you regulate the volume of a thought? Bemused, I promised to try and asked Dan, "Would you like something to drink?" I peered into the refrigerator. "Looks like we have Coke, orange juice, beer, water . . . "

"Thanks, but I know where Gwen stashes the booze." He opened a cupboard and pulled out a bottle of bourbon. "Want some?" He hesitated. "Oh, sorry. Forgot you're not old enough."

Just another reason for him to think I was a kid. Hell, he wasn't much older. Annoyed, I said, "No thanks—it tastes like gasoline." I poured myself a Coke.

He put some soft jazz on the CD player, turned the lights down low, and settled down on the opposite end of the couch from me with his feet up on the table.

"Gee, make yourself at home."

He looked somewhat embarrassed, "Sorry, I hang out at Gwen's a lot and this is how I unwind."

"It's okay," I reassured him.

He didn't seem to be able to relax, though, and looked as if some kind of hamster was spinning madly in his head. "Want to talk about it?" I asked.

"Nothing to talk about."

"Uh huh," I said doubtfully. "You learn your ex is a vampire and there's nothing to talk about?"

He sighed. "Well, one thing's for sure. There's no chance of getting back together."

Had he been hoping there was? I wondered at his disgusted tone. "You can't deal with dating a vampire?" I asked.

"It's hard to date someone who considers you food." He glanced at me. "Could you do it?"

"I guess not." Though it made me wonder what he'd think of dating a part-demon girl. Not that I was interested. Just, you know, curious.

A mental snort from Fang in the other room showed me what he thought of that rationalization. *Go back to sleep,* I thought irritably.

I didn't know you could laugh in someone else's mind, but Fang managed it.

Dan took another sip. "What I don't get is why. I mean, taking a step like that—turning into a vampire—has to be voluntary, right?"

"So far as I know. Unless the person who turned her somehow forced her to drink his or her blood. It's possible." Possible, but not probable. If that had been the case, she wouldn't be so cozy with them now.

Apparently, Dan had come to the same conclusion. "Why would she do such a thing? You think she was sick?"

I shrugged. "You'd know better than I would." I dearly wanted to know more, but he didn't seem very forthcoming and I didn't want him to think I was interested in him or anything.

Even if you are?

*Go to sleep, Fang.* Sheesh—I couldn't even be private in my own head.

Okay, okay. Don't get your knickers in a twist. I'll be silent as the grave.

Ignoring the hellhound, I said, "Maybe she wanted immortality. That's important to some people."

"No, I can't see it. But Alejandro could have enthralled her, forced her to want it."

I made a noncommittal noise. Again, it was possible. Maybe even probable, but more likely wishful thinking. Evidently, Dan wasn't over Lily yet. And who could compete with that?

He turned to look at me. "Hey, Alejandro said your sister came looking for you. What's that about?"

"I don't know." I took another sip. "The reason my parents

threw me out is because they thought I was a bad influence on her—she was all gung-ho on helping me kill vampires. But she's too young for this. Doesn't have the same . . . reflexes I do."

Dan stared at me curiously. "Yeah, how *do* you do it? It doesn't seem quite natural."

"Well, it is," I said defensively. Natural for me, anyway. To get him off the subject, I said, "Guess I need to find her tomorrow and beat some sense into her head."

He nodded. "I know how it is to have a stubborn little sister. Need some help?"

I grinned, remembering Jen's reaction the last time they'd met. "Yeah, sure. You, she might listen to."

He rose and placed his empty glass in the sink. "Okay, it's a deal. I'll come by early tomorrow and we'll put a scare into your sister."

"Good." I rose and followed him to the door. Trying for a joke, I said, "If the vamps don't kill me, Mom sure will." I didn't pull it off very well.

He glanced down at me. "Hey," he said softly. "You really are worried, aren't you?"

I shrugged. "Mom forbade me to see Jen again, but how can I protect her if she runs into danger on her own?"

"Don't worry—we'll take care of it."

He reached out to give me a hug and for some stupid reason, I dropped my guard for a moment and let him. It had been so long since someone had reached for me without holding thoughts of the demon in the back of their mind, without any thought but that I needed a hug. Human contact is a wondrous and scary thing. For me more than most.

Our energy fields intersected and clung. Heat flared between us—an odd, dancing energy—and my heart beat faster. Lola reached out to him and a surge of want and need flowed back and forth between us like a live thing.

I clutched his shoulders hard, tightening the embrace. The warmth of his body against mine, his woodsy, masculine scent, and the strange tingling in my own body were totally wonderful, yet frightening at the same time. Fearing he'd think I was acting too needy, I pulled back. Not all the way out of his arms, just far enough to look into his eyes.

Dan gave me an intense look, like he'd suddenly realized I wasn't just a girl, but a woman . . . and he wondered what that woman tasted like.

A strange heat flooded through me, leaving me feeling boneless and yearning. *Yes, please yes. Kiss me,* I willed him.

He lowered his head, staring at my mouth. Ohmigod. I didn't know it could, but my heart beat even faster and I felt energized— all warm and tingly—just like with Johnny Morton two years ago.

Uh oh. Draining your partner's life force was so not cool. I gasped and pulled away.

He looked stunned and I didn't quite know what to say or do. He didn't think of me as a kid anymore, that was for sure, but it was artificial, brought on by the demon within me.

"God, I'm so sorry," he said. "I don't—"

I cut him off as I struggled desperately to shove a disappointed Lola back into her bottle. "Don't worry about it. It was my fault."

"But—"

We heard a key in the lock then—Gwen must be home. Dan ran a hand through his hair, looking a little frazzled, and opened the door for his sister. "Hey, Gwennie. Val and I were just having a little chat, but I'm headed home now. See you." He rushed out the door.

Gwen glanced at her brother's back, then at me. She closed the door softly, asking, "What was that all about? Is there something going on between you two?"

"No, no," I assured her, not sure how she'd feel if there was. "It's just that he ran into his ex today, and he's not happy with . . . her new lifestyle."

"Oh," Gwen said in a flat tone and dumped her stuff on the dining room table. "You mean Lily?"

"Yeah." And this was the perfect opportunity to learn more about the woman Dan had loved at one time.

"How long have they been broken up?"

She grimaced. "Two months, thank God." Flopping down on the couch, she said, "I don't know what he saw in her—she's such a cold fish."

That was nice to hear. I sat down across from Gwen. "She seemed very . . . confident."

"Yeah. He's always been drawn to strong women, but we can't figure out why he chose *her*. The family's just glad she ended it."

If she ended it, that might explain why Dan still wasn't over her. "Family?" I asked.

"Yeah—my mother and my two brothers."

"I didn't know you had other brothers." Dan hadn't mentioned it. Then again, we hadn't talked about much except stalking the undead and my family.

"Yeah—Jack and Adam."

Two others like Dan? Whoa. "Older or younger?"

"Older. Dan and I are the youngest."

"Do they live here in San Antonio, too?"

"Yes—Jack is a cop and Adam's in civil service at Randolph Air Force Base and in the reserves."

I raised an eyebrow. "All serving their country in one way or another?"

She laughed. "Yeah, it's a Sullivan thing. It's sort of a tradition, a motto, amongst us that every family member serves and protects. My grandfather and father were both in the military—Dad died in Vietnam. The same with my cousins—police, military, firemen. It's what we do."

"I get it—you're all heroes," I said with a half smile. It explained a lot about Dan, why he was in the SCU to begin with.

She looked surprised. "No, that wasn't what I meant at all."

"I didn't mean it in a bad way," I assured her. "I think it's cool."

Gwen looked thoughtful. "That's interesting—I never thought of it that way. But you see why Lily wouldn't have fit in?"

"Yeah, she's more the predator type than the hero type."

"Exactly." Gwen wrinkled her brow. "You said something earlier about her new lifestyle. What did you mean by that?"

Uh, how did I explain this without mentioning the fact that she had gone over to the dark side—literally?

When I hesitated, Gwen's eyes widened. "Don't tell me—she's

turned into a vampire."

Whoa. "You know about them?" I knew she'd seen fang marks on victims in the ER, but didn't realize she knew what made them.

"Oh, yeah. Dan explained all about them. He wants me to be more careful. But I'm the only other one in the family who knows. Since you're his partner, I figure you had to."

"Yeah." It was odd talking about these things with someone outside my family. I'd had to remain close-mouthed for so long . . .

"So is she one of the walking undead now?" Gwen persisted. I nodded.

"Figures. Undead totally fits her personality. Well, good. Now maybe Dan will give up on the skank."

"He really loves her, huh?"

Gwen shrugged. "I don't think so. I think it was more of a pride thing—she ended it instead of him, but wouldn't give him a reason. I think he just really wants to know why. Plus he'd be upset if *anyone* he knew started playing on the wrong team."

Seemed like more than that to me. But what did I know? I wasn't bright enough to figure that out tonight. Not as frustrated as I felt. I was getting really tired of wanting things I couldn't have. Family, a boyfriend, a life.

Except . . . when I looked back on the last week, I realized I had more of a life now than I'd ever had before. Just because certain aspects sucked didn't mean it wasn't a life.

She yawned. "Well, I'm gonna hit the sack."

"Me, too." Though, as I crawled into bed with Fang, I wasn't sure if I'd be able to sleep. Remembering what had almost happened earlier with Dan was liable to occupy my dreams tonight, whether I wanted it to or not.

Inwardly, I felt like hugging the memory tight and living it over and over again.

Outwardly, I squirmed. Crap—I'd almost drained him, just like Johnny. How could I face Dan later today? How could I continue working in close proximity to him, wondering if the demon would break loose again, would try to enthrall him?

Unfortunately, I had no choice. I'd just have to keep a lid on it and make sure our energy fields never mingled again.

GOOD LUCK WITH THAT.

I glared at Fang on the bed. Man's best friend? Ha.

*

Later that day, as I waited for Dan to show up, I wondered if I should just take off on my own and blow him off. I was tempted, but I'd still have to see him at work anyway. Better just to tough it out, pretend it never happened. I shook my head. Well, nothing *had* happened except for a simple hug that had led nowhere. Unfortunately.

*No—don't even* think *that.*

It couldn't happen again, no matter how much I wished it would.

BOY, YOU'VE GOT IT BAD.

"Shut up," I muttered at Fang. "You're not helping."

He jumped up on the couch next to me and nudged my hand with his nose, offering comfort and probably an apology. IT'S NOT YOUR FAULT—IT'S THE SUCCUBUS PART OF YOU.

I scratched his fuzzy little ears. "I know. I just need to learn to control it."

YOU WILL.

Funny—the hellhound had more faith in me than I did.

When Dan finally knocked on my door about two in the afternoon, he looked none the worse for wear. Good—I was afraid he might have pulled a bender or something. But he looked as if he had everything under control, though his expression was a bit wary as he regarded me. After the way I'd acted like a frightened rabbit last night, I didn't blame him. Half the time I wasn't sure if I was a kid or an adult. Couldn't blame him for being confused, too.

I felt suddenly geeky and awkward, not knowing where to look or put my hands.

"You ready to find Jen and beat some answers out of her?" Dan asked.

He knew exactly what to say to make me feel at ease again—ignore the awkwardness, concentrate on pounding something. Now *that* I was good at. I laughed. "Sure."

Not knowing how long we'd be gone or if we'd be back before dark, I put on my holster with the stakes in back over my T-shirt and jeans, and covered them with my vest. "Okay, I'm ready."

I got into Dan's SUV and scooted as far away from him as I could get.

GEE, THAT'S NOT OBVIOUS OR ANYTHING. Fang jumped between us, making the distance seem more natural.

I resisted the urge to stick my tongue out at the dog. Sure, Fang was a great friend, but there were disadvantages to having an intelligent furry companion who knew you too well . . . and could make snide comments in your head.

"So, where can we find your sister?" Dan asked.

"She should still be in school this time of day." I gave him directions to the high school.

Luckily, I'd picked Jen up several times so the school officials knew me. But that familiarity did me no good.

She was at home, sick.

I had Dan call my parent's house but there was no answer. We tried the store next, but when Dan asked for Jen, pretending to be one of her friends, Rick said Jen was at school.

Dan turned off his cell phone. "Sounds like your little sister is playing hooky. Think she's out looking for you again?"

"Probably."

"So where would she be?"

I thought for a moment. "Maybe she's ditching at home, since Mom and Rick are at the store."

"Okay, let's try it."

It was tough driving up to the only home I'd known all my life and feeling like an outsider. I hated the thought of going in where I was no longer wanted, but I had to find Jen before she did something stupid.

"Is that her?" Dan asked.

Jen was just leaving the house, locking the door and looking around furtively. When I waved, she ran up to the car and beamed at me. "I've been trying to find you, but no one will tell me where you live or give me your phone number."

"Mom and Rick wouldn't give it to you because they don't want you seeing me anymore. You know that, right?"

"Yeah, yeah, but the 'rents have no idea how important this is." She glanced at the car. "Hey, can you give me a ride to the bookstore? I'm supposed to work there this afternoon."

Dan nodded, so I got out and motioned her to sit between us and Fang jumped in the back seat. As she got in, I gave Dan directions and he headed toward the bookstore.

Fang's nostrils flared. SHE SMELLS LIKE VAMPIRE.

*My little sister's one of the undead?* My heart stopped for a moment, until I realized Fang meant she smelled like vampire because she'd been hanging around them. Relief filled me, but annoyance soon followed. "What the hell have you been doing?" I snapped.

"Yeah," Dan all but growled. "Tell us why you've been flashing your sister's picture all over town, calling her the Slayer, nearly getting her killed."

"Killed?" Jen repeated. "I-I didn't know."

It was her favorite refrain, unfortunately used way too often, right after she screwed up. Truth be told, that's the part of Jen's life that made me angry. I was never allowed to say, "I don't know." Never allowed to be a kid. I tamped down the jealousy, telling myself for the zillionth time that it wasn't Jen's fault she could have a normal life, be a normal kid.

She glanced back and forth between Dan and me, looking frantic. "I-I thought I'd be safer around the . . . you know . . . if they thought I was under your protection. You have quite a reputation, Val."

"Yeah," Dan replied. "One you made for her. Until you put a name and face on her, the 'you know' didn't know who she was."

Jen looked miserable. "I'm sorry. I joined their movement to find out more about them for Val. I was just trying to help."

Dan had come to a stop a block past the bookstore and I spoke fast, not wanting Mom or Rick to see Jen with me. "You did *what?* How could you be so stupid? And why would you think that putting yourself in danger could possibly help me?"

She hunched one shoulder. "I'm not in danger. And I'm learning a lot—"

"I don't need your help—and they are *not* safe." Even if Alejandro meant what he said, I still didn't want my little sister hanging around them. "You have to promise me you won't talk to the vamps again—don't even go near them." She could be enthralled so easily.

She looked sullen. "All right, but what if I need to get in contact with you?"

"Call." I gave her my new phone number along with Dan's cell phone number, and Jen put them carefully in her purse.

Suddenly, Dan said, "Ah, hell."

What—?

But I didn't need to ask as my door was suddenly jerked open. I lurched a little, since I'd been leaning on it, but the seatbelt kept me in place. What the—

It was Mom, looking like a thundercloud about to dump a gutload of bad weather. Rick was right behind her.

"What are you doing here?" Mom demanded. "I told you to stay away from Jen."

"It's my fault," Jen said. "I asked her to—"

"I don't care what you asked her. I gave an order, and I expect it to be obeyed—by both of you. Get out of that car, young lady."

An order? Geez, what did she think this was? The army? Calmly, I unbuckled the seatbelt and motioned for Jen to get out. "Go on."

Jen looked pleadingly at me. "Can't I live with you?"

"No."

"You are *not* going to live with *her*," Mom all but shouted. "Get out."

Fang growled at Mom as Jen slowly got out of the car. Whoa. What a bitch. And I ain't talking about no female dog

Dan, looking pissed, got out of the car and glared at Mom and Rick over the hood. "Lay off. The truth is, your daughter Jennifer is skipping school, playing cozy with the vampires, and endangering Val to play some game of her own. She made her own stupid mistakes."

Well, they deserved to know the truth, but I wouldn't have put it so bluntly. I had to admit that Dan's version saved time, though. I slid back into the car and closed the door, hoping for a quick getaway. Dan got back in the car, too, having made his point.

Mom looked taken aback, but recovered quickly. "I should have known. It's all Val's fault—if she hadn't been hunting vampires, Jen wouldn't know about them to begin with."

Mom's face crumpled in distress, but I couldn't feel sorry for her, not with her blaming her demon daughter for every problem in the family.

I rolled my eyes. "Get a clue, Sharon. You run a freakin' new age bookstore fergawdsake."

Rick, looking stone-faced, butted in to ask Jen, "Where have you been going? Who have you been seeing?"

Like he could do anything about it. I grimaced. "Never mind. I'll take care of it." Then to my little sister, I said, "Don't tell him. He'll just do something stupid and get himself killed."

"I don't care," Rick said. "She's my daughter and it's my responsibility to—"

Dan butted in. "It's your responsibility to stay alive to take care of her," he said. "The rest is for us to do. I'm with the Special Crimes Unit of the San Antonio Police Department, and Val is now my partner. This is our job. This is what we're trained for. Let us handle it."

Mom did nothing but cry as Rick stood there, his fists clenched. "You can't expect me to stand by and do nothing when my daughter is out there in danger."

Yeah, their true colors were showing now. They didn't give a flick about what happened to me. Only their precious normal daughter. His *real* daughter. But I had no tears now, just anger.

I couldn't trust myself to speak, though. Luckily, Dan did it for me. "If you try something on your own, if you're stupid enough to jeopardize this investigation, we'll have you arrested for obstruction of justice and thrown in jail. Have you got that?"

Fang yipped. Go, Dan!

Rick and Mom stared at us both, stunned.

Yeah, they got it all right. I just hoped it stuck. "Let's get out of here," I muttered to Dan.

"Gladly." He started the car and peeled out, leaving them all gaping after us.

"Thanks," I said softly.

"No problem. That'll teach them to mess with the Slayer."

Fang chuckled, but I didn't think it was so funny. As my gut twisted in a knot, I wondered if I'd destroyed all chance of ever having a normal relationship with my family again.

It didn't matter. They might not care about me anymore, but I still cared about them. Only one thing was paramount now—finding out exactly which blood bank Jennifer had been going to and making sure she never went there again.

# CHAPTER EIGHT

It was almost time to go to work. Ramirez texted us on Dan's phone and asked us to check in. Though we could pretty much set our own hours so long as we produced results, we still tried to stay with night shift hours as much as possible. And, of course, give Ramirez a progress report every once in awhile.

Dan drove to the SCU headquarters and we found Ramirez in his office. The lieutenant waved us to the rickety seats and said, "So tell me what the hell happened last night. I hear you found the vein of vampires and caused a riot."

Dan and I exchanged a look of surprise, but then I realized some of the other scuzzies must have been at the rally last night. "We didn't cause a riot," I protested.

Ramirez let out a bark of laughter, but didn't sound amused in the least. "What do *you* call it, when twenty or thirty vampires have a rumble and trash a public place?"

"Fangbangers just wan-na have fun?" I asked.

Fang nudged my leg. OOH, GOOD ONE.

But Ramirez wasn't amused. "Don't be cute," he snapped. "Luckily, the vampires themselves must be helping the reporters forget, or there would be widespread panic by now." He scowled at me. "I hear you've been touting yourself as a badass vampire slayer, and that's what set them off. What the hell were you thinking?"

I squirmed a little. "That wasn't my doing. It was my sister's."

"Your *sister*? What the hell does she have to do with it?"

"You see, Jennifer has this dumb idea that she can help me, so she joined the Movement to find out as much as she can, but she used my reputation to keep herself safe while she's doing it." I paused, adding, "She's only sixteen."

Ramirez buried his face in his hands for a moment, apparently trying to control himself. Finally, he raised his head and asked,

"Your little sister is involved in this investigation?"

"Not really—I told her to lay off. She's probably grounded for the rest of her life by now."

"You really think that will stop her?"

I hoped so.

Ramirez turned to Dan. "And you. I hear one of the vamps was named Lily. I only know one Lily, and she disappeared on you."

Dan's face tightened. "Yes, I found her, but that was uncalled for."

Ramirez shook his head, looking weary. "You're right. I'm sorry. Sorry you found her, sorry that she was turned, and even sorrier that I'm going to have to pull you both from the investigation."

"What?" Dan and I exclaimed in unison.

"What did you think was gonna happen when you got personally involved?"

"We didn't get them involved," I protested. "They did that on their own. We had nothing to do with it."

"It doesn't matter how it happened," Ramirez said. "The fact is, they have now become a part of the investigation."

"You question our objectivity?" Dan's voice was quiet but part of me was tuned into him in a more intimate way since last night. I could feel anger pulsing just below the surface.

"Damned right I'm worried about your objectivity. Your emotions are involved now, and when emotions are involved, reason goes out the window."

"Not mine," Dan said. "Not Val's."

"You mean to tell me that you're not gonna let the fact that your ex is part of the group you're investigating influence you? That putting Val's sister in danger isn't a factor?"

Dan visibly reined in his anger. "Of course it affects us. How could it not? But it just means we'll work harder to make sure this new movement doesn't endanger the city or anyone else's family." When Ramirez didn't look convinced, he added, "We're going to investigate this organization one way or another. We have to. So we might as well help you while we're at it."

Ramirez ran a hand over his face, looking tired. "We're so short-handed, I can't afford to put anyone else on this. But there is one thing I'd really like to know."

"What's that?"

"Is it true you *rescued* the leader of this vampire movement?"

Fang chortled silently. YEAH, THAT WOULD STICK IN MY CRAW, TOO.

It did look kind of bad. I had to explain. "Yeah, and now he owes us a favor. The other vamps blamed Alejandro for me being there, for putting them all in danger. I couldn't leave him to be torn apart, not when it was my fault he was in trouble. Besides, we need him alive to find out what they're up to."

"So you did cause the riot," Ramirez said flatly.

"Not intentionally," Dan protested. "We had no way of knowing her sister had primed that particular pump to explode. Besides, their leader is intrigued with Val. Not only did she save him, but she's immune to his power. Her mental block is solid. That seems to fascinate him and they have already developed a rapport."

Wow—he was sticking up for me. I decided I liked having a partner.

"A rapport? Is that true?" the lieutenant asked me.

"I don't know about that," I protested. "But he was trying awfully hard to convince me his movement is all sweetness and light."

Ramirez sighed. "Okay, tell me about it."

We explained how the New Blood Movement was proposing to have vampires live in harmony with humans, to donate blood so they wouldn't have to hunt and feed.

Ramirez looked incredulous. "And you believe this crap?"

I shrugged. "He said that the people who become vampires aren't really evil—they just become more of what they were when they were human. According to him, bad people become bad vampires. Good people become good vampires."

The lieutenant looked thoughtful. "You buy that?"

"I don't know," I said. I tried to be objective. "It's possible that the independent ones we've run into on the streets are all the bad ones, and the good ones have banded quietly together under Alejandro. After all, he did make a point of saving all the humans before the riot started last night."

"Yet the riot did start," Ramirez pointed out. "In your estimation, is this movement a danger to the city?"

"Not right now," I said. "Alejandro's trying hard to convince us he's harmless, what with these blood banks around the city and the rally and publicity. He's risked a lot to out himself. Why would he endanger that?" When neither man responded, I continued, "So far, he seems to be targeting kids, Goths, misfits. He hasn't gone for the mainstream yet. I think he means what he says." Not that I wanted my sister involved in any of that.

Dan didn't look convinced. "That's how drug dealers start, too. They go for the kids with no support system or people who won't look too closely at the hand offering help or a high."

Ramirez's gaze swiveled to regard Dan. "You have a different opinion?"

"Let's just say I'm not convinced yet. I don't trust Alejandro. He's too smooth, too polished. He may be using this movement as a front for something else."

"Like what?"

"I don't know, but I plan to find out."

"Okay," Ramirez said, though he didn't look happy about it. "See what you can find out—with a minimum of damage to any innocent bystanders, please—and let me know what you learn. We need to get this locked down and settled."

"You seem remarkably well-informed for someone who doesn't work the streets," Dan said. "Who's your informant? Maybe he can help us."

"Informant? I had another SCU operative at the rally."

Dan nodded as if he'd expected that response, too, but didn't quite believe it. "And for the other info you've gathered?" he asked quietly.

I glanced at Dan in surprise. Good point. Where *did* the lieutenant get the info he'd been feeding us?

Ramirez frowned. "We occasionally get tips—anonymous ones from one particular source. But the information always checks out. Don't worry, I'll let you know everything I learn, too." He paused, then added, "But if it looks like your personal lives are affecting your work, I'm taking you off, you hear?"

"We hear," Dan assured him. Obviously dismissed, he took me by the arm and practically shoved me out of the office.

"Whew," I said, peering around to look at my backside. "My butt has a few teeth marks, but I think it's still there."

Fang laughed and so did Dan. "You think *that* was an ass-chewing? That was mild compared to some of the inquisitions I've sat through. We were lucky." He grabbed the keys to the truck. "Why don't we check out the blood bank?"

"Sure. Sounds like loads of fun."

He smiled then, looking all hot and sexy, and all of a sudden, the memory of last night, the memory I'd been suppressing all day, came back to me in full IMAX 3D.

My body reacted with a surge of need so strong, it left me weak in the knees, with all kinds of strange feelings I really didn't want to have. Not right now. Not with my partner.

Fang shoved my leg. GET A GRIP.

*I'm trying to.* I plastered myself against the door, as far away as I could get from him, and forcibly controlled Lola's reaction. If it was a choice between repeating last night's near kiss or kicking vampire butt, I'd feel safer in the middle of a fangbanger brawl.

"You okay?" Dan asked curiously.

No. That memory had blindsided me, releasing Lola without even a three-minute warning. But I couldn't tell him that. "Fine. I was just thinking that I, uh, didn't think to bring enough stakes." There was nothing like stabbing a cold, sharp implement into an undead body to keep the lust demon at bay.

"No problem. We have everything we need in the back seat."

I sighed. "Okay, let's go." Just where was a bloodsucking fiend when you needed one?

I put a lid on Lola as Dan drove to the blood bank on the south side. The renovated hotel where it was housed was brightly lit, an inviting oasis in the midst of a bleak neighborhood that appeared furtive and sordid after the sun went down.

I could understand why people in the area would gravitate toward the blood bank, but wondered how many actually stayed once they figured out its purpose.

He parked the truck as close as he could, though it was a

couple of blocks away, and loaded himself up with silver jewelry and concealed stakes as I stuck a few in my back waistband. Sure, the Movement preached tolerance and compassion, but you could never be too careful.

"Ready?" he asked.

"I guess. You have a plan?"

"Try to find out as much as we can."

"Sounds good to me."

Fang looked up at us eagerly. YEAH. LET'S GET SOME ANSWERS.

We entered the lobby area and, now that the lights were on, I could see it was as freshly renovated as the outside, kind of like a doctor's office, but done in warm brown and burgundy, with comfy chairs and dark wooden furniture. The waiting area looked about three-quarters full. At one end, a perky cheerleader type about Jen's age was trying to convince a man to accept a cup of juice.

He was about thirty-five—a mechanic if his blue work shirt and oval name tag were any indication—and had a weird satisfied look on his face, with fresh fang marks on his neck and a wet spot on his fly.

*Ew.* Gross.

GIVE YA THREE GUESSES AS TO WHAT HE'S BEEN DOING.

I didn't have to guess—I knew.

"Please, Mr. Johnson," the girl said. "You can't leave yet. You need to sit down and have some juice and cookies. The rules say you have to wait for at least half an hour after donating blood."

"So that's what they call it these days," Dan said for my ears only. "I wonder if Vice knows about this place. He looks like he's strung out on something."

Yeah. The seductive lure of the vampire's bite was a drug many would be unable to resist. Was Dan remembering what Charlene had done to him?

When Johnson tried to stagger away, the girl stomped her foot and said petulantly, "If you don't sit down now, you won't be allowed to come back."

That seemed to penetrate his sex-induced haze. "Not shee Lily again?" he slurred, then took the cup and abruptly collapsed into a chair.

Dan muttered something incoherent, and I wondered how he felt now that he'd learned Lily was not only a vampire, but obviously racking up a string of pseudo-boyfriends.

Fang sighed. NOT GOOD, BABE. NOT GOOD.

The cheerleader-type girl hurried back to the reception desk, and we stood in line behind a man who was waiting there. The name plate at the desk read Brittany.

Brittany gave the man in front of us an exasperated look. "Now, Mr. Archuleta, you know it's only been a week since you donated. You have to wait at least a month between donations."

I exchanged a disbelieving glance with Dan. They had standards? Maybe they weren't the pushers we thought after all.

After a few minutes of unsuccessful wheedling, the man left, disappointed.

"Hello," Brittany greeted Dan cheerfully. "Welcome to the blood bank. Which type of donation would you like to make?"

"None," Dan said with obvious revulsion.

Had to agree there. How could anyone watch their lifeblood flow into a plastic bag, knowing it was going to end up as someone's dinner?

I interrupted. "Do you know Jennifer Anderson?" I showed Brittany a picture of my sister.

"No, who's she?" The girl looked genuinely puzzled.

Well, crap. I guess this wasn't the right blood bank.

Dan said, "We'd like to see Alejandro. He said he'd be here tonight."

Good idea—get the info direct from the man in charge.

Her cheerful demeanor didn't waver. "I'm sorry, but Alejandro isn't seeing any more clients this evening."

"We're not clients. We're with the police." Dan flashed his badge. "And he invited us. Dan Sullivan and . . . Buffy."

Huh? Why was he calling me that? Oh yeah, that's the name I'd given Alejandro last night and, without asking why I didn't want my name known, Dan was honoring my decision. Cool.

Fang didn't know to give Dan high marks. He laughed inside my head. BUFFY?

I shrugged, feeling kind of embarrassed. *Hey, I don't give my name to vampires as a general rule, and Buffy was the only thing I could come up with at the time. Cut me some slack.*

Brittany looked uncertain for a moment, then used the fancy telephone system on her desk to hold a low-voiced conversation with someone. She hung up and beamed at us. "Alejandro is expecting you." Handing Dan a key card, she added, "You'll need this for the elevator, fourth floor, the executive suite."

I turned toward the elevator, but Dan paused to lean down and smile at her, asking softly, "Shouldn't you be home studying?"

Brittany's smile faltered. "I'm eighteen—I can do what I want."

She was the same age I was? She seemed years younger.

Fang added, AND WAY STUPIDER.

I had to agree. What a waste.

Dan snorted. "And you choose to spend your free time in the bad part of town, working for bloodsuckers, helping losers get their rocks off? Whatever they're paying you, it isn't enough."

Looking offended, Brittany said, "They don't pay me—I'm a volunteer. It's a good cause. Do you know how many lives we save by manning these blood banks?"

"Do you know how many addicts you're making in the process?" he countered.

*Whoa, Dan, tell us what you really think.* But I couldn't blame him—I wondered the same things.

"It's not an addiction," Brittany protested. "We take blood *from* these people, we don't put anything into their bloodstream, so how could anyone get addicted?"

Dan leaned in closer. "Think Johnson or Archuleta would say the same?" After his encounter with Charlene, he'd know, if anyone did, what a vamp could make you feel, make you want.

The girl waved that away as inconsequential. "They're just crushing on some of the women who work here. There's no addiction."

Dan leaned farther over the desk to peer at Brittany's neck and twitched her collar aside. "I don't see any fang marks on you. How would you know how it affects people?"

Indignantly, Brittany straightened her collar. "I know because Alejandro told me so. And they won't let the volunteers give blood in that way."

"Oh, yeah? Ever wonder why not?"

The girl sniffed. "You'll have to ask him that."

"Meaning you don't know," he said flatly. "Tell me, what else do the volunteers do?"

Crossing her arms over her chest, Brittany said, "I don't think I should talk to you anymore."

He straightened. "If you're not doing anything wrong, why won't you talk to me?"

"Because you twist what I say," she said petulantly.

Yes, and he did it so well . . . . "Never mind," I said. "C'mon, Dan, let's go see Alejandro."

As we got in the elevator, Fang said, CAN I BITE ONE? CAN I, HUH?

*Maybe. We'll see how it goes.*

We used the special key card to take the elevator up to the fourth floor. When we got off, Alejandro was there, beaming at us. "I am happy to see you accepted my invitation, Miss Shapiro."

Miss Shapiro? Alejandro had managed to learn my name in a very short period of time, despite my attempt to mislead him. I raised my eyebrows but said nothing as he escorted us to the suite.

The living area of the suite looked aggressively modern—all stainless steel, black and white leather, and the occasional bold red accent. But it didn't look really lived in, more like a staged magazine photo.

YEAH. KINDA MAKES ME WANT TO TAKE A LEAK ON HIS NICE WHITE RUG.

I suppressed a smirk. Evidently, this was *not* where Alejandro slept out his days. As we seated ourselves, I wondered idly if the vamp used a bed or a coffin.

"So," Alejandro said, producing his charming smile. "You happened to catch us on one of the nights we are at this particular location."

"Us?" I asked.

"Yes." Alejandro gestured, and two of his assistants—Lily and Luis—drifted in, looking incredibly pink and healthy. Obviously, dining on mechanic tartare agreed with Lily. No doubt Luis had just fed as well.

As Lily and Luis took up stations behind Alejandro, Dan's gaze seemed pulled toward Lily. But she was wouldn't return it.

"Did you come for the tour?" Luis asked. Though his English was perfect, his accent was even heavier than Alejandro's.

"No tour," Dan answered. "Just questions."

Alejandro spread his arms in invitation. "Ask."

Before I could, Dan asked, "Do you have a Jennifer Anderson working for you?"

Alejandro glanced at Lily. "Do we?"

Expressionless, Lily typed something into the PDA she pulled from her purse. "Yes, she's been working as a volunteer at the downtown blood bank for about a week."

"So why are you trolling the high schools for volunteers?" Dan asked.

"We do not do this 'troll,'" Alejandro protested. "They hear about us from their friends. They come to us. They find the idea of vampires exciting."

Maybe, but why weren't there more Goth or Emo volunteers? I would have thought they'd be first in line. Instead, the Movement seemed to go for the preppy type.

"Well, Jennifer is one you need to let go," I said firmly.

"But of course," Alejandro said, "if you wish it. But why?"

Dan gave me a hesitant glance, as if asking how much of my personal life I wanted to reveal. Well, since Alejandro knew my name, he could get the rest of it. Sighing, I said, "Jennifer is my sister. My half sister."

Luis let out a brittle laugh. "And you are trying to save your little sister from the big bad vampires. How sweet."

Dan glared at him. "We're trying to protect you as well. If she hadn't been working for you, your rally wouldn't have turned into a riot."

"I don't understand," Alejandro said in bewilderment.

"She's the one who was showing her picture around and calling her the Slayer."

"I see," the vampire leader said thoughtfully. "Of course, I did not know this."

I nodded. "Now that you do, you'll fire her?"

"It is difficult to fire someone you have not hired, but yes, we will ask her to leave her volunteer position." He glanced at Lily. "You will take care of it?"

"Yes, of course," Lily murmured.

That was weird—Lily's easy capitulation seemed at odds with that strong personality Gwen had mentioned.

"Thank you," I said and glanced at Dan, wondering why he hadn't moved yet.

He folded his arms and suddenly looked like someone even I wouldn't want to mess with. "I have a few questions of my own."

Fang said, OOH. THIS OUGHTA BE INTERESTING. THINK THEY'LL FIGHT?

Over Lily? I hoped not.

"Yes?" Alejandro asked with a raised eyebrow.

Dan ignored Alejandro and looked at Lily. "You couldn't stand the fact that I treated you as an equal? You had to become undead so you could play servant to your master?"

Lily just glared at him.

"She is no servant," Alejandro protested with a smile. "She is my trusted lieutenant, as are Luis and the other two you saw the other night. No one else has made it as far as fast as she has."

"Release her from your mind control and let her tell me that."

Luis snorted. "Mind control does not work on other vampires," he said in a contemptuous tone.

"He's right," I said, giving Dan an apologetic glance.

Dan shook his head and said to Lily, "Can we talk alone?"

"No." For the first time, some expression showed in her face—annoyance. "Look, I left because I didn't want you. You couldn't give me the life I deserved so I found someone who could."

Fang laughed. OUCH. THAT'S GOTTA HURT.

Yeah, though Dan looked more angry than hurt. "Okay," I said, rising. "Can we go now?" I asked him softly.

Dan rose. "Sure."

As we headed down in the elevator, I said, "So we both got what we came for."

Dan made a noncommittal sound. "Yeah. But I still don't get

how she—or anyone—would make that kind of choice."

Me either, so I just kept my mouth shut. We were headed out of the building toward the truck two blocks away when Fang suddenly growled and I heard the sound of running feet. Before I could really register that fact, something hit Dan in the back and slammed him face first onto the hood of a nearby car.

*Crap. A vamp.* Had to be—no one else was that fast.

But I didn't have time to help him, because two more vamps were headed my way. Fang leapt for the smaller one, and I braced myself as the other slammed me face-first against the building. Lola burst free.

Hating the way our energy fields intersected and caused his lust to leap to the forefront of his pants, I used my demon strength to kick backward and heard a yelp as my boot connected. His grip loosened and I whirled around and scrabbled for the stakes at the small of my back.

I whipped one out and fisted the stake with the flat end against my chest as the undead creep grabbed at the neck of my T-shirt. Sharp yellow fangs darted toward my neck and I pulled him forcefully against me with my free hand.

As he impaled himself against my stake, he gurgled and slid down my chest with a look of wide-eyed surprise.

Fang yelped. A LITTLE HELP HERE!

Fang had been harrying the other vampire to keep her off me, but she had the hellhound cornered and was bringing her foot back to kick him. *Hell, no.* No one messes with my dog.

Too pissed to think straight, I used brute force to slam into her. I got her away from Fang, all right, but I lost my balance, and we fell in a tangle of arms and legs.

She ended up on top and had her hands around my throat in a flash. To hell with biting me—she was determined to choke me to death. I grabbed her hands and was barely able to keep her from cutting off my air entirely, but I didn't dare let go to reach the stakes at my back.

Fang attacked her leg, trying to distract her, but she was so focused on killing me, I don't think she noticed. Maybe I could—

Suddenly, her grip loosened and she fell limp on top of me.

Surprised, I looked past her to see Dan standing above me with blood dripping down his arm onto the stake in her back.

Rubbing my throat, I croaked, "My hero."

Dan snorted. "Yeah, right."

Fang snorted. HEY, I HELPED.

*Yes, you did. You're my hero, too.*

AW, SHUCKS, TWEREN'T NOTHING.

Sounded like Fang was just fine.

He shook himself. I'M COOL.

I resisted the urge to chuckle and pushed the dead vamp off me, trying to avoid getting the blood on my shirt. Lola subsided, leaving me to deal with my aches and pains. Rising slowly, I told Dan, "No, really, thanks. For some dumb reason, I didn't expect that here. They took me by surprise."

"Me, too," Dan admitted, wincing.

"You're hurt."

Dan glanced down at his right wrist. It oozed blood and he cradled his right arm in his left as he tried to stop the bleeding. "Yeah. He wanted to rip open a vein in my wrist, but the silver stopped him, so he tried to tear off my arm instead."

I glanced down at his attacker. Silver burns marred his face from Dan's jewelry, and he sported a nice new accessory—a stake in his heart. Dan had really held his own, but he didn't heal as easily as Fang and I did. "We need to get you to a hospital."

"No need. Can you get one of those GPS locators from the kit?" I got it out of the truck and he showed me how to activate the beacon.

Dan slumped against the truck. "The ambulance the SCU pick-up team uses isn't just for show. All of them are trained EMTs, too—they'll fix me up and take the vamps with them when they go. Kill two birds with one stone."

Good, 'cause he sure wasn't going to be able help me haul them into the back of the truck with just one arm. I helped him rig a sling for his wrenched shoulder, and we managed to pull the three attackers into a pile and cover them with a tarp before anyone else came along.

As we waited for the ambulance to arrive, Dan said, "Did it

seem odd to you that we were attacked just after we had our little talk with Alejandro?"

"Maybe." I thought for a moment. "But wouldn't it be dumb for him to set his people on us, after trying so hard to gain our confidence?"

"Not if he thought we'd end up dead."

"Maybe," I repeated doubtfully. "But he has to know our superiors are aware that we're investigating him, and he would be the first suspect if anything happened to us. It doesn't make sense." I paused. "But what really bothers me is that there were three of them. Vamps don't usually travel in packs."

"Alejandro's people do," he pointed out.

"True, but I can't believe he's that stupid. It's not him I'm worried about."

"Who then?"

"It's the other vamps, the loners we've been staking one-on-one. They don't advertise their locations like Alejandro does. They're less predictable. What if they've started banding together?"

Dan frowned. "If they have, heaven help us mortals."

# CHAPTER NINE

I woke the next afternoon to the sound of the cell beeping. It startled me because I hadn't heard it go off before. Confused, I stared sleepily at it as Fang stirred beside me. Oh—it was a text message.

I fumbled with the phone, trying to figure out how to read it. I'd never had a phone before 'cause I never needed one. But Jen and her friends texted all the time. How hard could it be?

It took me a few minutes of pushing buttons, but I figured it out. The message said, "Ur sister ran away. Working 4 blood bank."

What? Who sent this? I checked to see who it was from, but there was no phone number listed, just an email address. Shoot, there went my idea of calling them to demand an explanation. I figured out how to reply and sent them a message. "Who r u?"

No response. I checked the email address again. It was from DU at a wireless company's service. DU? Who did I know with those initials? No one.

They knew I had a sister, knew about the blood banks, and knew my number . . . . I ran through the short list of people in my head who knew all that. None of them would have sent me this anonymous message.

The thought of my little sister in the clutches of bloodsuckers made me sick to my stomach. Yes, these were supposed to be the good guy vampires, but Jen was so impressionable, I worried that she might think their lifestyle was normal . . . enviable, even. I couldn't afford not to check it out.

I let Fang out of the bedroom then showered and dressed. I headed into the kitchen for something to eat first and saw Gwen and Dan eating lunch in the dining room. Strange—I hadn't heard him come in.

They were laughing about something and Dan caught Gwen in a careless one-armed hug. It was obvious they really cared about each other. My heart squeezed in envy. I wanted that—the in-jokes, the teasing, the love of a family. Did they have any idea how lucky they were?

Gwen spotted me and waved me over. "I made quesadillas for lunch. Want one?"

Fang popped in through the doggy door then, sniffing eagerly. I'LL TAKE ONE.

"Sure," I said. *I'll share*, I promised Fang

Dan turned around and he looked a little banged-up, with his right arm in a sling and a bandage around his wrist, mostly covered with a button-down shirt.

"How are you feeling?" I asked as Fang lifted his nose toward the bandage and sniffed.

He shrugged. "Well, I won't win an arm-wrestling contest anytime soon, but I'm fine. I think they disinfected it quickly enough. Can't imagine what was under that guy's nails."

I shuddered, imagining the possibilities. When Fang stopped sniffing and didn't look worried, I assumed all the vampire cooties were gone. "Hear anything on who they were or why they attacked us?"

"Not really. I talked to Ramirez. They all fit descriptions of those on his most wanted list, but none of them had worked together before that he knew of."

"Not the type to play well in Alejandro's organization?"

"On the surface, no. But who knows what the New Blood Movement is really after?"

I shrugged and told him about the text message.

He and Gwen both looked at it, but neither had any more clue than I did who it might be from. I decided to check it out before work.

After we ate lunch and Gwen admonished me to be careful, I looked up the address of the downtown blood bank and drove there on my Valkyrie. Unfortunately, there were no dogs allowed in the building.

I glanced down at Fang. "We'd better not push the service dog angle too much—it's hard to explain since you're not wearing a vest or even a collar. And there aren't any vamps out during the day, anyway."

True. And there's no way I'm wearing one of those sissy vests. As for a collar, forget it.

Couldn't blame him there. I helped him remove his goggles. "If Jen smells of vamp, can you tell which vamp it is?"

He jumped down to the ground and cocked his head. Maybe. Eau de vampire is pretty much the same from one undead to another, though there are some differences. I can try.

Good enough—and it was worth a shot. I found Jen easily enough. She looked about twelve years old in her blond ponytail and sweater set as she served refreshments. The donors at this blood bank came from a slightly better class. Then again, only the impersonal old-fashioned medical donation could be made during the day. The other kind that stained men's pants and made them look foolish had to wait for the vampires to rise for the night.

Jen's jugular was still unpunctured, thank heavens. And thank Alejandro's policy on volunteers.

"Val," Jen exclaimed and hugged me, though it was a bit stiffer than normal. "I'm sorry for the scene the other day. And I'm real sorry Mom and Dad kicked you out because of me."

"That's okay," I assured her. "It was time for me to move out, anyway. And my partner found me another place right away, so it wasn't a problem." Now, to get her within range of Fang's nose "Can we talk outside?"

"Why?" Jen asked suspiciously.

I cast around for a reason she'd buy. "Because I had to leave my dog outside and I don't want to leave him alone too long."

As I led Jen out the door, I added casually, "I hear *you've* left home as well."

Jen whirled on me. "Is that why you're here? I thought you of all people would understand."

"Understand what, Jennifer?"

"That I couldn't live there anymore, couldn't take their small-mindedness."

She had a point, but . . . "They're just concerned for you," I said in soothing tones. "They have a right to be." Odd that Jen would so completely rebel and go over to the dark side, reject her

parents. Just last week she'd been all gung-ho to help me hunt
down and kill every last vampire on earth. "You promised me you
wouldn't try to find out more about vampires."

"Yeah, well, I changed my mind," Jen said with a sniff.
"Besides, I'm not doing this for you anymore. I'm doing something
important here, helping the Movement save the lives of innocent
people by providing the people of the night with safer, more
convenient options for feeding their hunger."

I snorted. That was an interesting way to spin it. "But where
will you live? Volunteer positions pay nothing."

"Oh, but they're paying me now. Besides, one of the lawyers
here is helping me file for emancipation. Don't worry about me."

But I knew how complicated being on your own could be—I
was still trying to figure it all out myself. "I'm your sister. Of course
I'm going to worry. Maybe you can stay with me."

Jennifer shook her head. "Alejandro has a place for his people—
I'm staying there."

"You have got to be kidding me. You can't—"

But I broke off when Jen's pleasant expression turned annoyed
and suspicious. If I wanted to find out more about what was
happening with my sister, I needed to stay on her good side, not
piss her off. I changed the subject. "I thought Alejandro was
supposed to fire you."

Jen's eyes narrowed at me. "Was that your doing? Well, they
tried, but I refused to quit and they hired me full-time. They really
value me."

Wondering how to beat some sense into the girl's head, I said
gently, "It's not healthy for you to work there, Jen. Vampires are
unnatural creatures with a craving for human blood."

"I know that, and I think it's cool that they're trying to find a
way to make it work without hurting humans."

This wasn't working, so I took another tack. "At least you're
working during the daylight hours. I hope that continues."

It was more of a question than a statement, but Jennifer didn't
respond. She wasn't promising anything. I sighed. Was it possible
she was in thrall to someone in the Movement? If so, and I could
just figure out which one, I could force the creature to release my

little sister. Carefully, I said, "It sounds like you've made friends with one of them."

"Not just one—at least half a dozen. They're not as bad as you think."

"Do you have any *particular* friends in the Movement?" I persisted.

Jen frowned. "No." Then, more suspiciously, she asked, "Why?"

"No reason," I lied, then looked for a way to distract her. I led her over to my motorcycle. "Here, I don't think you got a chance to meet my dog the other day. His name's Fang."

Fang was still sitting by the Valkyrie. *Get a good whiff of her,* I told him mentally.

"Oh, how cute," Jen exclaimed.

She rushed to pet the part-hellhound dog who acted like a frisky puppy with her attention. I noticed he got a lot of sniffing in, though.

"I'm so happy you have new friends," Jen said when she was through petting the dog. "Just like me."

Not exactly . . . .

With one last caress on Fang's head, Jen said, "I'd better get back to work. Thanks for ignoring Mom and Dad's orders and coming by to see me."

She made me feel kind of guilty for having ulterior motives for seeing her. I gave Jen another hug. "It was nice to see you."

I wanted to haul her butt back home, but Jen had already proved she wouldn't stay there, especially if she was looking at emancipation. Better to stay on her good side so she'd come to me for help when she needed it. Now I was glad she'd used my reputation to protect herself. Alejandro's people would certainly think twice before they messed with the Slayer's sister.

But that didn't mean I wouldn't worry. "But if you need anything, call me right away, you hear? Any time, day or night. You still have the numbers where you can reach me?"

"Yes, I still have them," Jen said cheerfully.

As she left, I asked Fang, "Smell any vamps on Jen?"

WELL, DUH. SHE WORKS AT ONE OF THEIR BLOOD BANKS.

"Yeah, but I mean did you recognize any of the scents?"

No, but she has at least four different scents on her.

"Will you recognize them again if you smell them?"

Probably, though most smell pretty much alike. Besides, a bloodsucker doesn't have to actually be in contact with her to enslave her mind, you know.

*I know.* Crap. I'd hoped it would be obvious if she was enthralled and if so, by who. No such luck. I'd just have to find out another way.

I drove home and Dan was still there. I told him what had happened.

He frowned. "If she'd been my kid sister, I would have gone all Rambo on her ass and had her locked in her room for a year."

I shrugged. That's what I would like to do, but . . . "My parents tried that. It didn't work." Biting my lip, I explained, "I know Jen. If I try to force her, she'll dig her heels in and turn even more stubborn. It's better to help her find a way to change her own mind, by showing her the truth about the vampires she's now idolizing."

"Aren't you worried about her? Worried that she might be enthralled?"

"Of course, but if she is, the vamp can enslave her mind so she thinks only what he wants her to think. The only way to break the spell is to convince her master to let her go . . . or kill him."

"So our challenge is to find out if she's enthralled and if so, which one has her under control."

*Our* challenge? Then he really did think of us as a team. It gave me a warm feeling. Not as great as having a family, but it was nice. Really nice. I smiled. "Right."

"It's probably Alejandro."

Could be, Fang said. She smelled a little of him.

"Maybe. But it's probably someone subordinate to him. The way she spoke of him was more as a distant boss."

"Legally, she should be at home."

"Yeah, I know. But the best way to get her there is to play it my way. Besides, she's filed for emancipation from my parents."

He thought for a moment. "Okay. she's your kid sister. Your family. Your call."

Grateful that he was being reasonable, I smiled at him.

Dan snapped his fingers. "Speaking of family, that reminds me. I did some research on the net on Lucas Blackburn."

"You did?" I asked eagerly. "Did you find him?"

"Yes, sort of. I'm sorry, but the only Lucas Blackburn I could find died a couple of years ago."

I frowned, trying to hide my disappointment.

"But he had a son—a Micah Blackburn, who is still in San Antonio. If it's the same man."

It had to be. And if Micah was Lucas Blackburn's son, maybe he shared the same demon, too. It was worth talking to him, anyway. "Where does he live?"

"I'm not sure, but he owns a club on the River Walk called Purgatory."

I felt excited yet apprehensive at the same time. "You think we can find him there?"

"I assume so. He not only owns it, he . . . performs there."

"Really? When?"

"Most nights, I think."

"Then I have to go tonight," I declared. I had to see him, know if he was like me.

"Are you sure you want to?" He had an odd expression on his face, as if there was something he wasn't saying.

"Of course, why wouldn't I?" *Because I'm scared to death he'll reject me, too?* I shook my head. If I didn't go, I'd never know . . . and that would be worse than any rejection.

"Okay," Dan said doubtfully. "You, uh, want me to go with you?"

"Would you?"

"Sure."

"Then yes, I'd appreciate it." Just in case Micah turned out to be a real jerk.

But I had a feeling—a really good feeling—that he was nothing of the kind.

*

Later that night, I surveyed my closet and dithered over the choices. I felt a little nervous about meeting Micah, and going to a club. I'd never been to one before and didn't want to wear the wrong thing.

Faded jeans and T-shirts made up the bulk of my meager wardrobe, but it didn't seem right to wear my working clothes to a club. I pulled out a pair of nice jeans along with a black turtleneck and a dark red v-necked sweater Mom had given me and showed them to Fang. "Which sweater do you think is most appropriate for a club?"

I was kidding, but Fang took my question seriously and regarded the clothing with a critical eye.

NEITHER. He nosed through my closet and poked a long-sleeved white blouse with his nose. WEAR THIS WITH THE FLORAL VEST. IT'LL HIDE THE STAKES.

Good point—after being surprised by vamps last night, I didn't want to go anywhere unarmed. I put the outfit on that Fang had chosen, amused by the thought of taking fashion advice from a hellhound. Then again, it had to be better than my nonexistent style sense.

GWEN CAN HELP YOU WITH THE FACE PAINT. SHE'S GOOD AT THE GIRLIE STUFF.

True. And Gwen was more than happy to oblige. She helped me put on a little make-up and loaned me a cute pair of dangly earrings.

She stood back and looked at me approvingly. "There. You look more feminine . . . softer."

"You really think so?" I had no experience with these sorts of things, but I kind of liked this softer side of Val.

TOTALLY ROCKIN', BABE.

"Oh, yeah," Gwen said. "Trust me, you look hot."

No, no. That wasn't what I was going for.

BUT NOT TOO HOT, Fang amended. JUST RIGHT FOR A CLUB.

I relaxed a little. Good—I wasn't going there to find a boyfriend or anything . . . just Micah Blackburn.

So why was my stomach churning like a blender set on puree?

I knew my expectations were way too high. No one could be

the combination of family, mentor, and best friend that I longed for. Realistically, I'd be lucky if he would at least agree to meet with me. But I had to try.

"Thanks—I appreciate your help." I said to both of them.

"No problem," Gwen said. "Have fun."

I sent a question to Fang, asking if he was okay sitting home.

YEAH. CLUBS ARE NOISY AND THE PEOPLE THERE JUST ACT STUPID.

*Okay, I'll come by and get you if we go hunting.*

Fang settled in happily with Gwen, so I went to Dan's townhouse and knocked. He answered, looking really good in jeans and a soft navy blue sweater.

Dan took in my appearance. "Very nice. I've never seen you look so . . . feminine."

My face heated and I felt suddenly awkward. I wasn't real used to compliments and didn't know how to react. My eyes locked with his and I couldn't help but sway toward him, like he was a magnet and I was a hapless pile of filings.

Wow—he smelled great, with a musky, compelling, primal scent. Lola agreed, sending a warm tingling through my body, urging me to combine my yin with his yang.

No way. If his yang got anywhere near my yin, we'd both be in big trouble.

I backed up a step or two and took a deep breath, forcing my demon into submission. "Thank you," I said briefly. At least I assumed it was a compliment. I resisted the urge to tell him how great he looked in return. "Ready to roll?"

"Sure."

He insisted on driving again, saying his shoulder felt much better, and I didn't argue. Having him behind me on the motorcycle would be a very bad idea. Instead, we rode in near silence to Purgatory, both of us lost in our own thoughts, lost somehow in our own private purgatories. I knew mine had a demon in residence. I wasn't sure what populated Dan's private hell. Maybe doubt, questions about how a vampire life was better than a life with him.

The nightclub was in a large two-story building on the River Walk that was jammed with people, even on a Monday night.

Apparently, Micah was doing a thriving business. We entered, and were immediately engulfed in the world of Purgatory . . . dark, seductively lit with red lights, and throbbing with a heavy bass beat that I felt more than heard. It made the walls tremble.

Here, in the darkened foyer, the noise of merriment was muffled, and the dim light illuminated our options. The club was divided into four main areas—one each for jazz, rock, hip hop and rap, and ladies only. The club must be well sound-proofed, for I could barely hear the music from each one.

A man suddenly appeared from out of the darkness, looking like a clone of Bela Lugosi as Count Dracula, complete with white pancake make-up and fake fangs. "Have you been to Purgatory before?" he asked in a dramatic fake Transylvanian accent.

I suppressed a smile, wondering what the guy would do if ever confronted with a real vampire. "No, but we're looking for someone," I said. "His name is Micah."

The fake vamp laughed softly. "Yes, all the women look for Micah." He slanted a sly glance at Dan. "But the men would just as soon he not be found."

So Micah was a real ladies' man, huh? "This is different," I explained. "I want to talk to him about his father." When the vamp looked skeptical, I remembered what I'd told Dan and added, "I think we might be related." If lust demon blood ran through both our veins, we had to be related somehow, right?

The vamp shook his head and dropped the fake accent to sound pure Texan. "Nice try, but I've seen far more original attempts to meet Micah, and trust me, none of them work."

Exasperated, I said, "Look, Lucas Blackburn helped me out when I was a kid and I just want to talk to his son." When the man didn't look convinced, I said, "Just tell him, okay? He can decide if he wants to see me or not. My name is Val Shapiro."

The vamp shrugged. "Okay, I'll ask him after his set, but don't blame me if he refuses."

I didn't want to think about that possibility. "So he is here tonight?"

Smirking, the Bela Lugosi look-alike resumed his fake accent. "Why, of course. You can always find him entertaining in the Ladies

Lounge . . . ." And so saying, he backed into a dark corner and disappeared. Nice trick—must be a curtain or something there.

Dan frowned. "I was afraid of that. It's ladies only. They won't let me in."

"I'm sorry," I said, but it wasn't exactly true. Now that meeting Micah was imminent, I realized Dan's ignorance of my true nature might be a problem when I met another potential lust demon. "Would you mind waiting for me?"

He paused. "Are you sure you really want to do this? Maybe it would be better to call him during the day."

Why did he look so concerned? "No, I'm here now. I'd rather get it over with before I lose my nerve."

Dan sighed. "Okay. I'll just have a drink in the rock area." "Thanks."

Because I was under twenty-one, the guy at the desk stamped my hand with an X and put a red bracelet on me. At least they carded Dan as well. He got a green bracelet.

As Dan headed off to the rock lounge, I opened the door and went up the stairs to the Ladies Lounge, where a heavy beat and screams of feminine laughter filled the air. I was surprised to see three half-naked men on stage, bare chests glistening as they thrust their hips to the music. I'd heard of Chippendales, but . . . geez!

As I watched, one of the dancers ripped off his jeans to reveal a zebra-striped thong that barely covered his, er . . . package. A cheer went up in the room and a couple of women reached for him. He backed away as he continued bumping and grinding to the music. The other two men followed suit and the crowd went crazy.

Weirdly, Lola didn't react at all. Maybe generic commercial lust didn't do it for her. Or maybe I was just too embarrassed. I tried to look away, but was oddly fascinated by the men's hard bodies and the women who were all over them. Whoa. Guess my life was more sheltered than I thought.

My face grow hot. Yeah, I knew how odd it was for me of all people to feel uncomfortable around this, but I was still seven-eighths human. Heck, I'd just barely been kissed. This was totally out of my experience.

Another shout went up as a woman tucked some money into a dancer's thong. Ohmigod—I would never have the nerve to do that. Now I understood why Dan had seemed so uneasy. He must have realized what kind of place this was.

Was Micah one of those guys up on stage? I cringed at the thought. *I hope not.*

I made my way to the other side of the room where hunky bare-chested bartenders were dressed like comic book demons and other denizens of the underworld. Did everyone who worked here dress like something out of the *Encyclopedia Magicka?*

Shouting over the music, I asked one blond devil, "Is Micah on stage?"

"He'll be on later," the man yelled back. "What do you want to drink?"

I ordered a Coke with a twist of lime and sat down in the back to wait for Micah's appearance. Was he a stripper too? *Please, no.* But the odds were he probably was.

After a dancer dressed as a fireman lit more fires than he extinguished and a construction worker demonstrated the proper way to use his tools, the lights went out, then spotlights swept the stage.

A drum roll sounded, then a deep, amplified male voice came over the loudspeaker. "And now, Purgatory is happy to present the one, the only . . . *Micah!*"

*Finally.* I sat up straighter, making sure I had a good view of the stage. The sudden ear-splitting screams of the women in front told me they knew exactly who Micah was . . . and were *very* happy to see him.

Uneasily, I wondered what his act would be like . . . and if I really wanted to see it.

Abruptly, all the lights went out and the screaming stopped, anticipation hanging heavy in the air. A haunting piped melody filled the room, and a lone spotlight picked out the figure of a man on stage. He was costumed like a satyr, with horns, cloven hooves, a chest sprinkled with dark hair, and shaggy pants that made it appear as if he had fur from his waist to his feet. The crowd watched in fascination as he concentrated on playing the panpipes in his hands.

But none were as absorbed as me. I drank in his features, looking for any confirmation that he hosted a lust demon. He was tall, with a body that was leaner than the guys who had entertained earlier, more dancer than body-builder. With his dark wavy hair curling around his ears, full lips and firm chin, he looked very masculine and very seductive.

I could see his appeal to the other women, though he didn't do it for me personally. I squirmed a little, remembering the acts I'd just witnessed. Was I about to see a lot more of Micah than I wanted?

The haunting melody came to a lingering close, then with a wicked glance at the audience, Micah launched into a wild Celtic tune. An invisible orchestra picked up the melody and Micah abandoned the pipes to leap around the stage to the music, graceful as Baryshnikov, yet masculine as Schwarzenegger.

The women seemed spellbound as they watched his dance speak of passion, sensuality, and enticing erotic possibilities. A sudden dramatic pause in the music brought him to a halt in front of one audience member. He beckoned to her and she locked gazes with him then rose slowly to lay her trembling hands on his chest as the women around her sighed audibly.

Micah embraced her and lust surged in the room as the music swelled again and he whirled her in the dance. The woman, obviously no audience plant, was content to be moved in whatever direction Micah chose as he simulated a courtship. Then, when he was through with her, he twirled her back to her table. With her fingers lingering on his arm and gaze glued to his face, she sank bonelessly into her seat.

He glanced around for another partner and caught my eye. I shrank back and he looked startled for a moment, but recovered quickly and spun away to repeat the performance with another audience member.

Okay, this wasn't too uncomfortable. But that weird feeling in the air . . . what was that? It felt like . . . like satisfaction. Like a thirst finally slaked.

Lola stirred and I suddenly realized what had happened. Just as a succubus resided within me, Micah definitely hosted an incubus . . . and he was feeding it with the lust from the audience.

Shocked, I didn't know what to think. This had been forbidden to me all my life, yet he did it in full public view, almost like he was doing the dirty in front of an audience.

Finally, the dance ended with Micah frozen in a theatrical pose and the lights went out. Total silence reigned for a long moment, then the lights came up and the women went nuts—hooting and hollering as if it was the best thing they'd ever experienced. And perhaps it was, especially for those who had been seduced in the dance. Those few seemed stunned and completely satisfied, but at least he hadn't totally drained them of energy. They didn't seem to regret being singled out for Micah's special attention, either.

I felt a touch on my sleeve, and the Bela Lugosi look-alike was there, saying, "Micah will see you now."

I froze. Was I really ready for this?

Well, too late to back out now. Repressing a surge of elation tinged with apprehension, I followed Bela backstage to a simple unmarked room. Seeming a little embarrassed, probably for not believing me earlier, Bela showed me in, saying, "Micah will be with you shortly."

He left me alone in an office that was bigger than I expected. Not ostentatious, just simple and elegant, with comfy-looking chairs for guests. Not knowing what to expect, I stood in the middle of the space. After a few minutes, I heard the sound of a door opening, and turned toward it. Evidently the adjoining door was to a bathroom, for Micah stood there, smelling fresh from the shower, his hair wet.

Barefoot, but now wearing jeans and a shirt, he paused in buttoning his shirt to give me an enigmatic look, saying, "At long last, we meet . . . Valentine."

"Val," I managed. "I go by Val."

"I know. And I've been waiting a long time for you to find us." He held out his arms, offering a hug, and though I'd avoided personal contact with men all my life, I moved into his arms as if he were a long-lost brother.

Oh God, that felt good. Tears stung my eyes and I hugged him back fiercely. This . . . I had missed *this,* even though I'd never had it before. I'd never been able to hug men, not even Rick, for fear of the demon getting loose and sucking all of the life from them.

I didn't know if it was because we carried similar sorts of demons, but my succubus and Micah's incubus were quiescent, leaving me feeling like a normal person as I held him close.

What a wonderful sensation. In fact, I felt full of emotions, almost bursting with it, though I couldn't have said what those emotions were. Not romantic, not sleazy in any way, just overjoyed to find someone I could be myself with.

We broke the hug and Micah led me to a chair in front of the desk. As I seated myself, he leaned against the desk and smiled at me. "So what finally brought you to seek me out?"

I surreptitiously wiped the moisture from my eyes and said, "I just learned about your father a few days ago, how he helped my parents help me. I had no idea there were others like me. Are we related?" Did I actually have family on my father's side?

"It's very possible we're some sort of distant cousins, but your father didn't know much about his background. He was abandoned as a child."

I let out a bitter laugh. "I know how that feels." I gave him a curious look. "Did you know him?"

"A little. I was about nine when he died, but my father knew him better, and told me about him."

For the first time, I wondered what my father had been like, if he was really the monster Mom and my own imagination had made him out to be. "Will you tell me what you know?"

"I remember him as a smiling, happy man, always ready with a joke. But he had dark periods, when he struggled with his true nature."

That fit what I remembered of him. "Do you know what happened between him and my mother?" All I had was my five-year-old perspective, kind of limited. "Mom wouldn't talk about it."

Micah nodded. "I don't know the whole story, but you do know your father seduced your mother?"

"Yes." And Mom had been unable to resist the incubus part of him—a fact for which she had never forgiven him.

"Your mother was a very beautiful woman and your father fell in love with her the moment he saw her. He seduced her, then married her when he learned she was pregnant, hoping he could keep his nature under control. But your mother couldn't resist the incubus in your father, and it really bothered her when she lost all reason around him, so she divorced him and forbade him to see her soon after you were born."

"But I remember seeing him," I said in puzzlement. A few flashing memories of a handsome, laughing man who treated me like a princess.

"Yes, he still had visiting rights to see *you*—she wouldn't take that away from him. Then . . . something happened."

"What?"

"I hoped you could tell me that," Micah said seriously. "What happened when your father visited you on your fifth birthday?"

"Oh. That." Guilt filled me. I'd been trying to forget it for years, but horribly, it was the one clear memory I had of my father.

"Can you tell me?" Micah asked. "It's the only piece of the puzzle I don't have."

"I . . . it's difficult." As he waited patiently, I gathered my courage and told him. "I was a little over-excited since it was my birthday and my daddy had come to see me. For some reason, this time Mom didn't leave right away when he came." I shrugged. "I knew all the details of what happened, but didn't really understand it all until years later."

I paused, wondering how I could possibly put it into words. "He was . . . very glad to see Mom, very charming and cajoling. I think he was trying to convince her to come back to him, even though she'd already married Rick and had another daughter by that time."

When I paused, Micah nodded encouragingly.

"She kept refusing and trying to leave, but he wouldn't let her. Then . . . he did something. Something I didn't understand at the time. All I knew was that I felt something strange reach out from inside him toward Mom. I could tell Mom thought it was a bad thing, and I felt really afraid, especially since she seemed sort of scared, but sort of wanting it, too."

Micah nodded. "You would have just begun to recognize his incubus powers at that age, but you couldn't understand what was happening."

Glad he understood, I continued. "All I knew is that he was doing something bad and my mother was afraid. I asked him to stop, but he grabbed her and kissed her, and that funny feeling came again." I knew now I had sensed the incubus my father had been unable—or unwilling—to suppress.

"What did you do?" Micah asked softly.

"What could I do? I was only five. But . . . I beat on his leg with my fists and yelled at him to let her go." I still remembered the surprise on his face. "He did, and I jumped between them, holding my arms out to protect Mom, telling Daddy he was a very bad man and should leave us alone."

Micah kept silent, letting me tell the rest of the story my way. "He . . . he looked totally horrified. Stricken. Then he rushed out of there like the fiends of hell were at his heels." I blinked back tears. "I never saw him again." He had killed himself later that day.

Micah nodded. "It makes sense. From what others have said, I know that he often thought himself a monster."

I nodded. I knew the feeling. And though I knew I'd saved my mother from violation that day, I also knew I had the same possibilities lying dormant inside me. If my father, a strong adult, couldn't handle it, how could I be expected to?

Micah continued. "Obviously, he couldn't stand what he was doing to the woman he loved, especially when his five-year-old daughter chastised him for it."

I had to say what Micah must be thinking. "So I'm the reason he killed himself."

Micah looked truly horrified. "Is that what you've believed all these years?"

"It's the truth." It was always unspoken between Mom and me, but I knew I was the reason my father had committed suicide. If I hadn't jumped between the two of them, he might still be alive today.

Micah dropped to his knees to gather me in a hug once again. "It's not your fault, Val. He couldn't handle the two sides of our nature, couldn't reconcile the two and live with it."

Intellectually, I'd known that for a long time, but emotionally, I still felt I'd driven my father to suicide. I deepened the hug, letting the tears flow. "So you . . . don't blame me?"

He moved away from me a bit to look into my tear-filled face. "Of course not. How can you think that?"

I waved my hand vaguely. "You and your father knew about me, but never contacted me directly."

"It had nothing to do with you. Suffice it to say that your mother didn't want any reminders of your father around, didn't want anything that would jeopardize you fitting in with the rest of the world."

Yes, that sounded like Mom. "I wish you'd ignored her."

"We wanted to," Micah assured me.

"Why didn't you?"

"*Because* of you."

"I don't understand."

"You had a tough enough time growing up part demon in that household—"

"You know what my life was like?" I asked, surprised.

"Yes, we kept track of you as much as possible, helped where we could."

"How? Why?"

"Since my father and I shared your nature, we knew when the critical times would come, knew what would happen to you as you grew up. Father visited your parents to let them know what was coming, to help them help you deal with something they couldn't possibly understand." He smiled at me. "There aren't that many of us, and we need to help each other out. Besides, as you said, we're probably related somehow."

"But I still don't understand why you didn't contact me after I got older. We could have met outside the family, somewhere just the two of us, like this."

He regarded me for a moment, as if unsure what to tell me. "Because I lead a very different life than you do. I wasn't sure how you would react."

True, I really didn't know much about him. I laughed a little uneasily. "Why? Do you do more than dance with those women? You strip?"

He stood, looking uncomfortable. "That's not what I meant."

"Oh. You mean because you let the incubus control you and I keep the succubus repressed."

He cocked his head at her. "You speak of your gift as if it were a separate part of you."

Gift? More like a curse. "Isn't it?"

"No, it's not. It's part of who you are. You can't compartmentalize it, shove it aside. You have to come to terms with it, embrace it."

"But isn't that dangerous? I saw what it did to my father. That was a lesson I'll never forget—demon bad, human good."

"It doesn't have to be dangerous—"

"I don't believe that," I cut in. "When I was sixteen and kissed a boy for the first time, I almost drained him of his energy, his life force. I almost killed him."

"You were young and didn't understand your powers. It doesn't have to be that way. And it's dangerous to keep it suppressed the way you do. I can feel your power, straining to get out, caged like a beast."

Good analogy—that's how I often thought of the demon within me. "But I don't keep my 'gift' pent up all the time," I insisted. "I let it out by hunting vampires. That feeds the lust in a different way."

He shook his head. "But that way is so much less satisfying. The only way to truly satisfy your craving is to use it sexually. I told your parents that, but I guess they didn't find it a viable option."

Hardly. A bit uncomfortable discussing this, I said, "I can't do what you do." Then I would really lose all ties to my family. Besides, I was so not ready. "What if I take advantage of someone? What if I kill them? Heck, what if I take my father's route and kill myself?"

"Look," Micah said. "It isn't something you can just ignore

and hope it will go away."

"I know that." Only too well.

"You don't understand. You're like an uptight parent who thinks if they say, 'No sex' their teenagers will fall right into line, cross their legs and ignore their hormones. You can't ignore this. You can't take a pill for it. But you can keep it from destroying your life. When you bleed it off a little at a time, like I do, you don't get the cravings. You can control it easily, and you don't hurt anyone."

"Do you think those women you . . . seduced . . . feel the same?"

"Oh, I'm sure of it," Micah said seriously. "You saw the act. They all want to be with me, they all want to experience what I can give them. And I only take from those willing to give."

He sounded more resigned than pleased by the fact, and I realized he'd probably never been able to have a normal relationship either. It was kind of sad.

"It's different for me. I can't . . . do what you do."

"Too bad. You've kept it suppressed for so long that when you finally let loose, there's no telling what will happen."

That didn't sound good. "So, I can't ever . . . you know . . . ?"

He raised an eyebrow. "Be intimate with a guy?"

Well, yeah. I shrugged, my face hot.

"I take it you have someone specific in mind. Does he know what you are?"

"No, and I want to keep it that way."

Micah considered for a moment. "Well, you could let loose with someone else first, test it out and see what happens."

No way. "That's not an option."

"I didn't think so." He thought for a moment. "I've never been in this situation so I don't know how to advise you. But I'm sure you have a lot more control now than you did when you were sixteen. Maybe it won't be a problem. Maybe you can keep it under control."

Maybe. But could I chance it?

A knock sounded at the door and Micah answered it.

It was Dan. Lola perked up at the sight of him, but I forcibly restrained myself from having a reaction. It was just because we'd been talking about him and the possibilities, that was all.

"They told me where to find you," Dan said, his gaze darting back and forth between Micah and me as if trying to gauge what had happened. "Is everything okay?"

"It's great," I assured him. I introduced the two men, fibbing only a little to explain that Micah was my cousin on my father's side, then realized I couldn't continue this discussion in Dan's presence. "I guess I should let Micah get back to work."

Micah nodded and pulled me aside to talk to me privately. "This is the man. I can sense it, sense your response."

I nodded, not trusting myself to speak.

"Your reaction is strong. You realize you're either going to have to let loose with him or get him out of your life?"

"Aren't there any other options?" I asked wistfully.

"Not really."

It was a lose-lose situation. If I let loose, I'd probably lose his friendship forever. Either way, I'd never see him again . . . and that was just too depressing to contemplate.

The only solution was to keep on going as I had been and hope I never had to make that choice.

# CHAPTER TEN

I exchanged phone numbers with Micah and hugged him one last time. "Don't be a stranger. I plan on seeing you. Often."

Micah grinned down at me. "Glad to hear it."

As Dan followed me out of the club, he said, "I take it everything went well?"

"Very well."

"Good. His . . . dancing didn't bother you, then?"

"Not really." I slanted a glanced at him. "You knew what he did, and you didn't tell me?"

Dan shrugged. "I wasn't sure how to."

"Doesn't matter. He wasn't like the others. He, uh, didn't take his clothes off."

"That's a relief."

Dan opened the truck door for me, then went around to his side and got in. Looking curious, he asked, "Did you find out why your mother never told you about that side of the family?"

I shook my head. "Look, I'm sorry, but I really don't want to talk about this. I—I . . . don't know how I feel, and I just want to absorb it all, give it a chance to settle in." I cast him an anxious glance. "You understand?"

"Sure." He reached across the wide seat to give my shoulder a squeeze. "Let me know if you want to talk."

"Thanks." As he started the truck, I added thoughtfully, "It's strange. I never knew how much my family meant to me until I lost them."

"I'm glad you found Micah, then."

"Yeah . . . thanks to you."

He shrugged, looking uncomfortable with my gratitude. "Anyone could have done it."

"But you're the one who did, and I thank you for it."

He changed the subject. "Before we hit the streets again, why don't we go over our notes, make a few phone calls to see what we can find out? We can get a lot accomplished that way."

"Okay. Your place or mine?"

"Mine, I guess—I have my notes there."

When we arrived at the townhouses, I followed Dan into his, which was a mirror image of Gwen's. While he made a few phone calls to other SCU members, I called some of Jen's friends. Together, we managed to piece together a picture of what a volunteer did at the blood banks. Brittany was right—the Movement was scrupulous in not using their young workers as blood donors, and none of them had been harmed yet, or turned. Basically, all they did was hand out juice and cookies, direct traffic at the banks, and act as goodwill ambassadors to the public. I felt a little relieved, but not totally.

As Dan handed me a Coke, he said, "We've been distracted by Jennifer and Lily's situations and forgot that Ramirez tasked us with finding out if this vein of vampires is behind the killings."

"Yeah. We've found the vein, but don't know what they're up to."

Dan popped the top on his own Coke. "That's obvious. They're vampires, so what they're up to is murder, mayhem, and mass destruction."

Surprised by the harshness of his tone, I said, "You really think the Movement is responsible for the increased attacks? It could be another group we don't know about yet." Not that I had the warm and fuzzies for Alejandro's group, but I wanted to get it right.

"Vampire attacks have doubled since the Movement started. Is that a coincidence?" Dan sat on the couch and took a slug of his drink. "I don't think so."

I sat next to him, and we both slipped off our shoes to recline companionably on the couch together, our feet up on the coffee table. "But Ramirez says those three who attacked us weren't part of the New Blood Movement."

"So far as he knows."

He sure was cynical tonight. "His information has been accurate so far. Has your investigation shown something different?"

"Not yet. But don't you think it's weird that the lieutenant knows a lot about what is going on with the vampires in the city, but he doesn't know what the Movement is up to?"

I shrugged. "Maybe it means his informant doesn't know."

"So, the informant isn't in the Movement, but someone who knows what the other vamps are doing," Dan said thoughtfully.

"Another vamp?" I suggested.

"Maybe." He made an impatient gesture. "This is getting us nowhere. We need to find out what Alejandro is planning to do with the organization he's building."

"I think he's on the level. I think he built the Movement to do just as he said—improve vampire and human relationships."

Dan gave me a disbelieving look. "You believe that? Why? Because he's pretty and charming?"

That was insulting. "No, because everything he's said has checked out so far. He really does seem to be trying to make things better."

Dan snorted. "Yeah, right. That's why he turns people like Lily into bloodsuckers . . . because he's such a nice guy."

"Lily is responsible for her own decisions. Why are you trying to act like she had no choice?" I asked, then mocked him with his own words. "Because she's pretty and charming? C'mon Dan, she's just as undead as he is."

Running an impatient hand through his hair, Dan said, "Yeah, It's just hard to believe anyone I know would choose a life like that."

"Are you sure that's all it is?" I asked skeptically.

"Yes, I'm sure. Damn it, I don't want her anymore. She's dead to me now. Literally. You've shown me that." He slanted me a glance full of meaning.

Meaning what, though? Heat suffused my face as I wondered . . . hoped . . . he meant he wanted *me* instead.

No, I couldn't go there. "I'm glad to hear I helped you come to your senses," I hedged.

"That's not what I meant." He moved closer. "There's something between us—chemistry, something, I don't know. Don't you feel it?"

I scooted away as he advanced, until I came up against the end of the couch and couldn't go any farther.

His face inches from my own, he stared into my eyes. "You do, don't you?"

Lola yelled, "Yes!" but I blurted, "No!"

"Why not?" Dan asked with a smile as he caressed my cheek with the back of his fingers.

Ohmigod. I didn't know I could feel like that, all kind of tingly and warm and weak. This wasn't demon-Val—she was more likely to just want to get physical. This part was all human-Val, wanting something all mixed-up and emotional.

But Dan had just asked me why we couldn't share a little tenderness. I was having a hard time figuring that out myself, but I searched for something he would buy. "Because we work together?" I hated the way that came out sounding more like a question than a statement. But he was sorely testing the limits of my hold on Lola.

"So?" he asked as he leaned even closer. "We're both professionals. We won't let this interfere with our jobs." And his slow smile made me feel boneless as he cupped the back of my head with his hand and leaned closer.

Ohmigod. I could sympathize—*really* sympathize—but I had to control my emotions before it was too late to control the demon. How could I stop this? "You're on the rebound," I protested, pressing myself as far into the couch cushions away from him as I could and pushing my hands against his chest.

"Not really. Lily and I haven't been together for two months, and before that it wasn't . . . good."

He leaned down and kissed my neck. Something inside me did a loop the loop of pure joy. Oh, no. I wanted him to do more. I wanted him to stop. I didn't know what the heck I wanted. But the succubus inside me was very clear—it was warm, willing, and waiting . . . for *him*. All I had to do was cooperate.

But how could I? Lord knew I wanted to, but could I rein it in? Could I keep the demon from pulling too much energy while enjoying it on a non-physical level? Unsure, I fired my strongest weapon. "I-I don't want this."

Dan laughed. "The hell you don't." And with that, he kissed

me, his lips soft and gentle. I sank into him and he moved his mouth against mine, coaxing me to respond.

I had so many odd feelings going on inside me, I didn't know what to do. That kiss with Johnny Morton had been a pale thing compared to this. Johnny was a boy, but Dan was definitely a man. Was I ready for this?

And he sure knew how to kiss. I couldn't help but react, and the power curled within me, responding to Dan's sensuality. But it didn't try to take charge, didn't try to force him. Instead, Lola seemed content to let Dan rev me up.

Not that he needed any help from the demon to make me go all weak at the knees—he was doing fine all by himself. He broke the kiss off to say in a hoarse voice, "Tell me you don't want this."

Heaven help me, I did—badly. I'd controlled Lola so far, maybe it was possible to keep her from taking over. And why shouldn't I try? Every other girl my age had done this, why couldn't I? I really wanted to know what it was like to make out with a guy.

Feeling as if I were drowning in sensation, I admitted, "I can't tell you that." I dragged his head back down to mine and kissed him with all the pent-up frustration I'd held inside for so long.

He responded in kind and soon we were both breathless, lying half on, half off the couch. Dan rose to his knees and tugged his sweater off over his head, tossing it aside.

"Oh, wow," I breathed. If I hadn't succumbed before, the sight of Dan's chest would have made me drop my defenses in a flash. Lightly sculpted with the sleek muscles of a man who trained in martial arts, his chest was sprinkled with light brown hair and a couple of old scars.

And I thought he was hot before . . . . A surge of hunger licked through me, prowling through me like a predator on the hunt.

He reached for my blouse but I grabbed his hand and held it away. My face was way too hot, and the rest of my body wasn't doing much better. I couldn't go any further, couldn't risk the demon getting loose, though I was surely tempted. What would it feel like to have his hands on my bare skin? On those parts that were aching with need?

As if Lola sensed I couldn't be trusted to give her what she wanted, she burst free, sending greedy tentacles of power whipping into Dan.

*No, no, no.* As I watched in helpless horror, desperately trying to gather up the shredded remains of my control, Dan reared back, his body bowed with surprise. Dan's eyes widened and he gripped my arms tighter as he shuddered in ecstasy.

No, no, no. This couldn't be happening.

He released me and collapsed back onto the couch, and I used everything in my power to keep the succubus from drinking in all that delicious energy and draining him. I scrambled away from him to a chair in the far corner, hoping that the distance would make it easier on both of us. When I finally had it back under wraps, I asked, "Dan, are you all right?"

He lay sprawled back on the couch, trying to catch his breath. "My God," he gasped. "What . . . what the hell was that?"

"A really good make-out session?" I ventured. But the anger in his eyes told me he wasn't buying it, and I'd better come up with a plausible explanation—fast.

Dan scowled. "The hell it was. That was something different. It felt like . . . like when Charlene had her hooks in me. Are you a vampire?" he asked tightly.

"No!" He wasn't thinking clearly. "You saw me handle silver and sunlight with no problem." But he was probably feeling manipulated and controlled right now . . . violated. Who could blame him? I watched him anxiously.

He narrowed his eyes. "Okay, so you're not a vampire. But you're not quite human, either, are you? I saw your eyes flash some weird purple light. What are you?"

I bit my lip, looking anywhere but at him. How could I tell him?

"Are you some kind of . . . of . . . hell spawn?"

Oh yeah, right. That's *so* not the first thing I would have thought. "So far as I know, there's no such thing as hell spawn," I said indignantly.

"Quit avoiding the question. What are you?"

I squirmed a little, then admitted, "My . . . my great-grandparent was a demon."

"I've been kissing a *demon*?" He scrambled to his feet.

"Only one-eighth demon," I said, my eyes pleading with him to understand.

"So . . . what?" he asked, retreating to a chair. "You go all bumpy and scaly now?"

Damn it, I knew it. I knew he'd think of me as a monster. Why had I been so stupid? "Don't be ridiculous. Do I look like a lizard to you?"

"No . . . But how am I supposed to know what you'll do?"

I sighed. "There are all kinds of demons."

"What kind are *you*?"

"I-I'm part succubus."

"What the hell is that?"

Still avoiding his gaze, I said, "A succubus is a female . . . lust demon. I call mine Lola."

"*Lust* demon? You mean you forced me to feel the way I did?"

He sounded betrayed. I met his gaze then. "Not entirely. Our attraction to each other just made it stronger."

"What is 'it' exactly? What does a succubus demon do?"

"Absorbs the energy generated by lust."

He stared at me for a moment as he took in the implications of my confession. When he finally regained his powers of speech, he asked, "You *fed* on me?"

"A little," I admitted. "But I stopped it as soon as I could."

"You've been feeding on me all this time?"

"You make it sound like I seduced you against your will," I protested. "You started this."

"Maybe," he gritted out. "But you're the one who finished it."

"Not me," I said, hating the way I sounded so desperate and pleading. "It was the demon inside me. I thought I could control her, keep her hidden, but you were such a good kisser, I lost it."

He rejected my flattery with a sharp movement of his hand. "You said earlier you were one-eighth demon. Now you're trying to tell me it's living inside you like a separate being? What does that mean? What Lola wants, Lola gets?"

I hunched a shoulder. "No. I have her under control . . . most of the time."

"So can you get rid of her?"

"I wish I could, but it doesn't work like that. Lola really is a part of me." I shook my head sadly. "I'm so sorry. Micah thought I might be able to control it—"

"Wait," Dan said, "Micah is a succubus too?"

"Actually, a male lust demon is called an incubus."

"Whatever. Is he one, too?"

"Yes. He inherited it from his father. I inherited from my father." I clutched a pillow to my stomach, feeling miserable. "He couldn't control the incubus, so he killed himself."

"Well, that explains a lot . . . . Does Ramirez know what you are?"

"Yeah. I don't know how, but he does."

"So that makes four lust demons so far, two living. How many are there in the city?"

"I-I don't know. Until I found Micah, I thought I was the only one."

He looked thoughtful. "You said there's more than one kind of demon. Those costumes in Purgatory . . . they weren't costumes, were they? Those were real demons."

That forced my head to snap up. Were they real? "I don't know. If they were, I didn't know it either. Fang could tell you—"

I broke off suddenly, wishing I could rewind what I'd just said.

"*Fang?*" he repeated. "The *dog* is a demon?"

"To some extent," I said lamely. "Like me. He's part hellhound, which is why he can sniff out vampires and other demons." Plus he talked to me in my head, but I wasn't sure Dan was ready to hear that yet.

Dan shook his head in disbelief. "Does *everyone* have supernatural blood but me?"

"Of course not. And just because we're part demon doesn't mean we're all bad, you know. Just like you, we try to live normal lives. We eat, sleep, drink—"

"Suck blood, feed on sexual energy . . . "

"That's not fair," I protested.

"Fair?" he repeated, his voice rising. "What the hell is fair about any of this? How can I tell what's real now? How can I tell what feelings are really mine, and which are caused by Lola?" He glared at me. "Turn it off."

"What?"

"Turn off your powers. I want to know what I really feel without them."

I shook my head slowly. "It's not like a faucet. I can't turn it off. I can only keep it subdued . . . like now. Anything you're feeling at this moment comes from you, not me."

"How do I know that?"

"You have my word on it."

He snorted. "Your word. Right. The word of a woman who's passing for human and lying about being a demon to her own partner?"

"I had a good reason for not telling you," I snapped.

"Yeah—so you and Lola could suck me dry without my knowing it."

"No, if I'd wanted to do that, I could have done it the first time we met. But I knew you wouldn't understand."

"What's there to understand? No wonder you're so good at killing the monsters—you're one of them." He turned away, running a hand over his face. "I'd appreciate it if you'd leave now. I'll ask Ramirez for another partner first thing tomorrow."

Whoa. Talk about a slam in the gut. I don't know why, but I hadn't expected that. I guess I thought we could work it out, find some way to continue working together. Guess not.

And it was all my fault. Life had just been starting to turn good again, but I had to go and ruin it all.

No, that was wrong. Lola had ruined it, and now Dan thought I was some kind of monster. There was nothing else I could do or say. As tears blinded me, I blinked them back, gathered up my things, and left.

## CHAPTER ELEVEN

I woke from a restless sleep the next afternoon after a night of chewing myself out. Though I didn't get much sleep, I felt stronger than I ever had before, more vibrantly alive. I'd have liked to attribute it to healthy living, but knew it was because Lola had fed on Dan's energy.

I was just relieved I'd stopped it before she had gone too far. But what if I hadn't? I shuddered. That would have been a catastrophe. Dan was already angry with me. If I'd taken any more from him, he would really be pissed . . . or dead.

But what I hated most was how good I felt, like I'd been thirsty my whole life and had just gotten a tiny sip of the nectar of the gods. The only problem was, I didn't want just a sip. I wanted to drink and drink until I filled up all the parched, empty spots in my being. Yeah, mostly it was demon-Val feeling that way, but I feared a lot of it was human-Val, too. Was that sick, or what?

Fang nudged me with his nose, offering comfort. You're not sick. You're normal. It's the whole teenager hormone thing, you know.

Maybe. I smiled at him. "Thanks for trying." I just wished I could believe him.

He snuggled closer and licked my hand as I stroked his soft ears.

From now on, I was sticking to dogs. They were sweet, uncomplicated, and loved without reservation. Guys were just too much work.

I should have known better, should have trusted my instincts and never gotten close. I'd thought I could handle it, keep Lola under control. But the succubus had betrayed me at the worst possible moment. And now I was paying the price.

That was the killer. The price was way too high for a few moments of bliss. It had cost me Dan's friendship.

I blinked back tears. People all over the world were pairing up. Would it ever be my turn? Would I ever be able to be myself and find someone to love without giving up my humanity to do it?

The tears did escape then. This just confirmed that I could never get close to a guy again. Not in that way, anyway. Not unless I took Micah's advice and found someone I could take advantage of to feed Lola first.

Yeah, like that would ever happen.

Forget it. I'd just dwindle into an old maid with nothing but hellhounds to keep me company in my senior years.

VAL, I LOVE YA, BUT ENOUGH WITH THE PITY PARTY, ALREADY.

I wiped a tear away and hugged the snarky little mutt, knowing he was just trying to help. Thank heavens I had Micah now. The only person who could possibly understand me, care about me, was one who was exactly like me. I'd just have to be content with having Micah and Fang as my only family.

My cell rang then, and I stared at it, wondering if I should answer it. I didn't really want to talk to anyone right now.

Then again, it could be Micah.

I answered the phone, surprised to hear Ramirez's voice on the other end.

His conversation was short, but not very sweet. "Get your butt down to my office in half an hour."

"Why?"

"I'll tell you when you get here."

"But . . . I'm not even dressed yet." And I really didn't want to talk to anyone in my current mood.

"Forty-five minutes then." His tone was uncompromising.

"But—"

"If you want to keep this job, be here within forty-five minutes." Without waiting for a response, he hung up.

I stared at the phone in disbelief. Dan sure hadn't wasted any time. At least, I assumed that's what had Ramirez so ticked off. Well, there was only one way to find out. I crawled out of bed and headed for the shower. I'd lost enough important things in my life lately, I didn't want to lose my only source of income, too.

I made it to the West Substation with three minutes to spare.

The desk sergeant gave Fang a dubious glance, but must have gotten approval from Ramirez, for he sent us both on back.

I swung open the door to the lieutenant's office and stopped dead. Dan was there, sitting across from Ramirez.

Ah, hell. I was so not ready for this. I figured it would just be Ramirez and me. I didn't realize he'd force us to be in the same room together.

Fang growled at Dan as if he were a vampire. I suddenly felt a lot better. Now who was the monster? And, taking my cue from Fang, I decided to not let my pain show. I wouldn't give Dan the satisfaction.

"What is *she* doing here?" Dan asked.

Ramirez said, "Have a seat, Val. I promise Dan won't bite."

Fang snorted. YEAH, BUT *I'M* NOT MAKING ANY PROMISES.

Dan made some sort of strangled sound again, but kept his mouth shut. Giving him a wary glance, I sat in the only other chair available . . . next to him.

This time, I was so disappointed in him, so angry at his narrow-minded attitude, that the succubus wasn't even tempted. Lola and I both deserved better.

But as Fang settled protectively between us and Dan tried to scoot farther away, some impulse made me whisper, "Lola says hi."

Dan shot to his feet. "Can I go now?" he asked Ramirez.

YOU GO, GIRL, Fang said, laughing silently.

The lieutenant scowled. "No. Sit down." He glared at both of us as Dan took his seat once more. "Now, what's this about you not wanting to work together any more?"

I shrugged, feigning nonchalance. "Ask him. It was his idea."

I could practically feel Dan grow rigid in the chair next to me. "We don't work well together," Dan bit out.

"You have up until now," Ramirez said calmly. "What's different?"

"We're not . . . compatible," Dan explained.

Ramirez scowled. "What the hell do you think this is? *The Bachelor?* I'm not asking you two to live together, just work together."

Dan's chin came up and he matched the lieutenant scowl for scowl. "Well, I can't do that anymore. I want another partner."

I was in full agreement. I didn't want to work with someone who didn't even consider me human.

Fang snuffled my knee. YEAH. THE ONLY PARTNER YOU NEED IS ME.

"I can't do that," Ramirez said. "Everyone else in the unit is already paired up and working well together."

"Then I'll work alone," Dan said.

"I'd prefer it, too," I said, just in case the lieutenant thought he was trying to spare my feelings or something.

He disabused me quickly of that notion. "You will *not* work alone, either of you. It's too dangerous out there without backup."

I shrugged. "I did it before. What's different now?"

"I'll tell you what's different. We have vampires coming out of the freaking woodwork. Attacks have doubled in the last week, and from what I hear, more and more bloodsuckers are being made every day."

"Maybe that's because of the time of the year," I said, offering a possible explanation. "Halloween, Days of the Dead . . . "

"Maybe," Ramirez conceded. "Except now that the Days of the Dead are over, vampire activity hasn't lessened any. Fortunately, some vampires must still be keeping the media under compulsion not to notice—or not to reveal what they know. Otherwise, there would be wide-spread panic by now." He leaned forward, spearing us both in turn with his intense gaze. "It's dangerous out there, and we can't afford to lose either of you. Either you work together, or you find another job."

"Then I want a transfer," Dan blurted out.

Ramirez leaned back in his chair and raised an eyebrow at Dan's vehemence. "So, you finally learned what she is, huh? Finally learned about her gift?"

"Gift," Dan said derisively. "That's rich."

Well, he was right, there—it was more like a curse.

"Yes, gift," Ramirez insisted, giving Dan a hard stare. "Without it, you might be dead right now. I'll bet she and Fang have saved your butt more than once, haven't they?"

Dan shrugged, but wouldn't admit it.

"I'm sure you've helped her too. And that's exactly why you two need to stay together. You make a damned fine team . . . when you aren't acting like prima donnas, that is." When Dan and I didn't answer, Ramirez added, "You two have the potential to be the best team in the SCU. I can't afford to lose you to something this stupid. I need you. The *city* needs you. Bad."

I didn't know what to think, but Dan had no problem verbalizing his thoughts. "How can we work as a team when I can't trust her?"

"Has she let you down yet?" the lieutenant countered.

"Not as a partner."

That hurt. "What does that mean?" I snapped.

But Dan responded to Ramirez, not me. "I'm talking about her powers. I can't trust her to keep her lust to herself."

Fang glared at him. *THFPTTTTT.*

I had to agree with Fang's mental raspberry. What a pig-headed egotist. I laughed. "Don't flatter yourself, Sullivan. You're not irresistible." Not anymore.

Ramirez regarded Dan thoughtfully. "This isn't something she has control over, you know."

"No kidding. I found that out last night."

The lieutenant raised an eyebrow, as if he would have liked to ask how, but wisely chose not to go there. "But it does give her an edge. She's the best weapon we have to fight the vampires, and you're the best we've got to find out what's causing this and what they're up to." His voice hardened. "Now, are you going to hunker down and do your job or am I gonna have to kick your ass?"

Fang wagged his tail. NOW *THAT* I'D LIKE TO SEE.

I raised my hand. "I vote for—"

"Shut up," Ramirez said, cutting off my smart-aleck response. "You're no better. You wanted a chance to fight the vampires, wanted the ability to feed your demon with the lust of the hunt. I gave that to you . . . and now you want to cave because it got a little difficult?"

How did he know all that? "No—"

"Good. Then you're in."

Ramirez was right. I needed this job. Not only for the money, but for the outlet to keep Lola under control. If Dan couldn't handle it, that was *his* problem. "Yeah. I'm in."

Ramirez nodded, as if he'd expected nothing less, then swung his gaze to Dan's. "Sullivan?"

"I'll do it," Dan bit out. Left unspoken but hanging there in the air was what he left unsaid—he'd do it, but he wouldn't like it.

"Good. Now let me explain what we've learned." And as if nothing had ever happened, the lieutenant briefed us on what the other SCU members had experienced throughout the city as Dan and I took notes. Increased attacks on tourists, vampires traveling in small groups to do more damage, and lots of missing victims who turned up undead the next day. Ramirez was right—it did sound bad.

When he was done, Dan said, "I just have one last question." He sounded so belligerent that I had the feeling I wasn't going to like this.

"Shoot," the lieutenant said.

"How did you know about her demon? And why didn't you tell me?" He tried to keep his voice calm, but obvious anger seethed beneath the surface.

"I didn't tell you because it's Val's business, not yours."

Fang grunted. YOU GOT THAT RIGHT.

I'd wondered how he knew, myself. "Will you tell *me*?" I asked. "Privately?"

Ramirez nodded. "Sullivan, we're done here. You can wait outside."

"Gladly," Dan gritted and left.

Once Dan was out the door and out of hearing range, I asked, "How did you know so much about me?"

Ramirez hesitated, then said, "My informant told me about you, encouraged me to seek you out in fact. But you crossed my threshold before I could find you."

So that's why the lieutenant had recruited me so quickly. I'd wondered. "Who is it? Who knows that much about me?" When he hesitated, I said, "Please, I have to know." Was this person discreet . . . or would the whole world soon know what I was?

Ramirez answered my unasked question. "Don't worry—your secret is safe."

"Is it?" I asked doubtfully. "How do I know that? How do *you* know that?"

He sighed. "I'm not sure if you're ready to hear this yet, but my informant isn't anonymous. He's the leader of the demon underground."

The *what?*

The lieutenant nodded as if he'd heard my stunned question. "Yes, San Antonio has a demon underground. You're not the only one in town, you know."

"I know, but . . . there are more?" More people like Micah and me?

"Yes . . . more than you'd think."

"So how did he know about me?"

"He makes it his business to follow the lives of every person with demon blood, to help where he can, offer assistance when it's needed. If you ever need it, he'll be there for you, too."

Sounded like this mysterious leader had already helped me out at least once. "Lucas Blackburn . . . The leader sent Lucas Blackburn to my parents, didn't he?"

"You could say that."

I relaxed a little. "But . . . how do you know all this?" A suspicion bloomed in my mind. "Are you one of them? Are you . . . part demon, too?"

Fang nudged me. NO, I'D KNOW IF HE WAS.

Ramirez shook his head and said softly, "No, I'm not . . . but my wife is."

I stared at him, open-mouthed.

He smiled ruefully. "I don't have to tell you this is confidential . . . ."

"Of course," I assured him. Stunned by the secret he'd just placed in my care, I vowed to do everything in my power to keep his trust.

That was the easy part. Now for the hard part—trying to find a way to work with Dan that wouldn't make me feel like a monster . . . and wouldn't engage the monster within me.

I found Dan in the parking lot. He kept his body distant and his face hard. But I was so over it already. The anger had drained out of me and now all I felt was sad. Sad that it had come to this, that any potential we might have had as trusted partners—of any kind—was now gone.

Dan ran a hand over his face. "We need to talk about what we're going to do next."

"Okay, where?"

He hesitated for a moment, obviously trying to think of a place that would be private enough not to be overheard, but not intimate. "How about your place?"

"Okay. See you there."

Luckily, Gwen wasn't home. Dan pointedly took a chair on the opposite side of the living room from me, and Fang just as pointedly parked himself between us and eyed Dan with an odd expression that was definitely undog-like.

"What exactly is a part-hellhound dog?" Dan asked uneasily, looking at Fang as if he thought the cute little mutt was as much of a monster as I was.

I shrugged. "Fang's abilities seem to lie primarily in the area of sniffing out vampires, demons, and other unworldly creatures."

I'M THINKING OF ADDING EMASCULATING STUPID COPS TO MY TALENTS.

"So why is he looking at me like that?"

I decided not to relay Fang's threat to Dan's genitals. "He's also very intelligent."

"What does that mean?" Dan asked, looking a little offended.

I sighed. "He understands English, and though he can't speak it, he can communicate telepathically. With me, anyway."

Dan glanced down at Fang, whose jaw had dropped open in what looked like canine amusement. "You understand me?" Dan asked skeptically.

No, DUH. Fang rolled his eyes then deliberately nodded.

Dan looked taken aback. "Do I smell like vampire to you?"

Fang shook his head.

"Then why are you staring at me?" he asked the dog.

BECAUSE I'M HUNGRY AND YOU LOOK LIKE LUNCH.

I snorted. "What do you expect him to do, spell out an answer on the rug? You'll either have to trust me to translate or limit your questions to those he can answer with actions. He doesn't have vocal cords like humans. If he was in demon-hunting mode, you'd know it—his eyes flash purple, too. But I think the reason he's staring at you is because you've been so hostile and he wants to make sure you're not going to hurt me."

You got it, babe.

Fang let loose with a yip and a glare that left Dan in no doubt that the hellhound was agreeing with me.

"Me hurt *you*? That's rich."

Tired of this whole Val-is-a-monster thing, I said, "Are we done with the insults? Can we get to work now?" Focusing on work would be the best all the way around. Maybe then Dan would forget what I was . . . and I would forget he thought of me as something less than human.

"Okay," he said grudgingly, though he didn't apologize. "What's next?"

"You still think Alejandro is the culprit, don't you?"

Dan nodded. "Things got worse just as his movement started growing. I don't see how that could be a coincidence. We can't overlook the fact that he might be responsible for the increased activity. Let's talk to him again, see if we can learn any more."

"Yeah, before my parents barge in and do something stupid." I paused, remembering. "I'd also like to find out where Jen is staying, if I can."

"Well, I did some research on him earlier to see if I could get a home address."

"And?"

"No luck. His blood banks are all in the name of the New Blood Movement and he's not listed as officer or board member on state's corporate records. It's hard to find out more information without knowing his last name. Alejandro is a common name here in San Antonio." And before I could ask, Dan added, "I checked under Lily's name, too. Nothing's changed since she was . . . turned."

"Could she still be living in the same place she was when you were dating?" I asked.

"No—she left and someone else has already moved in. But she hasn't registered a change of address anywhere that I could find."

I nodded slowly. "And we don't know the last names of any of his other people. Wonder if they do that on purpose?"

"Probably. Most cults try to get people to submerge your identity in theirs."

That was an odd thought. "This isn't really a cult, is it?"

"Not yet . . . but you want to bet it won't turn into one?"

"Yeah, I guess it could, even if Alejandro doesn't want it to. So what do we do now?"

Dan shrugged. "We investigate, see what leads we can find, see if we can find a connection between the three vamps who attacked us and the Movement."

I nodded. "Makes sense. How?"

"See what the word is on the streets."

"Ask the gangs, you mean?"

"No, I don't think they'd know much about this. I mean we should ask the bloodsuckers themselves. Find a couple and question them."

Fang perked up. NOW YOU'RE TALKING.

Dan continued, "It'll be dark soon. Let's catch a bite to eat, then catch them before they can get a bite."

GROAN.

I agreed with Fang, but at least Dan seemed to be trying to overcome his prejudices. "You make it sound so easy."

"Hey, how can I lose with a hellhound and a demon vampire Slayer by my side?"

He kept his tone light, but there was an undercurrent to it, as if he resented having to rely on us for help. "All right, let's hunt down some vamps."

# CHAPTER TWELVE

Dan rose to his feet. "So, dinner first, then where? The blood bank to check on your sister? Or would you rather go hunting first?"

I thought for a moment. From all indications, Jen didn't seem to be in immediate danger. "Hunting."

According to Dan's notes, the River Walk was attracting more vampires lately, so we decided to go there first. Dan went to pick up the SCU truck, but I decided to drive the Valkyrie and meet him at a restaurant. We both needed some space.

We walked down the stone steps to the river. During the day, it was a lot more colorful. The beautiful jade green river was lined with dozens of tables topped with brightly colored umbrellas, bustling with tourists. We chose to eat outside at a restaurant on the water so Fang could join us. He wasn't too pleased at having to be on a leash, but it was required at the River Walk.

Conversation was sparse since we couldn't talk about our job in public and we didn't have much else to say to each other. By the time we finished eating, the sun was down.

It was never really dark in this area of the River Walk, though, not with the twinkling fairy lights in the trees and the busy restaurants and hotels along the river. Two groups of partiers floated by on red dinner barges, barely passing each other on the narrow river and adding a brief burst of laughter and gaiety to the evening.

It reminded me that this was what we were trying to preserve— the right for people to live their lives and enjoy themselves without worrying about the dark things that lurked in hiding. It wasn't all about combating the lust inside me or killing vamps. I needed to remember that.

Dan flipped through the notes he'd taken in the lieutenant's office. "It looks like most of the sightings have been downstream. Start there?"

I nodded. That's where I'd killed the vampire the night I'd found Fang.

After we paid and left, we headed past the touristy area, down to the darker side of the River Walk, strolling the flagstone path like any other normal couple. That was, any other normal couple who kept two feet of distance and a small hellhound between them.

I hated the fact that it was necessary, but knew it was the wise thing to do. So far, my anger at Dan had kept Lola at bay, but I couldn't count on it to continue. A little vampire action tonight would help take care of her.

As if my wish had made it so, Fang suddenly paused and sniffed the air. With that telltale purple eye flash, he growled and sprang into action, jerking the leash out of my hand and bolting toward the embankment.

VAMPIRE! he told me, unnecessarily.

Dan ran after him with me close behind, my demon blood sizzling with the anticipation of action. Dan leapt over something, but I didn't notice in time and tripped. As I went sprawling, I had one moment to feel grateful that the large soft thing had kept me from scraping my hands or face on the ground, then realized the thing I'd landed on was a body. A warm, unmoving one.

In horror, I scrambled off it. No, not it. *Her.* I'd seen plenty of dead vamps in my short life, but humans . . . that was something else entirely. I froze for a moment. This wasn't something I'd had to deal with before.

Dan and Fang rushed on ahead, and I chastised myself. *You're a professional, a slayer. You know what to do.*

Yes—I had to see if the woman was still alive. I knelt down to feel the pulse at the side of her neck. Unfortunately, there was no pulse, only a pair of neat punctures, oozing sticky wet blood. Poor woman.

Dan and Fang came back, a little slower than they'd left. *Lose the scent?* I asked Fang, wiping the blood off on my jeans.

YEAH. HE MUST HAVE TAKEN TO THE TREES OR ROOFTOPS, 'CAUSE THERE WAS NOTHING LEFT ON THE GROUND.

"Lost him," Dan said. He glanced down at the woman I'd

tripped over then at me. "Don't you know better than to contaminate a crime scene?"

"Very funny," I snapped. "I'm sure the dead woman appreciates your humor." And dead very recently, too, if the warmth of her body was any indication.

Fang thoroughly sniffed the body. He'd know that vampire's scent again if he encountered it.

Dan removed the dead woman's wallet from her purse then called Ramirez on his cell, advising him to get a team down there ASAP, before any tourists took a stroll this way. "The victim is a Caucasian female, name Lorena Kott, with a Louisiana driver's license," he told Ramirez. "She's probably a tourist." He pulled out one of her business cards. "Says she's a molecular virologist."

I gazed down at her with regret. It wasn't often I actually *saw* the victims. "She looks like a nice woman. I wonder what she was doing on this part of the River Walk by herself?"

"Oh my God, Lorena," a woman exclaimed from the sidewalk behind us. She stared at the body in horror and hurried over.

Dan and I spent the next twenty minutes trying to calm the hysterical woman, and I was grateful when the team arrived and took over. This had to stop. I never wanted to have to do this for some poor person's loved ones ever again. What if it had been Jen? The thought made my blood run cold, making me even more determined to learn as much as I could.

After the team took over, Dan and I were free to do some more hunting. Unfortunately, with all the sirens and flashing lights, I figured any vamp would be long gone by now.

Ramirez was right—the vamps were getting bolder, getting closer to crowded areas, which was so unlike them. "Let's go somewhere else," I suggested.

Dan agreed and we headed out toward the seedy west side of town where there had been increased vampiric activity, me on my motorcycle with Dan following in the truck. But as we passed HemisFair Park with its distinctive Tower of the Americas silhouette, Fang suddenly nudged me with his nose, hard. I glanced back and saw he was snarling, his fur hackled.

I SMELL VAMP. TAKE A RIGHT.

I did as he asked and thrust an arm in that direction to let Dan know where I was going.

The hellhound directed me through the park, finally saying, STOP HERE.

I had barely come to a skidding halt when Fang leapt off the motorcycle and took off for the trees, still wearing his goggles. Taking a moment to shove down the kickstand, I ran after him, figuring Dan was close behind.

As the demon leapt joyfully into play, I ran as silently as I could so as not to alert the vamp. No, make that *vamps*, plural, I realized as I suddenly came upon two of them in a clearing.

A boy about Jen's age lay on the ground, and two male vamps tugged a girl between them like a wishbone they were about to pull apart. The girl was making helpless whimpering noises as the boys, who didn't appear to look any older than their victims, fought over her.

"Stop," I yelled. *You, too, Fang. We need info.*

Fang halted, and the vamps turned toward us. They howled with laughter, then the redheaded one on the right said, "What? Or your ferocious four-eyed dog will attack us? Ooooh, I'm so scared."

The other snarled, trying to look bad-ass and failing as he said in a dramatic voice, "You have no idea what you're dealing with."

Fang snorted. ARE WE IN THE MIDDLE OF A BAD B MOVIE, OR WHAT? WHAT ARE THEY, TWELVE?

Luckily for me, the redhead made the mistake of trying to control my mind. He must have been very newly made, because as soon as he connected I was able to learn exactly what kind of person I was dealing with. "Oh, really?" I whipped two stakes out of my back holster and spun them like an old-time gunslinger, letting them come to rest with the sharp ends pointed toward their hearts. "Care to bet on that, Billy? Or you, James?"

I grinned—I'd been practicing that move for awhile and had finally gotten the hang of it.

They cast uncertain looks at me, obviously wondering how I knew their names. "Who are you?" Billy, the skinny redhead, asked.

"Ever heard of the Slayer?" I might as well get some use out of the stupid nickname.

"Ye-es," James, the more solidly built blond, admitted.

"Then you know what I do to creatures like you who hurt people. Let go of the girl." I took a menacing step forward, wondering where the heck Dan was.

The vamps snarled, still not understanding the danger, still thinking they were immortal. "Make me," Billy said mockingly.

I heard a twang and a swish, and Billy was suddenly pinned to a tree by a quivering quarrel bolt. As the vamp screamed, I glanced aside to see Dan just stepping out of the shadows, reloading his crossbow.

Fang woofed. GOOD SHOT.

"Nice toy," I said admiringly. So that's what had delayed him.

"Nicer than you think," he said, aiming at James. "The bolts are coated in silver."

No wonder Billy was still screaming . . . and unable to pull himself loose.

"Let go of the girl," Dan called to James. "Or the next one goes in your throat."

James didn't even try to resist and was too dumb to think of using the girl as a shield. He dropped her, and she crawled toward the boy on the ground, sobbing.

James backed away, his hands up as Fang advanced with a menacing growl.

LET ME TAKE JUST ONE LITTLE BITE, PLEASE.

*Not yet. Let's see what else we can find out, first.*

"Don't shoot," James begged. "We weren't going to hurt her—we were just gonna have a taste."

Billy stopped screaming long enough to gasp out his agreement.

"Like you did to that boy on the ground?" Dan asked, his voice hard.

"He's not dead—just fainted," James said. "Ask her."

The girl, who had been frantically pawing at the boy, finally spoke. "He's alive, but no thanks to *them*." If her eyes had been weapons, James and Billy would have been slain on the spot.

They were telling the truth. "They're newly undead," I told Dan, holding one hand in staking position as I approached James.

The vamp stared at me from fear-filled eyes, his mouth wide with shock as he backed as far as he could. When his back came up against a tree and he could go no farther, Fang growled.

WHAT A WIMP. A DISGRACE TO VAMPIRES EVERYWHERE.

I stifled a smile. Fang had his fierce gaze on James's crotch, like a child eyeing a Christmas package he couldn't wait to unwrap. "Good boy," I said. "If he moves, eat the dangly bits first."

James visibly gulped and lowered his hands to shield his bits, which had probably shriveled by now. "How . . . how do you know when we were made?"

"I know because I'm the Slayer," I said and gave him a cold smile. "Go ahead, try to control my mind."

The idiot did, and at the first probe of his mind, he opened up a connection between us that I now owned—I could read his every thought. "Ask your questions," I told Dan.

"When were you turned?" he asked.

"Last . . . last week," James said.

"Who turned you?"

"I-I don't know. It was one of those initiation things. Everyone was masked."

Dan shook his head like he didn't believe it, but I said, "He's telling the truth. So far." But this was the first I'd heard of someone being turned by a group.

"Who do you work for?" Dan persisted.

"No-no one," James gasped out.

"Then why are you working together?" Dan demanded. "Most vamps work alone."

"We're best friends, we always do everything together." James glanced tearfully at his friend who was still pinned to the tree. "Why did you do that to him?"

Fang took a step closer as Dan menaced James with the crossbow. "You should be more worried about what we're going to do to you if you don't answer my questions."

The vamp didn't seem able to decide which threat was more dangerous—Fang or Dan. "What? Ask me anything, just let him go."

For the next twenty minutes, Dan grilled James. We learned

that he and his friend had contacted the vamps themselves, thinking that becoming undead would solve all their problems. But James didn't know who had "initiated" them, didn't know anything about the three who had attacked us, and didn't have a clue who was behind the sudden rash of new vampires springing up around San Antonio. The only order their initiators had given them was to avoid the New Blood Movement and the blood banks at all costs.

"He's telling the truth," I confirmed

"How many people have you killed?" Dan asked, his voice hard.

"None, I swear it," James said as his friend sobbed out a denial. "We'd never do that—we only take a little. But we have to have blood somehow or we'll die."

Dan glanced at me. I said, "James is being a good little vampire and telling the truth." I backed off a little when I realized that. These idiots had gotten in way over their heads. But it wasn't like they could suddenly change their minds and decide they didn't want to be undead after all.

"Are you going to let us live?" James asked, hope dawning on his face.

"Why should we?" Dan asked harshly.

I moved closer to Dan, and said softly, "They haven't killed anyone. Maybe we should let them go."

Dan scowled. "But they have terrorized people. And we don't have holding cells for vamps."

"Yes, but we can't just kill them." Not when they were helpless. When he continued to frown, I added softly, "They remind me of Jen. It's the kind of stupid mistake she'd make . . . that she might still make. Remember what Alejandro said—not all vamps are evil. They become more of what they were when they were alive." After touching the minds of these fledgling vamps, I believed that. "Maybe you can scare them into staying on the straight and narrow."

Dan relaxed a little. "Okay, you have a point."

I relaxed muscles I hadn't realized I'd tightened and Fang sighed mentally. WELL, SHOOT. I WAS LOOKING FORWARD TO THOSE DANGLY BITS.

Dan glanced at the terrified baby vamps and raised his voice.

"You're lucky. My partner is feeling charitable today and wants to let you live."

"We won't do it again, I swear," Billy said.

"Will you join the New Blood Movement?" Dan asked. "Take blood only from those willing to give it?"

I listened carefully to James's mind to see what that meant to him. All I got was fear.

"But they told us to stay away from the blood banks," James protested.

"Or what?" I asked.

"Huh?"

"What did your sires say would happen if you went there?"

"Sires? You mean our fathers?"

I rolled my eyes. These clueless guys knew absolutely nothing about the culture they'd joined. "Your sire is the vampire who turned you. What did yours say would happen if you went to the New Blood Movement?"

James seemed genuinely puzzled. "Nothing—they just said not to go there."

Dan looked incredulous. "They made you, said don't go to the blood banks, then let you trot off without guidance or supervision?"

"Yeah, I guess." James glanced back and forth between Dan and me as if wondering what it signified.

"Doesn't that seem strange to you?" Dan asked.

"Uh . . . yes?" He said it as if asking Dan if he were giving the right answer.

I sighed. "Trust me, it's odd. I doubt they are tracking you or even have a clue what you're doing."

"Right," Dan grated. "But I can guarantee you one thing. If we ever hear either one of you have attacked another person again, we will personally hunt you down, stake you on a sheet of silver, and feed you to the sun. Have you got that clear?"

"Yes, sir!" James snapped as smartly as any military recruit. Billy nodded.

"Good—use the blood banks. That's what they're for."

Dan removed the bolt from Billy's shoulder. The vamps sped

off into the darkness, terrified out of their minds. Good. Maybe this incident had knocked some sense into their heads.

THEY MUST BE GETTING DESPERATE FOR SOMEONE TO TURN, Fang said, his tongue lolling out as he looked very pleased with himself.

As well he should. *Thanks for sniffing those two out for us.*

MY PLEASURE. WHEN I SMELLED THE HUMANS, TOO, I KNEW SOMEONE HAD TO BE IN TROUBLE.

Oh, yeah, the humans. I glanced around, but the two victims had vanished, apparently having made good their escape while their attackers were distracted.

"So, lust demons are lie detectors, too?" Dan asked as he carefully disarmed the crossbow.

I shrugged and answered him warily. "Not really. But if they try to control my mind, I can read theirs. That's what gives me an edge in a fight. And those two were so new, they couldn't hide anything."

"Nice ability. Any reason why you didn't tell me earlier?" He sounded a little miffed.

"Because then I would have had to reveal my true nature . . . and look how well *that* turned out."

"Anything else I should know about you?"

"Let's see," I said mockingly. "Lust, reading minds, inhuman speed, super hearing, fast healing . . . nope, that about covers it."

"Good."

"So glad you're satisfied. Now, let's talk about what we learned."

"Like what?" Dan asked. "Did you get more out of that than I did?"

"I shared everything I learned."

"Then all we know is that some mysterious vampires sired them and told them not to go near Alejandro's organization."

"Yeah. Kind of makes it look like he's in the clear. On this anyway."

"Maybe. Maybe not," Dan said. "Kind of sounds like classic game theory—the quickest way to get humans on board with blood banks is to show them the alternative. People will be lining up to give blood in a nice civilized fashion once this gets out. He's probably getting desperate, too, since the news isn't picking this up."

"Or maybe someone else is trying to make him look guilty because they know that's what people would think."

"I doubt it."

"That remains to be seen."

Dan looked exasperated, but I could tell he wasn't entirely convinced by his own arguments. "Let's do it then. Let's find out."

"All right." Next stop—Alejandro's blood bank. And he'd better have some damned good answers.

\*

I glared, exasperated, at the perky Brittany. "Yes, I understand Alejandro isn't here, but can you tell us where he is?" This was the third blood bank we'd visited, with no luck.

"No, I'm sorry, I don't know," Brittany said, apparently determined to be cheerful despite my annoyance.

"What about one of his assistants? Like Lily or Austin?" What were the names of the other two? Oh, yeah. "Or Rosa, Luis."

"They're not here, either."

"Look," Dan said. "You know we were here before and met with Alejandro and the others. Can you get a message to him, letting him know we'd like to talk to him?"

A frown marred her pretty face. "I-I can't. I don't know how to get in touch with him. It's a secret."

Dan and I exchanged glances. *A secret?* "Why?"

Brittany glanced around the full waiting room nervously. I checked to see if anyone was watching, and saw one guy in the waiting area who looked interested in our conversation. Blond and good-looking, he appeared familiar, but I couldn't place him.

Brittany must have noticed him, too, for she lowered her voice and leaned forward to confide, "Alejandro has to be more careful. There's been . . . trouble lately."

"What kind of trouble?" Dan asked in a voice equally as low.

"Some of the other vampires are resisting the Movement. They've been attacking people outside the blood banks, especially when Alejandro is there. So, he's had to lay low for awhile."

I nodded. That tracked with what had happened to us the last time we were here.

"Do you have Alejandro's home address?" Dan asked.

Brittany looked shocked at the suggestion. "He doesn't give that out to anyone."

"How about his cell phone number?" Dan persisted. "I know he has one."

"Maybe, but I don't have it."

Looking as exasperated as I felt, Dan asked, "Then how do you get in touch with him if something goes wrong?"

"I don't. I contact the manager and he gets in touch with Alejandro."

"Okay," Dan said patiently. "Can we talk with your manager?"

Brittany waved an arm at the full waiting room. "You'll have to wait in line. He has a lot of people waiting to see him."

"Never mind," Dan said and gave Brittany our cell phone numbers in case she saw Alejandro. "Thanks for your help."

As Dan pulled me away, I asked, "Why didn't you wait? Or flash your badge or something?"

"The manager's a vamp—he won't be any more forthcoming."

True.

Though we had kept our voices low, that blond guy was still watching us. I nodded toward him. "Do you know who that guy is—the blond, in the blue shirt? He's been watching us. I recognize him, but can't place him."

Dan glanced in that direction. "No, but I recognized someone else in the last blood bank we visited."

"Who?"

"A waitress from Micah's club."

I glanced at the blond again. Take off his shirt and add devil horns . . . . "That's it. He's a bartender at Purgatory." We exchanged glances. "Think it's a coincidence?"

Dan shook his head. "I don't believe in coincidences, not when it comes to police work. We're not getting anywhere in finding Alejandro. Let's check it out."

I reluctantly agreed to visit Micah's club. Though I wouldn't mind seeing him again, I wished it wasn't under these circumstances. I didn't trust Dan not to bully him. So, when we got there, I said, "Let me do the talking, okay?"

Dan raised an eyebrow. "Why? Because he's your cousin?"

"Yeah." Sort of. "And you don't have a great track record in dealing with those who are . . . different."

Dan looked as if he would have liked to respond to that, but he wisely kept his mouth shut.

We approached the door of the club and Fang followed.

I'M TIRED OF WAITING OUTSIDE.

*They may not let you in.*

DOESN'T HURT TO TRY.

To my surprise, the Bela Lugosi doorman we'd met before glanced at Fang but made no objections as he ushered us in through the back way to Micah's office.

Micah was between sets, doing some paperwork, when we walked in. Fang ran over and greeted him like a long-lost friend, and Micah responded in kind.

"That's Fang," I said with a laugh. "We must smell alike or something. I've never seen him do that to anyone else."

I LIKE HIM, Fang said, sounding a little guilty. What did he have to feel guilty about? He could like who he wanted.

Micah smiled and rose to give me a hug. "It's good to see you again."

I returned his embrace. It felt good to just be held by someone who didn't judge me, didn't want something from me. I released him reluctantly, and we all seated ourselves, Fang surprisingly crawling into Micah's lap.

But before I could say anything, a woman stuck her head in the door. Slight, with an elfin face and exotically slanted eyes, she looked like a pixie. "I have some info for the scuzz—" She broke off as she spotted us in the room. "For that, uh scuzzball."

Micah frowned at her. "Thank you, Tessa. I'll get it later." Tessa nodded and withdrew, and Micah said, "Sorry about that. What can I do for you?"

I squirmed a little. "I'm afraid this isn't a social call. We have some questions for you."

Micah glanced toward Dan, then questioned me with his eyes.

"He knows," I said simply.

"Knows what?"

Dan answered. "I know what you both are—incubus, succubus, the whole demon thing." His tone was bland, but that didn't fool me. He sounded too casual, as if contempt was seething just below the surface.

Micah's raised eyebrow showed that he must have sensed it as well. "I take it the revelation didn't go well."

I pursed my lips. "You could say that." I turned to Dan. "Maybe it would be better if you let me talk to him alone."

"Forget it."

"But I'll share everything I get," I promised.

"Then there should be no problem in letting me hear it first-hand." Dan shook his head. "What's the problem, Val? You trying to protect your cousin and his demon friends?"

"What makes you think he needs protection . . . or even *has* demon friends?" I asked in exasperation.

Dan just shook his head, as if my question was too dumb to answer. Okay, maybe it was. I didn't know if Micah actually had any demon friends, but if he did, I planned to keep Dan out of it. I slanted an apologetic look at Micah.

"It's okay," Micah said as he continued petting Fang. "What do you want to know?"

"There have been increased attacks by vampires recently, and we're trying to find out who's behind it. You've heard of Alejandro and his New Blood Movement?"

"Yes. But what does that have to do with me?"

"We saw some of your employees at the blood bank . . . ." I trailed off, knowing it was a long shot.

"What my employees do on their day off is their own business. We don't regulate morals here."

Dan made a disbelieving sound. "Two employees, two different blood banks. Don't you think that's a hell of a coincidence?"

Micah shrugged, looking unconcerned. "Perhaps the atmosphere at Purgatory lends itself to my employees being more accepting of the supernatural."

"Perhaps," Dan said doubtfully. "Or maybe they accept it better because they're demons, too."

I scowled, not liking the way my partner was harassing my cousin, no matter how distant the relationship. I turned to Micah, prepared to apologize, but he didn't look angry. In fact, his expression was totally bland as he continued to pet Fang. The hellhound had a blissful look on his face from all the attention.

Hmm . . . odd. If Micah was part-demon like me—and he definitely was—then he should be used to dogs sensing his demon and shying away. Why had he assumed Fang was different? He hadn't been surprised when Fang jumped in his lap, and they seemed awfully cozy together. A sudden suspicion bloomed within me. "How do you know my dog? How did you know he was friendly?"

Both Micah and Fang froze, the picture of guilt. Then Micah relaxed. "You mentioned him last time I saw you. I figured if he didn't object to your nature, he wouldn't object to mine either."

"But I didn't mention him." I was certain of that.

Micah shrugged. "I must have heard about him somewhere, then."

Fang got down off his lap and came to lie at my feet, looking abject as only a dog could. I LOVE YOU BEST.

That wasn't the issue. Come to think of it, there were some other odd things, too. "And your employee Tessa. She started to say scuzzie, first, didn't she? Before she changed it to scuzzball. Scuzzie is what others call members of the SCU."

Dan narrowed his eyes at Micah, whose expression gave nothing away.

I followed through on that line of thought. "And Ramirez knew what I was, without me telling him. The only thing I can figure is that Ramirez got the information from his informant." I speared Micah with a look that dared him to lie to me. "Someone here at Purgatory is the informant, isn't he? And the leader of the demon underground?"

"The what?" Dan asked, looking surprised.

Well, shoot. I shouldn't have mentioned that in front of him. But I couldn't worry about that now as all my attention was focused on Micah.

He sighed. "You are persistent, aren't you? I should have expected that."

"Yes, you should have," I agreed. "But stop stalling and answer the question. Who is it?"

He stared at me for a moment, as if thinking. "I can't tell you. You don't need to know."

"Yes, I *do* need to know. He's Ramirez's informant. He probably has information we need. If he can help, you can't keep his identity a secret. We need him."

Micah sighed. "You're right." He paused, obviously reluctant to give up the secret, then finally relented. "The leader is . . . me."

For some reason, that shocked me. He seemed too young to be the leader of anything. "You? Why didn't you tell me?" Okay, I knew it was unreasonable to expect him to have told me his secrets, but I'd bared my soul to him, so I guess I expected he should have done the same. Irrationally, I felt left out.

"You didn't need to know yet. And Sullivan *sure* didn't." He shot Dan an annoyed glance.

"Sorry about that." I hadn't meant to reveal his secrets—especially since I hadn't known they existed.

"How did you find out about the underground in the first place?" Micah asked.

"Ramirez told me."

Dan looked startled, but that was one secret I'd keep to myself. If Ramirez wanted Dan to know about his wife, the lieutenant would tell him.

Sudden realization made me turn to Micah. "So that's what you meant when you said you've been helping me where you could. Ramirez said something similar. Did you get my job for me?"

"Not exactly. I told Ramirez what you were when it was clear you were being interviewed by the SCU, but it was Ramirez's decision to hire you."

"And Fang?" I demanded.

"Fang is a fairly new member of our organization," Micah admitted. "I sent him to meet you, but it was his decision to stay."

Fang nudged me with his nose, looking soulfully up at me. I CHOSE YOU, he assured me. LOVE YA, BABE.

Well, at least the dog was truly my friend. And apparently Micah was, too . . . secretly. How strange that he had done all that without my knowledge. "So you did help me." I didn't know whether to be grateful . . . or annoyed that I hadn't accomplished everything on my own since my newfound liberation.

"That's what the underground is for," Micah said with a wary glance at Dan.

"Don't worry," Dan growled. "I won't reveal your secrets."

Micah nodded, though he didn't look convinced. "We help other part-demons and magic users find jobs, network with others like themselves."

"Hide from the rest of the world," Dan said flatly.

"Live normal lives," Micah corrected him. "We just want to be like everyone else without having to worry about being persecuted for our differences."

"Why you?" I asked. "Why are you the leader?"

"My father was the former leader. He trained me to take his place and rescue others like you and me."

"So why didn't the two of you rescue me?" I asked, wondering why I had never had the comfort of knowing there were others like myself in the world. It would have helped so much . . . .

"We didn't need to. Your parents did that for you. No matter what you might think of them now, they helped you learn to deal with your powers, enter the mainstream. Do you know how many would envy you for the life you've led? You didn't need rescuing."

Intellectually, I understood, but emotionally, I wasn't quite there yet. I'd felt like a freak for so long, like a total outsider to that mainstream. He could have welcomed me in to a world where I belonged. Instead, he'd let me continue staying in that house, knowing what he knew, and not cluing me in. I felt a little abandoned, as if my best friend had just let me down.

Fang poked me with his nose. NO, I'M STILL HERE.

The fuzzy mutt did make me feel better. "Okay, but why are you an informant?" I asked Micah. "Why do you work for the SCU?"

Micah flicked another wary glance at Dan, but decided to answer. "The purpose of the underground is to help our kind become accepted in normal society. But there are those, like many vampires, who don't want to blend or live peacefully alongside everyone else. They make it worse for the rest of us, so between us, Ramirez and I try to keep the malcontents under control."

"How?"

Dan snorted. "Obviously, he has a network of spies everywhere. That's why we saw his two employees at the blood banks, and why Ramirez knows so much about what the vampires are doing."

"I wouldn't call them spies," Micah said. "Watchers, maybe. When we learn of something that endangers the city, we let the lieutenant know."

It all made sense now. And maybe he could help with the argument Dan and I had. "So is the New Blood Movement bad or good? Are they behind the increased vampire attacks on humans?"

Micah grimaced. "I wish I could answer that, but it remains to be seen. I've tried to get some people into their inner circle, but haven't had any success yet." He cocked his head, looking curious. "Why is this so important to you?"

"Because not only do we need to stop this sudden crime wave, but my sister has gotten mixed up with them." The light dawned. "Wait. DU . . . demon underground. Are you the one who sent me the text message about Jen?"

Micah nodded. "My people did, anyway. We've been keeping an eye on you and your family, so when it became clear that your sister was getting involved with the blood banks, I thought you ought to know."

"Thanks—I appreciate that." Another mystery solved. "But we need more information. Do you know where Alejandro lives? He must have some place where he goes to rest at dawn each day."

"I don't know offhand, but we have an extensive database on the activities of those we've been watching. It might be in there, but I don't have time to search for it right now. I have another show."

"Can I take a look?" Dan asked.

When Micah looked reluctant, I said, "He's really a whiz with a computer. And if Ramirez trusts him, maybe you could, too."

"I'll only search for information on Alejandro and his

lieutenants—I won't touch anything else," Dan promised.

"I'll watch him, make sure of it," I added.

"Okay," Micah said, and turned toward the computer. He pulled up a program and turned it over to Dan, giving him a piercing look. "I'm trusting you on Val's word. Don't let us down."

"I won't," Dan said. "Word of a Sullivan. Trust me, it's good."

"Okay."

Micah left us alone with the computer, and Dan rubbed his hands together before settling them on the keys. "Now, to find Alejandro . . . ."

# CHAPTER THIRTEEN

After about half an hour of searching, Dan said, "Got it!"

"What?" I asked, peering over his shoulder at the computer.

"This record says one of Micah's . . . operatives followed Alejandro and his people one night to a house, and they stayed there all day and didn't come back out until moonrise."

"Great—that must be it, then. Where is it?"

He scribbled down the address. "It's in Alamo Heights."

"Oh, really? That's a pretty ritzy neighborhood."

"Yeah. No telling how many years he's had to accumulate money."

True—it could have been centuries for all we knew—vampires didn't age after they were turned.

Micah came back in then, wearing a brief Tarzan-type costume and looking like he'd just had a workout. It was one thing to see him perform on stage, but quite another to see him mostly naked and sweaty in his own office. Dan looked as uncomfortable as I felt.

Apparently sensing that, Micah slipped on a robe and asked, "Have any luck?"

"Yes, we did." Dan rose and stuck the address in his pocket. "Found his address in your system and we're going to check it out tonight. Thanks."

"You're welcome." Micah leaned casually against the doorframe, but his eyes were intense as he regarded Dan. "Anytime you need information—on anything to do with demons—" he flicked a glance at me "—just ask."

Real subtle. But Dan obviously didn't want to know anything else about Lola. He grimaced and said, "Thanks."

"Good luck," Micah called as we went out the door.

As we headed out toward the parking lot, Dan said, "Why don't we take the truck? It's less conspicuous."

He had a point. With Fang sitting on the back of my motorcycle in his goggles, we were more likely to draw attention than divert it.

Yeah, that's 'cause I'm smokin'!

I suppressed a grin. And here I thought it'd be difficult to get Fang to wear those goggles . . . .

We arrived at the address and all three of us sat there for a moment or two, gaping at the mansion. Done in Spanish-Mediterranean style, it boasted three stories on at least five acres, dozens of rooms, and gated security.

Talk about conspicuous consumption . . . .

"Looks like there's room there for a whole nest of vampires," Dan said.

"Yeah . . . and a few humans as well." And it would be real attractive to Jennifer who always wanted more than our parents had been able to provide. I released my seat belt and gave Dan a doubtful glance. "Are you sure this is the right place?"

Dan consulted the paper in his pocket. "It's the address that was in Micah's database."

"How do we find out if it's Alejandro's hideout? Knock on the front door and ask if they have vampires living there?"

He gave me a wry glance. "How far do you think that will get us?"

"Probably not far."

"Yeah. Even though Alejandro invited us to ask questions, he probably wouldn't be happy we showed up at his house." Dan thought for a moment. "Well, we can either charge right in and see if we can find her, or do some reconnaissance, see if this is the right place and if Jennifer is even in there." He glanced at his watch. "We have about forty-five minutes until dawn. If there's any activity inside, it'll likely stop by then. If we want to learn anything, we'd better do it now."

"Okay," I said. "Let's take a look."

Fang growled and looked behind us. Company, he warned.

A dark limo was approaching. We all crouched down in the seat to be less visible, but Dan watched out of the side view mirror.

"What's going on?" I whispered.

"They're entering numbers on a security box." After a moment, he said, "Okay, they've gone in. Let's check it out."

Dan peered at the box on a pole next to the gate. "It's a cipher lock."

I glanced down at Fang. "Were there vamps in the limo?"

He sniffed the air. NOT MUCH TO GO ON, BUT YEAH, SOME FOLKS OF THE UNDEAD PERSUASION WERE DEFINITELY IN THAT LIMO.

Okay, so we probably had the right place. I nodded at Dan.

Dan glanced up at the wrought iron fence where the *fleur de lis* designs on top came to a sharp point every six inches or so. "We can either try to make it over that, or wait for another car to come through. At this time of night, there might be more returning to the nest."

"You could," a man said from behind us. "Or you could use the code and get in that way."

I grabbed a stake and whirled toward the source of the voice, seeing Dan do the same. But Fang was wagging his tail as he ran over to greet the newcomer.

CHILL. HE'S A FRIEND.

Dan and I relaxed as the man, who stayed in the shadows, bent down to pet Fang. "Howya doing, pal?" He straightened, saying, "They call me Shade. Micah called me, asked me to come by and give you a message."

Shade stayed hidden, making it difficult to make out his features, especially since he was wearing a hood that obscured his face. But there was something odd about him, something not quite right. Since he came from Micah, he was probably some kind of demon. Best to let the guy retain his secrets and anonymity.

I put away my stake and Dan did the same. "What message?"

"I've been watching this place, and Micah said to tell you whatever you need to know. I figure you need the code—78209."

How original—it was the zip code here. "Is there a camera pick-up?"

"No, just voice for visitors to request admission."

"Thanks." I pulled a picture of Jen out of my back pocket. "Have you seen this girl go in there?"

Shade took the photo and pulled it into his darkness. "I've

seen her, once or twice." He handed the photo back to me, never letting a glimpse of his skin show.

"Is she there now?"

"Maybe. I don't know. I can't be here twenty-four seven."

Damn. I wish there was some way to know for sure.

Dan asked, "How many vamps are in there?"

"It varies. Sometimes as few as eight, or as many as twenty. More sometimes when there's an event going on."

"Is one going on now?"

Shade turned toward the house as if searching out its secrets. "No, not enough lighted windows."

"Still, eight is too many," Dan said.

"You don't think Ramirez would authorize us to take an army in there?" I asked dryly.

"I doubt it. And to be completely legal, we need a search warrant." He turned toward the spy. "What can you tell us about the security at the house?"

"Not much, but I haven't seen any sentries patrolling the grounds. I guess they figure they don't need them."

True. How many people would be dumb enough to sneak into a nest of vampires with super-sensitive senses?

"What about electronic security systems?" Dan asked.

"I don't know. I just watch from afar, keep track of the comings and goings when the situation warrants. There hasn't been much activity tonight, though."

"Is Alejandro inside?" I asked.

"I think so. I haven't seen him leave, anyway."

Dan nodded. "Thanks—you've been a big help."

"You're welcome." And Shade, true to his name, slipped back into the darkness.

"So," I said. "Do we go in on foot or take the truck?"

"I'd rather not take the chance that anyone would see the truck. It might be out of place among their other vehicles—especially if they have more limos."

"Okay, on foot it is." I strode to the gate and keyed in the numbers Shade had given us. Just as promised, the gate opened, then closed silently behind us.

We kept to the wooded areas at the sides as we approached the house and crept up to one lighted window. We crouched down to peer in, but all I could see was the curtain covering it. Most of the windows on the ground floor were that way, except for one. It looked like a dining room and was empty of people. Made sense— vamps wouldn't have much use for a dining room.

I leaned over to whisper in Dan's ear, "I'll check out the second story."

He frowned at me. "Okay, but be careful."

There were several live oak trees along the side of the house, and I shimmied up one of them, then climbed out on a limb to check out the light in the second story. Yes, there were a couple of people inside, though I still couldn't see much through the sheer curtains. I gave Dan a thumb's-up and edged out a little more. But I was paying so much attention to the window that I wasn't paying attention to my feet. One foot slipped and I lost my balance for a moment.

Dan, looking alarmed, rose to catch me, but I grabbed a branch and regained my footing quickly.

Unfortunately, Dan was now clearly visible from the windows.

Fang yipped. WATCH OUT!

"Intruders," someone yelled.

Suddenly, the bottom window was thrust open and a vamp I'd never seen before flew out at Dan, smashing him against a tree.

Two more followed him out and as Fang tried to hamstring the one attacking Dan, Lola broke free with glee for the hunt. I jumped down to land on the other two, hoping we could fight free of these three before any more joined the fray.

Shoot, I hadn't thought to draw a stake before jumping and was too occupied with using my feet and fists to keep these two at bay to get one now. I caught a glimpse of two more vamps peering out the window. *Aw, crap.* We were in trouble now.

*Fang, hurry, go get Shade. We need backup.*

But before the hellhound could leave, a buzzer sounded and all of the vamps froze. Suddenly abandoning the fight, they dove back into the house through the window and hurriedly closed it.

"What the—" Dan's words were cut off as shutters slammed

down on every window all over the house, completely obscuring the view inside.

WHOA. THAT WAS LUCKY.

*No, that was dawn.* I gestured toward the first few pink rays of light. "The shutters cut off the light, and the buzzer must have warned them dawn was imminent. I guess they didn't want to get caught outside in the sunshine." Thank heavens. Lola seemed a little disappointed, but now that the threat was gone, I locked her down good and tight. Didn't want Dan getting all freaked out again.

Dan started to move but moaned.

Fang glanced up at him. THAT DOESN'T LOOK GOOD.

"What's wrong?" I asked, coming to take a closer look at him in the darkness. There was a dark stain on his shoulder, the same one he'd injured before. "Is that your blood?"

"I'm not sure . . . ." But the pain in his voice indicated it probably was.

I peered closer and gasped. "There's a small branch piercing your shoulder. Hold on, let me help you."

Fang winced. OUCH. THAT'S GOTTA HURT.

I pulled Dan away. The pain must have been excruciating as the branch came out, but he didn't show it, though his whole body tensed around the pain.

"Come on," I said. "Let's get you to a hospital."

"Okay, but not Gwen's," he gritted out. "She'll worry."

Shaking my head, I helped him back to the truck.

*

The emergency room fixed him up, but the doctors said it would be days before he could use his right arm at all, weeks or months before physical therapy would bring it back to full use.

We had a short tussle about who exactly was going to drive the SCU truck back, but I won since Dan wasn't in any condition to drive.

Fang snorted. YA THINK?

Ignoring Fang, I concentrated on driving the truck, which was bigger than anything I'd driven before.

Dan slumped in his seat. "I can't believe I was so stupid," he muttered.

"How do you figure?"

"If I hadn't stood up in front of the window, they wouldn't have spotted me, and we wouldn't be in this mess."

"That was my fault. After all, you stood up to keep me from falling." Which was kind of sweet, come to think of it.

Dan grunted, but I couldn't tell if he was grunting yes or no.

Fant arched a doggie brow. SOMETIMES A GRUNT IS JUST A GRUNT. AND DOES IT REALLY MATTER? THE GUY'S IN PAIN, PROBABLY NOT THINKING STRAIGHT.

True, he'd refused to take any more medication until he got home.

When we got back to his townhouse, I followed him inside.

"No need to stay," he said, scowling.

"Someone needs to," I shot back. "You're right-handed, aren't you?"

"Yeah. So?"

"So you can't use your right hand or your right arm at all for several days—the doctor said so. You'll need help."

"I'll manage."

Fang belched. HE'S A BIG GUY, HE CAN HANDLE IT. HOW ABOUT YOU FEED YOUR FAITHFUL HELLHOUND INSTEAD?

That's right—in all the excitement, we hadn't eaten lately. I regarded Dan doubtfully. "Tell you what, I'll take Fang home and get him something to eat, then I'll be back to see how you're doing."

"That's not necessary—" Dan began, but I was already gone and out the door before he could object further.

I gave Fang some leftover pizza and decided to take the rest to Dan's. Fang flopped down on the bed and refused to leave the room, declining to help me play nursemaid. I hurried back to Dan's and didn't knock, not giving him a chance to turn me away. From the sounds of it, he was in the kitchen.

He didn't realize I was there yet so I watched as he got a can of Coke out of the refrigerator and tried to open it with his left hand. When it slipped away from him, he set it on the countertop and braced it against the refrigerator. But when he tried to pop the top, it shot across the slick side of the fridge like a greased pig.

He tried to grab it with his right hand, evidently forgetting his injury, and cursed in pain as the Coke spewed all over the kitchen floor.

Time to make my presence known. "I'll get that," I said and grabbed some paper towels.

"I can do it," he snapped.

"I'm sure." I glared up at him from my position on the floor. "But I can do it faster and easier. Stop playing macho man and go sit down in the living room. I'll bring you a Coke."

He glared at me, but stomped off anyway. I heated up the leftover pizza, put it on a couple of plates, and brought it in along with a fresh soda.

He regarded the pizza suspiciously. "What's that for?"

"Eating."

He flashed me a look of annoyance at my sarcastic tone, and I added, "The doctor said you'll need something on your stomach when you take the pain pill. Don't want you throwing up on top of everything else. Besides, we didn't get dinner and I'm hungry."

I took a piece and bit into it, then handed him his plate.

He took it, muttering, "You don't need to wait on me."

"Then who will?"

"No one. I can take care of myself."

"Oh, really? Then how do you plan to get dressed? Shave? Take a shower? Drive? Cook?"

"Okay, you've made your point. I'll find someone."

But obviously, it wasn't going to be his partner. No, he was too afraid of Lola breaking out and ravishing him or something. Idiot. His precious virtue was safe with me.

"Fine. As soon as they get here, I'll leave. Who will you call?"

"I don't know. Gwen maybe?"

"Oh, that'll be a lot of fun for her. But she's still at work now, you know."

"She'll help," he said stubbornly. "Or my mother will."

"Okay, but until then, you're stuck with me." I stared at him, shaking my head ruefully.

He swallowed a bite of pizza. "What?"

"Ramirez won't be pleased when he learns you're out of commission."

Dan took a slug of his drink. "Who says I'm out of commission?"

I gestured at his bandaged shoulder. "That says so."

"No, it doesn't. I'm supposed to be the brains in this partnership, right?"

"Yeah, but—"

"Well, I sure as hell don't think with my shoulder."

"What *do* you think with, then? 'Cause right now, it sure isn't your brain."

Before Dan could answer, the doorbell rang.

I answered it, surprised to see Shade, still looking all dark and mysterious beneath his hoodie. With gloved hands, he pulled his unusually deep hood around his face so I couldn't see inside. What was up with the guy? He glanced around, seeming a little nervous in the daylight. "Can I come in?"

I let him in and Dan grunted a greeting. Though I sat down and offered him a chair, Shade remained standing and spoke from the depths of his hood. "I saw your accident and reported it to Micah. He sent me to help."

"As what?" I asked. "My new partner? How are you at staking vamps?"

"No," Shade said. "I'm here to help your existing partner get back on his feet."

I grinned. "Here's the nursemaid you wanted, Dan."

Dan shot Shade a look that clearly said, "No way."

"Not exactly," Shade said, sounding unperturbed. He paused and turned his hood in my direction. "Is it true you're related to Micah?"

Yeah, but what did that have to do with anything? "Yes. At least, we think we're distant cousins since we both have the same . . . demon." Powers? Curse? I didn't know what else to call it.

Shade made a questioning gesture toward Dan.

I shrugged, figuring I knew his unspoken question. "Oh, him? You can trust him." After all, he'd kept my secret, even from his sister, even though he seemed annoyed by Lola

Shade hesitated, then said, "You know I'm . . . like you?"

"Part demon, you mean? I guessed it." His mysterious manner was kind of a giveaway, plus the fact that he knew Fang and Micah. "What kind of demon are you?"

"A shadow demon."

A what? "Sorry, I guess I haven't been doing my homework lately. What exactly is a shadow demon?"

In answer, Shade pushed back his hood. Everywhere there should have been skin, there was . . . something else. He looked like a faint hologram outlining the shape of a man. But the insides shifted and swirled with dark streamers of light in all shades of gray. Clothing concealed most of the turmoil, but his features were totally obscured by churning ribbons of light, making it impossible to read his expression. Or even see his face for that matter.

It was a little unnerving, and I expected at least a comment from Dan, but there was nothing. Maybe it was the drugs, or the mesmerizing movement, or maybe because Dan had been asked to believe too many impossible things before breakfast, but this didn't even seem to faze him.

The oddest thing was to hear a completely normal voice issue from that maelstrom. "Shadow demons can occupy more than one dimension. Since I'm part human, I exist mostly in this one, but still shift in and out of others as well."

Fascinating. I'd have to read up on his kind.

"How will that help us?" Dan asked.

"I can pull energies from other dimensions—healing energies—but only if you both agree."

Dan seemed torn and glanced at me doubtfully. I couldn't read his mind, but I could guess about what was going through his head. He had thoroughly rejected my demon. Would it be hypocritical of him to accept the help of Shade's?

"Do it," I told him. The situations were entirely different, and we couldn't afford the time for him to heal. "It's not any different than going to an alternative healer, is it?" At least, I hoped so. I had no idea what Shade could do.

"Okay," Dan said. "I'll do it."

That was a bit of a shocker. I'd expected a lot more argument out of him. But he probably hated feeling helpless, at my mercy. Yeah, that'd do it.

Shade's endlessly moving face was still unreadable. Must come in really useful when playing poker. "Do you agree, Val?" he asked.

Looking puzzled, Dan asked, "Why does she need to agree? It's me you're healing."

"Because to use this healing method, I must ground myself in a being of this world, one whose uninjured shoulder will not only act as a template to heal yours, but who will supply energy for the healing. As a partial demon herself with strong powers, Val is ideal."

"Will it hurt her?" Dan asked.

He'd managed to surprise me again. Did he really care? Then again, it must be that hero thing again—his protective instinct coming to the fore. Kind of made me wish I needed protecting.

Shade shook his head, and the energies coiled wildly where his face should have been. "Not at all. It will drain her of some vitality, but nothing that can't be repaired by a good night's sleep."

Kind of like what I had done to Dan. It seemed fitting to pay him back in this way. "Fair enough. Will it hurt you or Dan?"

"It won't hurt me," Shade assured us. "I am merely a conduit. However, the process of healing will be painful for the one being healed, and the act can be more . . . intimate than either of you might care for."

Dan looking suddenly suspicious. "What do you mean, intimate?"

Pain didn't bother him, but the thought of letting Lola sink her virtual tentacles into him again obviously did. Idiot. I wanted to yell at him to get over it already. I wasn't about to let that happen again. I'd locked it down so tight, it would take a crowbar to let Lola loose again around Dan.

Shade shrugged. "I mean simply that since I will be drawing upon Val's powers to heal you, you may learn more about each other than you really want to."

Dan looked relieved. "Okay. No secrets here."

I hesitated. Did I really want Dan knowing how I felt about him? Not that I *cared*, you know, but I didn't want him knowing how much his rejection had hurt. Then again, if I could keep Lola caged up, I guess I could keep that hidden, too. Besides, I needed him in good working condition. I couldn't take on a whole vein of vampires with no one but Fang for backup. I could do this—I'd just have to be very careful. "I'm in."

"Good." Shade moved toward Dan. "How many painkillers do you have in your system?"

"They gave me a shot at the hospital, but it's just about worn off, and I haven't taken any pills yet." He'd obviously been waiting for me to leave.

"Good. This will work better if your mind isn't clouded."

"What do I need to do?"

"Stay where you are." Shade beckoned to me as he moved around behind Dan and took off his gloves. "Come sit next to him on the couch so I can touch both your shoulders. We'll need to get the bandage off."

I sat next to Dan, then helped him remove the bandage. Once it was off, I glanced uncertainly at Shade, realizing I didn't know how my inner demon might react with his. Would it distract him? Offend him? "Um, when our energy fields overlap, my succubus—"

"No worries," Shade said. "Knowing where the lust comes from will help me handle it. Besides, once my power kicks in, all of you—including your demon—will be too occupied to do anything about it."

Shade had us face each other on the couch, then touched my shoulder. It was as if the shadow demon drew substance from me. He solidified, becoming real, human. Without the spooky special effects, he looked like a normal guy—a little older than me, maybe. He had long blond hair, blue eyes, and was totally gorgeous, but normal.

Shade glanced at Dan, and for the first time, I could read Shade's face—he looked concerned. "If this becomes too much, tell me and I'll stop."

Then he touched Dan's neck and I didn't care what he looked like. All I could care about were the strange . . . things going on inside me.

Now I knew what he meant about being totally occupied. Energy ebbed and flowed, from me into Dan, then back into me. There was no room for anything else, not even Lola—we were both just swept along by the tide. Whenever I surged into Dan, I obtained a small glimpse into his psyche, a private view of his world, his mind. As Shade had warned, it was incredibly intimate and I was learning a great deal about Dan, straight from the source where I knew only truth existed.

I obtained flashes of his past, learning about his pride in being a Sullivan and a protector, his strong love of family, his annoyance at losing Lily to the vampires, and his fear of Lola. But not the way I thought. He was having enough problems controlling his attraction to a girl he considered too young to have even had a life yet, and Lola made it a heck of a lot more difficult to stick with his good-guy code.

Really? That made me feel better.

In return, I could tell he was learning about me as well. Though I tried to snatch them back, my memories leaked out of me. My isolation as a child when I watched other children play in the street but couldn't join them. My mother's caring, but wariness of the demon child she'd spawned. My first kiss that almost proved fatal for Johnny. My training to control the lust, and my sorrow at being different and losing my family.

Worse, my constant battle to balance my need for people with the side of me that reached out for the kind of contact I might not be ready for. Dan learned his big scary lust demon was a great big virgin chicken.

When Dan veered too close to things I didn't want him to learn, I tensed, but it wasn't necessary.

Shade moved his hand to the wound on Dan's shoulder and I felt Dan's reaction as hot pain scalded him. There was no more give and take, there was only my power and strength flowing to Dan as Shade used it to reattach ligaments, repair torn muscle and regrow shredded skin tissue.

It took longer, much longer, to heal the damage than it had to create it, and was infinitely more painful for Dan as he felt every minute detail of the healing. I opened my eyes once to beg Shade to stop, to stop torturing Dan, but seeing the shadow demon flicker in and out of human form, seeing Dan stoically endure as his face tightened in a rictus of pain and his skin turned pale and pasty, I couldn't do it.

Finally, after eons of mind-numbing agony for Dan, it abruptly ceased as Shade removed his hands from both of us.

The relief was incredible, and though I felt exhausted, I leaned over to look at Dan's shoulder. "Ohmigod . . . it's completely healed."

"Yes." Shade paused in pulling on his jacket. "He was very strong and was able to endure until the end. I've never seen anyone tolerate that much pain for a wound that size." He settled the hood over his head once more and pulled on his gloves.

Yeah, that was Dan, all right. After being in his head, I could see everything he did was heroic.

"Thanks, man," Dan said hoarsely. "I owe you one."

Shade nodded, his expression enigmatic behind the hood and the flow of interdimensional energies. "You do. And someday, Micah will collect."

That sounded ominous. Dan raised an eyebrow, but didn't object.

Shade continued, "How many know of your wound?"

"Only Val, you, and the people in the ER."

"Then I suggest you don't end up in that ER again anytime soon. It would be difficult to explain your sudden healing."

"Don't worry. I plan to avoid the hospital at all costs."

Yeah. Two injuries in one week was more than enough for any guy, no matter how heroic. Especially in the same shoulder.

"You two rest," Shade suggested. "I can see myself out."

I felt too exhausted to move and Dan looked even worse than I felt. "I'm sorry," he said gruffly. "I didn't realize how much this would drain you."

I made a feeble motion with my fingers—all I could manage at the moment. "S'okay. I agreed."

"Yes, but . . . I used you, used your powers. Kind of like—"

He broke off, but we were still connected in a way, so I suspected what he'd left unsaid. "Kind of like Lola used you?" I said softly.

"Yeah. But I saw . . . inside you . . . saw that you couldn't help it, that it was involuntary. I'm sorry for being such a jackass."

I nodded, the smallest possible movement of my head. "Apology accepted. We're even now."

Did that mean we could be friends again? I hoped so.

## CHAPTER FOURTEEN

Though we both fell asleep on Dan's couch, I stumbled home to my own bed at some point, and woke to find Fang nosing me.

YOU GOING TO SLEEP ALL DAY? I'M HUNGRY.

I checked the clock. Nine hours had passed, and the sun had gone down again. I was beginning to feel like a vampire myself, what with sleeping during the day and working during the hours of darkness. Luckily, I didn't have a thirst for blood, just Coke. And, as Shade promised, I felt as if I had fully recovered my energy.

I got up and dressed, seeing that Gwen had left us some food. I fed myself and Fang and snuggled up on the couch with my Coke as I thought about the events of the night before.

Shade had been strange, yet fascinating, and he'd done wonders in healing Dan. Idly, I wondered if Shade had healed more than his shoulder. How else could I account for Dan's apology?

I relived the moment in my mind. Yes, I was certain he was sincere, especially after I'd touched the innermost part of him last night. He was an honorable man, so if he said he was sorry, then he really meant it.

Dan knocked on the door then, and I let him in. "How are you feeling?" I asked.

He stretched his shoulder experimentally, swinging it a few times. "Better than new. How about you? Did you get enough sleep?"

"Yes, I'm fine. What are the plans for today? Shall we try to find Alejandro at his home? Try the blood banks?"

Dan thought for a moment. "I'm not sure what the best approach is, especially after last night. Maybe—"

A low buzz interrupted him and he broke off and held up one finger as he took his cell phone out of his pocket. "Hello?" He raised an eyebrow. "Alejandro?"

I signaled to let me hear as well, and he tilted the phone slightly so I could hear both sides of the conversation. Luckily, my hearing was excellent.

"You have been trying to reach me?" Alejandro asked.

"Yes—"

"I understand the two of you had a slight altercation with some of my people last night."

"Us? What makes you say that?"

"One of my people recognized Ms. Shapiro and I deduced you must have been her companion in the altercation."

Dan rolled his eyes. "That unprovoked attack, you mean?"

"Oh, not unprovoked, surely," Alejandro corrected smoothly. "After all, you were on private property, uninvited, peering into windows like a schoolboy. No wonder we assumed you were an enemy."

Dan grimaced. Guess he didn't like being called a schoolboy. "And now? Do you still assume we are enemies?"

"Misguided perhaps, but not enemies." Before Dan could say anything more, Alejandro added, "My apologies. If I had known it was you, we would have invited you inside. Why didn't you just knock?"

I guess he was thrown off balance by the vampire leader's apology, because Dan said, "We didn't think we'd be welcome."

Alejandro paused. "That close to dawn . . . perhaps you were right to worry. There would be more danger of overreaction. But not now. Would you care to join me?"

"Join you where?" Dan asked warily.

"At the mansion. Come, and I will show you around, answer your questions. You know the address . . . ."

Dan questioned me with his eyebrows. I shrugged. Why not? It couldn't hurt.

Dan accepted the invitation, but he called Ramirez and briefed him on what we were about to do, just in case.

When we arrived at Alejandro's mansion this time, we were admitted with gracious Old World charm by the leader of the New Blood Movement himself. He accepted Fang as a matter of course, though the hellhound bristled at so many vampires around, and Alejandro showed us through the beautiful mansion.

Being undead must pay pretty well, 'cause it was awesome, like the "after" pictures in those television decorating shows. He hadn't gone for the über modern look here. Instead, lots of tile, wood, and earthy colors, combined with stone and wrought iron accessories, made it very warm and inviting. Kind of like I imagined a villa in Spain might look.

The only place he didn't take us was the basement, and I assumed that was because they slept there during the day.

Unfortunately, I didn't see Jen anywhere, nor did Fang alert me to her presence. I didn't force the issue on the basement since Fang didn't seem interested in following his nose down there.

No humans go there, he confirmed.

Once the amenities were over, Alejandro took us to his study. More warm tile here, with thick rugs and the obligatory masculine leather chair and desk. But it was the mural completely covering one wall that captured the attention. It showed a lush green hillside covered with wildflowers leading down to a turquoise sea. But what was most remarkable about the mural was how everything seemed drenched in sunlight. Probably the only daylight he ever saw.

Alejandro waved us to a pair of leather chairs and offered us refreshment. Not knowing what people who only drank blood might have on hand to munch on, I declined and Dan did as well.

As if by prearranged signal, Luis and Lily drifted in to take up stations on either side of their boss—an attractive pair of bookends leaning on either side of his throne-like chair.

"So," Alejandro said, folding his hands in his lap and looking the picture of the considerate host. "You wished to see me. How may I help you?"

Dan gestured at me to go ahead. Deciding not to offend Alejandro within his own home with accusations of murder and mayhem, I said, "I'm looking for my sister."

One eyebrow rose. "And you think I have her?"

"Yes. You, or one of your people."

"But as you requested, I gave orders that her employment was to be terminated."

Lily nodded. "It was. I told her to leave."

"But she didn't," I said patiently. "And you're paying her now."

Alejandro spread his hands as if in supplication. "If she will not go when asked, what do you expect us to do?"

"Maybe the *reason* she didn't quit is because she is enthralled by a vampire who won't let her."

"I find that hard to believe. That is forbidden in the organization."

"Oh, really," Dan said flatly as Luis and Lily exchanged enigmatic glances. "Then what do you call what you were doing to the audience the night of the rally, what you do to every person you meet?"

He shrugged. "I use my charisma to persuade, not to control. And that is what every member of my organization learns—they may use their power to sway men's minds to make giving blood more pleasurable, but may not use it to harm others or use them as slaves."

Lily and Luis exchanged another enigmatic glance.

What did that mean? They didn't seem to be as confident of Alejandro's assurances as he was. Perhaps the man didn't practice what he preached. Or maybe some members of the organization weren't as much under his control as he assumed.

"Maybe not everyone who works for you feels the same," I suggested.

A small spark of anger lit in Alejandro's eyes. "If so, I assure you I shall find the culprit and force him to release your sister. I will not be defied."

I wanted to believe him, but I couldn't, not when Jennifer was in danger. But, the big question was, if Alejandro didn't know she was enthralled and he actively opposed it, why would one of his underlings risk ticking off the boss? Did Jen know something that made controlling her a necessity?

Freeing her suddenly became even more imperative. "Do it soon," I said, my voice cold. "Or I'll find another way."

Luis spoke for the first time since coming in to the room. "How? If we are not able to make this determination, how can you?"

I rose, preparing to leave. "Simple. I'll just kill you one by one until I find her controller and Jennifer is released."

Lily let out a brief laugh.

Dan rose as well and glanced at her. "Val's not kidding. She'll do it."

Fang growled. AND I'LL HELP.

Lily's amusement faded and Alejandro cocked his head, looking mildly curious, but unsurprised. "Would you really?"

"Damn skippy," I said and left.

Fang followed me. OOH, PITHY. WORTHY OF A HELLHOUND.

Once we were out of the mansion and back in the truck, I glanced at Dan. "Did you really believe I would kill them all or were you just backing me up?" I wasn't sure which one I hoped he'd choose. One made me out to be a monster, and the other a liar.

He gave me a half smile. "I was in your head last night. I know how much your family means to you, even though they don't deserve it. You'd do anything to keep them safe." He paused, then added quietly, "I would, too, if it were my family."

Relief washed over me at the realization that Dan meant it. Wow, so this was what it felt like to be understood and accepted. I liked it.

"But I thought you were all gung-ho on proving Alejandro is one of the good guys," Dan added.

"I am. I still think he is. But I'm not so sure about his underlings. He may think he has them all under control, but, judging from their body language, Luis and Lily aren't as confident. How much you want to bet the lieutenants are having problems they're not telling Alejandro about?"

"No bet here."

I shrugged. "I figured a threat would help smoke out the real culprit. Any ideas on what we should do next?"

He paused, thinking. "We don't have any other leads in finding the source of the increased activity. Besides, whenever we look for your sister, trouble always seems to find us."

Fang snorted. HE HAS A POINT.

"True."

"Maybe I can take another look at Micah's records, see if I can find any reference to Jen."

"Good idea. I think I'll take another look at the blood banks, talk to some of her friends, check out her regular hangouts, and see if I can find her that way . . . or if Fang can sniff her out."

Since all three of us were in agreement, Dan dropped me off at the townhouses and headed once again to Purgatory.

I had no luck at her usual hangouts and no one seemed to know where she was, so I returned to Purgatory. Tessa, Micah's assistant, let me into his office.

Fang and I walked in just in time to hear Dan ask Micah, "Does it work on all women?"

"Does what work?" I asked behind him.

Dan turned around, surprised. "I was just asking Micah if his powers work on all women."

Tessa rolled her eyes. "If they have a pulse."

"Even other demons?" Dan persisted. "Even vampires?"

"Of course," Tessa said with an impatient wave of her hand. "What do you think *I* am?"

"You're a vampire?" he asked in disbelief.

"No, genius, I'm part demon."

Micah and I unsuccessfully tried to hide our smiles.

Fang danced a step. I LIKE HER.

Micah cocked an eyebrow at Tessa. "I'd like to give him a little demonstration of my powers, if you don't mind."

Tessa grimaced. "Is that necessary?"

"I'm afraid so."

"Okay, go ahead." She stiffened, as if preparing herself for battle.

Micah grinned. "First, tell him how it is to work for me."

She shrugged. "You're an okay boss. You pay well, you're not judgmental, and you don't chase me around the office."

Sounded like she had some history there.

"Thank you." Micah rose and took her hand, despite the apprehensive expression on her face. "Now for the demonstration."

I felt his incubus rouse and reach for Tessa. All of a sudden, her face relaxed into a goofy smile, and she stared adoringly at Micah.

Micah smiled down at her. "Now, tell him, Tessa, how it is to work for me."

She reached up to stroke his cheek with one hand and snake her other arm around his waist. "You're the *best*, the sexiest man alive. But you never chase me—"

"Now it ends," Micah said, releasing her hand and taking a step back.

His incubus flowed back into him, fully under his control. He made it seem effortless. I wished I could do that.

Tessa backed off, wiping her hand against her jeans. "I really hate it when you do that—it's demeaning."

Surprisingly, Micah didn't seem offended. "There will be a bonus in your next paycheck." He turned to Dan. "You see? She is only attracted to me when I am consciously using my power. When I am not, her mind and her feelings are her own."

Ooookay. Real subtle there, Micah. Just what kind of discussion had he and Dan been having before I came in?

Tessa backed away, and Dan looked thoughtful as he glanced at me. "If it works even on vampires, then that's how you can find out if Alejandro is telling the truth—use your powers on him, Val."

"No way." Did he even realize he was asking me to do something he hated having done to him?

"Why not?" Dan persisted. "It will help you find your sister."

"If I do that, then I am no better than the vampire who has enthralled her mind."

"Not exactly. You'd be doing it to help free your sister, not enslave her."

Maybe. But it would also let Lola loose, and the last time that had happened, I'd enjoyed it way too much for my liking. I shook my head. "You of all people should know better."

Dan shrugged. "Maybe we'd better go."

We said our good-byes, then on the way out the door, I accidentally brushed against Tessa.

She grabbed my arm as her eyes flashed purple. Shutting them tight, she furrowed her brow in concentration. After a moment or two, she said, "To obtain what you most desire, you must accept what you most hate."

I pulled away. "What does that mean?" Had Micah been coaching her?

Tessa opened her eyes. "What did I say?"

I repeated it.

She frowned, muttering, "Why do I always have to sound like a stupid fortune cookie?"

Micah smiled. "The message sounds pretty obvious to me."

Did it? Well, I didn't get it.

"Thanks, guys," Tessa said. "It's been real." She seemed a little shaken, but tried to hide it with a casual wave of farewell as she left.

"That's Tessa's gift—prophecy," Micah said. "You're lucky. She rarely shares it with anyone outside the inner circle. But trite as her predictions may sound, Tessa is always right."

His phone rang then and Micah answered it. When he hung up, his look at me was part sad, part pitying.

Fear leapt through me, like a wildfire. "What is it? Has something happened to Jennifer?"

"Not your sister. Your stepfather."

"Something happened to Rick?"

"Yes. He's missing."

No, it couldn't be. I couldn't lose another one. And Rick had always treated me well—better than my mother sometimes. "What do you know?"

"That's all. I've had people watching your family, but he hasn't been seen since last night. Your mother seems worried."

And she hadn't called me? That hurt. I turned to Dan. "You coming?"

"You bet. Let's go."

\*

Dan stopped the truck in front of my childhood home and turned off the engine. I hesitated, unsure if I really wanted to deal with my mother. Dan just waited, allowing me to gather my scattered thoughts, but Fang nosed me, looking anxious.

YOU OKAY, KIDDO?

I scratched his ears. "It's okay. I just need a moment." But no amount of time could prepare me for the scene I was sure I was about to endure. Sighing, I got out of the truck and headed for the front door. Dan and Fang followed but I didn't stop them. I'd take a cue from the cops and accept backup.

Boy, it felt weird to knock on the door I'd used so freely throughout my childhood.

Mom answered the door, looking hopeful. But when she saw me, her face fell. "Why are you here? Have you found Jen?"

Gee, way to make me feel welcome. "Can we come in?"

She waved us into the living room, looking a bit distracted. A small, ginger-colored cat wandered out, saw me, and bristled up to twice its size. Fang curled his lip, took one step forward and snarled. The cat took off like hell itself was nipping at its heels.

"You have a *cat* now?" I didn't mean to sound accusing, but Mom knew how animals reacted around me. Always before, she'd been careful to keep them away, to avoid hurting my feelings. What did it mean now that she had one in her house? Had she thought I'd never come here again? Or did she just not care?

I hadn't thought anything else Mom could do would hurt me, but for some reason, this did.

Mom looked slightly embarrassed. "Jennifer was always bugging me for a cat. I thought if I got her one, she might come back . . . ."

"Uh-huh," I said doubtfully, though I had to admit I felt a little better for the explanation.

Mom made an impatient gesture. "Why are you here? Have you found Jen? Is she okay?"

"Not yet," I said soothingly. I'd never seen my mother look so fragile, so worried. "Why don't you sit down?"

"I don't want to sit down. I want my daughter back. You said you'd find her."

*My daughter.* The words were like a spike in my heart. Did Mom think of Jennifer as her *only* daughter now?

Fang nuzzled my leg. SHE DOESN'T DESERVE YOUR LOVE.

Fang was right. Every time I saw Mom, she killed a little more. But it was difficult to stop loving someone all at once, no matter how badly they treated you. And it was clear now that no amount of wanting would make Mom love me. I just had to accept it and move on with my life.

Something inside me hardened, walling away the hurt, forcing me to grow up a little. Taking a shaky breath, I said, "I'm doing what I can—"

"Well, it's not good enough. God only knows what those creatures are doing to her."

Dan stepped forward and opened his mouth, probably to defend me, but I stopped him with a look and an upraised hand. Mom was understandably upset, and I was willing to cut her some slack. "I *will* get her back," I promised.

"Then what are you doing here? Why aren't you out there looking for her?"

Couldn't I have just come to see my family, to be there for her, have her be there for me?

Apparently not. "Because I heard Rick is missing."

"Rick isn't missing. He's out there actively looking for his daughter, and he won't come home until he finds her."

That's what I'd feared. "Damn it, I told him not to. I told him I'd take care of it." Why couldn't he have trusted me?

"What do you expect? His little girl is gone. He had to do something."

I closed my eyes in disbelief. Rick was usually the smart one, not the macho type. Sure, I understood his reasoning, but why couldn't he have waited? I opened my eyes. "He hasn't called?"

Mom shook her head. "He won't until he finds Jen."

Maybe. Then again, maybe he couldn't. Rather than add to Mom's worries, I asked, "When did you last see him?"

Mom pushed her hair aside, looking extremely weary. "Last night. He went looking for Jen right after the store closed. But he hasn't been home. He's probably sleeping in his car or something."

She sounded more worried than she let on. "Do you know where he went?"

"A friend's daughter heard at school that Jen was working at a different vampire blood bank, had just moved from one to another."

"Did she say which one?" Dan asked, leaning forward.

"Yes—the one out by Fort Sam."

"Good," I said. "That gives us a place to start looking."

Mom raised her head, her expression apprehensive. "You don't think Rick is dead . . . or enthralled, do you?"

Either was possible, and I wasn't going to lie. "I don't know."

"Oh, God." Mom wrapped her arms around herself and whispered, "I can't lose him, too. I just can't." She turned a ravaged face to me. "I-I love him so much."

"I know," I said softly. "So do I." I'd heard horror stories about other stepfathers, but Rick had been nothing but kind to me. In fact, he supported me more than Mom had. I didn't want to lose that . . . or him.

"So you'll bring them back to me?" Mom persisted.

I wouldn't lie and make promises I might not be able to keep. "I'll try."

I *would* find Rick and Jen, one way or the other. I just hoped they were still alive and unharmed when I did.

"What about Val?" Dan asked, but there was steel beneath his deceptively quiet voice. "Aren't you worried about losing her, too?"

Exactly what I was wondering.

It was nice to hear some people thought I was as important as Jen and Rick, but I wasn't certain I wanted to hear Mom's answer. I tugged on Dan's arm. "It's okay," I whispered. "You don't have to do this."

"Val can take care of herself," Mom said defensively. "Besides, it's her lifestyle that got us into this mess. It's her responsibility to clean it up."

Was she singing that old tune again? Okay, damn it. Mom had just reached the end of her allotted slack. I was tired of being the scapegoat for every problem in the family, tired of being the one who always tried to smooth things over. I couldn't make things okay anymore, couldn't buy my way back into the family by playing nice. It was time to give up old habits that didn't work. It was time to let go.

I released Dan's arm, giving him tacit permission to let loose.

He took it. "*Her* responsibility?" he repeated incredulously. "What about your responsibility as a mother? When did you abdicate that?"

"I didn't—"

"The hell you didn't," Dan bit out. "Val has done nothing but try to help you and you treat her like crap."

"I do not." But her protest was faint. Was that because Dan wasn't the kind of guy you argued with when he was so righteously angry . . . or because Mom knew he was right?

"Yes, you do," Dan insisted. "Not only have the lot of you continued doing idiotic things when she expressly warned you against them, but then you blame her for your own stupidity! You can't even trust her to do her job, the one thing you know she's damned good at. And what the hell happened to unconditional love?"

I'M BEGINNING TO LIKE THIS GUY.

My eyes stung. Damn, it felt good to have a champion for a change.

Mom seemed to crumple. "Val has always been the strong one. She never needed me as much as Jen did."

That's what she'd like to believe, but I knew better. However, I realized Mom needed a scapegoat and her eldest daughter was the chosen sacrifice. Maybe once all this was over, she'd be more sensible. But for now, there was no sense trying to reason with her. "Let's go," I said to Dan.

Dan and I turned toward the door. I just wanted to leave, get away from all this emotional bloodletting. Fang snarled at Mom, then followed.

As we exited, Dan turned around for one parting shot at Mom. "You're just damned lucky Val is decent enough to ignore the way you've treated her and help you anyway."

Mom just shook her head, looking sad, and closed the door.

I sighed. It was no more than I expected. But no matter what Mom thought, I was going to find her missing family members and bring them home . . . to the home where I suspected I'd never be welcome again.

Well, to hell with them. I'd just carve out a new life for myself— better than anything I had in the past. I deserved the kind of love and respect the Sullivans seemed to have for each other, and damn it, I was going to find it, no matter how long it took.

# CHAPTER FIFTEEN

As we drove to the blood bank, the injustice of Mom's finger-pointing nagged at me until I was totally pissed. It woke the dormant Lola, and lust began to sizzle beneath the surface. I deliberately focused it away from Dan and into the anger fueling my quest for Jen and Rick.

When we arrived at the blood bank, I climbed out of the truck and slammed the door, not knowing or caring if Dan and Fang followed me. I shoved open the door to the building and glanced around. The place was full, but no Rick, no Jen. I stalked toward the desk and the young man sitting there. He paled when he saw my expression.

I glanced at his nametag. "Hello, Jerry." It came out as more of a threat than a greeting.

He gulped and scooted backward, out of range. Smart guy. "H-hi," he stammered.

"Is Jennifer Anderson here?" I didn't even try to soften my voice. I finally had a lead and I was going to follow it until I found Jen and Rick, or someone was going to pay.

"Not tonight."

Dan appeared by my side, along with Fang. Jerry glanced down at the terrier. "You can't bring dogs in here—"

Fang and I both snarled at him, and Jerry backed off even more. "Okay, okay. So long as he's good, I'll overlook it this time."

"When will Jennifer be here?" I demanded.

"Wh-why do you want to know?" He looked terrified as he glanced back and forth between Dan and me, but still had guts enough to defy us.

"She's my sister."

"Oh." He gulped. "I-I'm sorry, but even so, I'm not allowed to give out that infor—"

He broke off when I came around the desk after him. Holding

up his hands to fend me off, he said, "Please, I can't. You have no idea how much trouble I'd be in."

But the lust within me needed an outlet, needed someone to pound on. Clenching my fists, I restrained it, saying, "You'll be in more trouble if you don't tell me."

"But . . . they're vampires," Jerry said, as if it trumped my threat.

I shoved my face into his. "Yeah, and I'm the vampire *slayer.*" As the anger surged within me, I saw my purple eye-flash reflected in his pupils.

"Oh, crap." Jerry's voice was a mere squeak and he closed his eyes as if death were imminent. Too, he must be really confused by the lust that surged through him with my proximity.

Dan appeared behind Jerry looking amused. But he kept his voice serious as he said, "I don't think Jerry knows enough to be helpful, do you, Jerry?"

Jerry's eyes flew open and he grabbed on to Dan's words as if to a lifeline. His fear overcame his lust as he blurted, "No, no. He's right—I'm totally ignorant."

Fang snorted. If I weren't so ticked off, I'd find him amusing, too. I glanced at Dan to see where he was going with this. This was the best lead we had to find both Jen and Rick.

Dan came around the chair so he could smile down at the kid. "But I bet you know who can give us the information."

"Su-sure. One of the bosses."

I backed off and the relief on Jerry's face was almost comical.

"Okay," Dan said. "You let us talk to one of the bosses and she'll let you live."

"They're all accepting personal donations." Ick—he meant the fang to neck kind. "You'll have to wait in line—"

I took a step forward and Jerry raised his hands again. "But for you, I'll make an exception," he babbled.

I relaxed and glanced around the waiting room. About ninety percent of it had cleared out during our little altercation, and I raised an eyebrow at the remaining men and women. "Anyone mind if we go first?"

There was a chorus of hasty no's, except for one irate middle-aged woman who said, "I do—"

But the man sitting next to her clamped a hand over her mouth and said with a sickly smile, "Please, go ahead."

Fang growled and I glanced over to see what he was staring at. A vampire and his latest drooling "customer" had come out of the back room.

The vamp looked like a smirking college frat boy playing dress-up in a costume of a flowing white pirate shirt and tight black leather pants. He glanced down at Fang, then stupidly ignored him, dismissing the dog as no threat. "Who's next?" he asked arrogantly.

"Lorenzo . . . " the woman who had objected said with a sigh of longing.

Ignoring her, I smiled a predator's smile and focused on Lorenzo. "We are."

"We?" Lorenzo looked back and forth between Dan and me. "It's a little kinky, but what the heck."

As he led us back to a suite of rooms, Dan muttered, "You okay? You look like you're about to lose it."

I took a deep breath. "Yeah, I think so."

"Chill. I'll handle this part."

I nodded, realizing he was right—I needed to calm down.

Lorenzo gestured at three doors. "What's your fancy? Victorian bordello, woodland scene, or dungeon?"

I gaped at him for a moment until I realized he was asking where I wanted to experience the pleasure of his "kiss."

"Woodland," Dan said.

Good. I didn't want to think about the sort of person who chose the dungeon. Besides, we needed to question him in private, not out here in the hallway, but didn't need to be too distracted by our surroundings either.

We entered the large room. It was dark inside, but my eyes soon adjusted, and the illusion was so complete, I felt as if we'd entered another realm. Moonlight played over the pastoral scene, several sheltering trees shaded a bower that looked soft and inviting, and the scent of some fragrant, musky flower wafted by on a warm breeze.

Lorenzo lounged with practiced ease on the blanket, patting

the space next to him invitingly.

Fang growled. LET ME AT HIM.

I waved him back. Lorenzo hadn't done anything wrong . . .
yet. He thought we were willing blood donors, looking for a thrill.

I surreptitiously drew a stake from my back waistband and
held it behind me as Dan said, "We aren't here for the game you
think we are."

"Oh? And what would your game be?"

"The game is, we ask the questions and you give the answers."

Annoyed, he snapped, "That's not the way it works here. What
are you playing at?"

I glanced at Dan and he nodded, knowing what I needed to do.
I dropped to my knees on the vamp's chest, shoved my forearm
across his throat so he couldn't move, and held the stake in my
other fist, poised over his heart. "No, *we* ask the questions."

Anger flashed in his eyes as he tried to buck me off. When it
didn't work, he tried to control my mind, even as his body
responded to Lola's seductive force field.

Now I had him. "Okay, Dan, ask."

Dan sat on the vamp's legs so he'd stop kicking. "Do you know
Jennifer Anderson?"

Lorenzo fought the lure of the succubus, which wasn't too
difficult since Lola wasn't all that interested. "Go to hell," he
snarled.

But the answer was clear in his mind—he did. I nodded at
Dan to signal that the vamp did know Jen. It was easier if he
asked the questions while I concentrated on reading the vamp's
mind for the answers.

"Do you know where she is?" Dan asked. "Who's controlling
her?"

I read the answer clearly. "No, he doesn't," I said. "And
Alejandro has put the word out to find out who's doing it."

Lorenzo gaped up at me. "Who *are* you?"

"The Slayer." Dan loved to say that, apparently. Seeing
recognition in the vamp's eyes, Dan added, "But if you're a good
little vampire and tell us what we want to know, we may let you
live."

Lorenzo frowned but stopped fighting. I read in his mind that Alejandro had told them to cooperate with me. He didn't want to, but he said, "Depends. What do you want to know?"

Since the vamp was being reasonable, I let up on my stranglehold.

I nodded at Dan who asked, "Did Jennifer's father come looking for her here last night?"

"Yes."

"What happened?

"He made a big scene, tried to drag her out of here, but she wouldn't go."

I nodded to signal Lorenzo was playing it straight.

"So you killed him?" Dan asked.

"No! Alejandro wouldn't allow— That is, it wouldn't be right."

"So what did you do?"

"He was annoying the customers, scaring people away, so we tossed him out, told him never to come back."

He was telling the truth, but there was something else . . . . "What aren't you telling us?" I asked.

"Nothing," Lorenzo assured me.

But he lied. There, clear in his mind, was what had really happened. Lorenzo had watched out the window as three vampires he thought of as the disenfranchised ones grabbed Rick. As they dragged him off, they laughed, saying they were going to bless him.

Bless him? What the heck would blessing mean to a vampire? Crosses and holy water were pure torture to them. With fear leaping in my chest, I asked, "What does that mean? What is a vampire blessing?"

Lorenzo gave up the information readily, obviously hoping it would hurt us. "That's their slang for bringing him over." Then, in case we didn't get it, he explained, "They plan to make him one of us."

My skin turned clammy and my head spun. *Ohmigod. They turned the only father I've known into a vampire.*

I had foolishly feared he would be dead, lying drained of blood somewhere. I thought that was the worst thing that could happen.

But this . . . No, I couldn't even conceive of this.

My own blood drained from my face and I felt cold and clammy, a bit nauseous, and totally shell-shocked. I must have looked it, too, because the vampire just sprawled there staring at me, apparently pleased with his bombshell.

Dan questioned him some more, getting descriptions of the vampires, then took me gently by the arm and led me out a side door to the truck. Feeling numb, I sat huddled against the door, trying not to think, not to feel. I barely noticed when Fang cuddled up to me and licked my arm.

"You okay?" Dan asked.

"Yeah," I lied. "I just want to find them—somehow." I couldn't think beyond that. Wouldn't think beyond that. I stared straight ahead and Dan finally cranked the truck.

We drove around all night, trying to find more leads at the blood banks, on the streets, anywhere we could. No luck. Finally, exhausted and disappointed, I realized it was nearly dawn and the vamps would be holed up somewhere until the sun went down again, so we went home.

Depressed, I felt as if I were wandering in a fog. It didn't lift until Dan settled me on my sofa and sat next to me. "Talk to me, Val."

But it wasn't his words that penetrated my daze, it was his gentle touch as he brushed the hair from my face.

I glanced down at Fang who had curled up next to me on the couch. My hands had tightened in his fur without even realizing it. I loosened my death grip on the poor dog and stroked his wiry fur. He hadn't even complained. "It's all my fault," I said in a tight voice.

Dan took me into his arms. "Don't be ridiculous," he murmured as he held me close. "It's not your fault."

Oh wow, this was so nice. I snuggled into him like a child seeking comfort. But he was wrong. "Yes, it is," I said, my voice muffled in his chest. "If I had found Jen, none of this would have happened."

"You don't know that," Dan protested.

"Oh, please," I said and pulled away slightly. "Like being turned into a vampire is something that happens to just anyone."

"Didn't you say becoming a vampire has to be voluntary, since they have to drink the blood of the person who turns them?"

I stiffened. What was he getting at? "Usually, though it's possible that it could be forced."

"Then . . . maybe it was his choice," Dan suggested.

I expected Fang to respond to that, but he was so tuckered out, he'd gone to sleep.

I pulled away to look Dan in the eye. "What are you saying? That my stepfather *wanted* to become a vampire?" Ridiculous.

"Maybe. Maybe they gave him no other choice."

"You mean die or become one of the undead?"

Dan nodded.

I thought for a moment. "No, I can't believe it. He helped me learn about them, helped me learn how to fight them. He would never *become* one. Who would make that kind of choice?"

"A lot of people have. From what we hear, more each day."

"Not Rick," I said with conviction.

Dan stroked my hair again. "Well, maybe he's not a vampire yet. Maybe he got away."

I'd like to believe that, like to believe it was possible, but I'd stopped believing in Santa Claus, the Easter Bunny, and magic wishes a long time ago. And I could tell Dan didn't believe it, either. He was only trying to calm me. "Nice try, but I doubt it."

"Don't worry, we'll find out, one way or the other."

Yeah, that's what bothered me. I closed my eyes against the pain. How had everything gotten so messed up? Just when things were looking up, when I'd gained a wonderful dog, a partner who stood up for me, and an incredible new family member who liked me for myself, fate had to dump on me and rip away my joy.

Worse, just when I'd finally found someone to care about, the universe had ensured he was the one guy who would never care about me.

*What the heck did I do to deserve this?* Was it payback for thinking I was stronger, faster, better than others? Or for being not quite human?

Dan kissed my forehead and longing surged within me. Not

desire, but a yearning for normality, for a lasting bond with someone, like the one he shared with his sister.

Even if I couldn't have my cake, I was willing to settle for a few crumbs.

I tentatively put my arms around him, accepting the comfort he seemed to be offering. When he returned the favor, I clung to him, soaking in the wonderful feeling. In his arms, I felt safe, cared for . . . almost human.

Lola wasn't interested in these kind of feelings, but I could feel the desire rising within him—undoubtedly a purely physical reaction. "Aren't you afraid?" I asked into his neck.

"Afraid of what?"

"Of Lola. Of what she could do to you."

"No, Micah explained some things. I know that if you wanted to, you could force me to make love to you."

"Actually, I could only force you to feel desire. What you do with that desire is up to you." It was important he understand that I hadn't made him *do* anything.

"Point taken."

"But of course I wouldn't ever force you intentionally," I assured him earnestly.

"I know that now."

He sounded sad and more than a little tired. All of a sudden, I realized how horrible this must be for him. I sighed heavily. "I'm so sorry, Dan."

"For what?"

"For getting you involved in my messy life."

His gave me a little squeeze. "Don't worry about it. I'm not. You need me now."

"Thanks." This was getting way too emotional and I sounded like some wimpy crybaby. I wanted him to feel safe, to not worry that I might be crushing on him or anything.

Reluctantly, I pulled away and injected some mischief into my voice. "Friends are good. But maybe Micah can introduce me to a nice part-demon boy, one who can tolerate Lola. Shade is kind of cute, when he's not all dark and swirly. You think he might be interested?"

I glanced up at Dan who looked a little weirded out by the whole idea.

I laughed. "Never mind." I woke Fang and headed on home to get some sleep before I had to be the big bad vampire slayer again.

In bed, worry settled over me like a blanket. Was Rick really a vampire? Had they turned Jen as well? If not, what did they want with her? Were either of them still even alive? And how the hell was I going to find them?

I knew one thing for sure. I'd rise before the vampires and be there for Jen . . . the way no one ever was there for me.

# CHAPTER SIXTEEN

I woke up in the early afternoon to a knock on the door. It was Dan. He hadn't even taken time to shave, and the dark shadow on his face made him look dangerous and rather sexy.

He thrust a crumpled piece of paper at me. "Someone threw a rock through my window. This was attached to it."

TELL THE SLAYER TO STOP HER INVESTIGATION NOW, OR SHE'LL LOSE MORE FAMILY MEMBERS.

The sender of this note probably intended to cause fear, but all I felt was rage.

Dan's expression turned grim. "You aren't giving up."

I shoved the door closed behind him. "Not a chance."

"Good for you."

"Any idea where it came from?"

He shook his head. "Anyone could have printed it off on a computer."

"Yeah. I—" I broke off as I noticed the hellhound sniffing the note. "What is it, Fang?"

I SMELL HUMAN.

I relayed the info to Dan and asked Fang, "Do you recognize the scent?"

NO.

"Could you follow the scent?"

I AIN'T A HELLHOUND FOR NOTHIN', BABE.

"He can," I told Dan.

Dan frowned. "If the guy who left this used a car, you might not get very far. And it's still daylight, so it must have been left by a human servant, not your sister's actual controller."

All true, but . . . "It's worth a try."

I dressed in record time and we hurried over to Dan's townhouse. I turned to Fang. "Go to it."

The terrier put his nose to the ground beneath the window and sniffed, then sped eagerly across the small lawn to the curb where he stopped and ran in circles for a few moments, whining.

Stopped already?

Dan sighed. "I was afraid of this—"

I'LL GET IT, I'LL GET IT. JUST HOLD ON.

"A hellhound's nose is supposed to be far more sensitive than a normal dog's," I explained. "If the scent isn't too old, maybe he can still follow it."

YEAH, I GOT A LINE ON IT. LET ME TRY.

"Come on, let's use the Valkyrie. It'll be easier."

We had to take Fang's seat off the back to accommodate Dan, but he held onto Fang. They both gave me directions as I slowly followed the scent trail on the motorcycle, ignoring the rude comments of the other motorists who objected to our slow speed.

It didn't take long to figure out where we were going. "Betcha we're going to end up at Alejandro's mansion," Dan yelled above the wind.

Sure enough, we did. When we got there, Fang jumped down and sniffed furiously around the gate. "Did he get out here?" I asked.

YES, BUT HE DIDN'T GO INSIDE THE GATE. THE SCENT STOPS OUTSIDE IT.

I relayed the info to Dan, asking, "What does that mean?"

"Maybe he stopped here and got out, but didn't go in."

"Why?"

Dan shrugged. "Could be he picked up the note here and we followed him to his point of origin."

"Or he got into another car."

"Possible. The problem is, we don't know if we were following his trail back to where he came from, or after he left the note off."

I glanced down at Fang. "Can you tell?"

NOPE. SORRY.

"Should we continue following the scent?" Dan asked. "Either way, we might find him."

"No." I glared at the mansion, which looked innocuous and innocent in the daylight. "Everything always seems to come back to Alejandro. Let's see if we can get some answers."

I punched the code in and the gates opened. Either no one had bothered to change it or Alejandro thought he had nothing to hide.

Two beefy no-neck guards clad all in black met us at the end of the drive, arms crossed and expressions glowering. And if I wasn't mistaken, they were packing quite a bit of firepower under those loose jackets.

"Hi," I said cheerfully, staying on the bike. "Guards are new. Is Alejandro having some problems he hasn't told us about?"

The guard on the right said, "This is private property. You're trespassing."

"How can we be trespassing if we had the code to get in?" I asked, still keeping my tone light.

That seemed to stump him, but guard number two said, "Alejandro didn't say he was expecting visitors today."

"True, we're not expected, but can't old friends drop in and see each other? He said we were always welcome."

"Not during the day," number two said. "No one is welcome until after dark. If you want to see him, come back then."

"But—" I dropped what I was going to say when number one reached inside his jacket.

Dan tightened his grip around my waist. "We'll be back at sunset."

"So long." I played along, waggled my fingers at them and did a one-eighty on the bike to leave the property.

About a half block away, I stopped and looked back. Was Jen inside? Was Rick?

"Don't even think about," Dan warned. "There are probably two more at the back of the house, and there's no way we're getting in through those shuttered windows. Do what he said—come back tonight."

"Okay." The really dangerous time was after the sun went down, but it griped my butt to have to wait. "Why do you think he has so many security guards?"

"Either the attacks at the blood banks have escalated and he fears for his life or he's doing something he shouldn't."

"You think the increased precautions have something to do with Jen and Rick?"

"There's no way of knowing. I'd rather worry about something I *can* control. Maybe we can follow the rest of that scent?"

Fang tried, but lost the trail when it crossed Loop 410. There was just too much traffic on the highway and too many exhaust fumes to follow one individual scent.

Just in case I'd ticked off the person who sent that threatening note, I called Mom. I warned her not to leave the house and to not, under any circumstances, invite anyone in.

When I was certain Mom understood how important this was, Dan and I got the latest skinny from Ramirez and Micah, then stocked up on weapons. I wasn't really planning on fighting my way into the mansion, but I wanted to be ready if I had to.

When the sun set behind the horizon, Dan, Fang and I were already waiting at Alejandro's. Once the shutters on the windows opened, we figured it was safe to make our move.

The two guards glared at us but didn't stop us from ringing the doorbell.

After a few minutes, Alejandro's lieutenant, Austin, answered and tipped his cowboy hat. "Howdy, ma'am . . . sir. Nice to see you again."

He was so pleasant, I suddenly wondered if I'd overreacted. "Can we see Alejandro?"

"Yes, ma'am." He opened the door wide and let us in.

I couldn't resist shooting a triumphant glance at the no-necks guarding the door outside. But the glance was wasted—their attention was turned outside, to the grounds.

Austin led us to the very masculine study where we had been before. When Alejandro spotted us, he broke off his conversation with two underlings and waved them away. Smiling, he gestured us to chairs. "To what do I owe this honor?" he asked, charming as always.

Dan deferred to me with a glance.

"My sister is still missing," I said without preamble. Alejandro's smile faded a little as he shook his head sadly. "I'm afraid you were right about her being controlled."

Dan sat forward like a dog on point. "How do you know?"

"A human can only be controlled by one vampire at a time. So, to test her, I had one of my lieutenants try to control her."

"Which one?" I demanded.

"That would be me, ma'am," Austin said.

"And?" I asked.

"I couldn't get her to do a darned thing."

"Confirming that she's being controlled by someone else?"

Alejandro and Austin both nodded.

"Then who?"

Alejandro spread his hands. "I'm sorry, we have no way of knowing that, but I'm doing everything I can to find out."

Dan scowled. "How about her father? Are you aware he came to one of your blood banks and was thrown out?"

Alejandro nodded gravely. "Yes. What would you have us do? He was causing a scene."

"Were you also aware that some vampires grabbed him and said they were going to force him to join your little undead club?"

The vamp leader seemed truly surprised. "You do not think my people did it, do you?"

In answer, I handed him the note.

Dan added, "That was thrown through my window this afternoon. We followed the scent of your delivery boy back to here."

Alejandro stared at us incredulously. "Surely you do not think I left such a note?"

Maybe. On one hand, he had readily agreed to see us, which argued that he was innocent of any wrongdoing—in this, anyway. On the other hand, all clues seemed to lead here.

Fruitlessly, I wished I had thought far enough ahead to have something of Rick's for Fang to sniff. If I had, we might be able to tell if Rick was here or not. Jen wasn't. Fang had pretty thoroughly used his nose all the way in. If he'd smelled my sister, he would have let me know.

"I don't know what to think," I said honestly as I rose in preparation to leave. "But I can tell you this. If any of my family is harmed in any way, I will personally hunt down the monsters responsible and feed them to the sun. Is that clear?"

"Just let us know if you need any help," Austin offered.

I took a step back in surprise. That wasn't the response I'd expected at all.

Fang looked up at me. YEAH, AND I DON'T TRUST IT.

Alejandro rose and took my hand in both of his. Strange how they had no warmth in them. "Austin is quite right. We are fighting for an accommodation with humans, fighting to assure our place—peacefully—alongside you. The beasts who have done these heinous acts are not welcome within our organization, nor this city. We will root them out and destroy them."

"O-okay," I said. That was exactly what I wanted, but again, they had managed to surprise me with the unexpected.

Alejandro's hand tightened on mine. "If we hear any word, get any lead, we will let you know."

"Good, good," was all I could say. I pulled my hand away and followed Austin out the door.

As all three of us got on the motorcycle, Dan asked, "Do you believe him?"

I sighed. "Yeah, I think I do."

"I think we're making a big mistake."

"Maybe. But what can we do? Everything we've learned points to Jen and Rick not being there."

"We can do some more good old-fashioned detective work."

"Okay." None of our other leads were panning out, so it was our only choice. But I had a feeling I'd better find them soon . . . or it would be too late.

We decided to head back to the blood bank. It was a long shot, but maybe Lorenzo could give us more information about the vampires who took Rick.

About three-quarters of the way there, Dan tapped on my shoulder and signaled for me to pull over. I swerved over to the side of the road and gave him a questioning look.

"Phone," he said briefly. He answered it and listened for a moment, then handed it to me. "Micah gave Shade my number. He wants to talk to you."

I had been kidding about Shade being a potential boyfriend, but surprisingly, the disapproving glint in Dan's eyes indicated he thought I was serious. Interesting.

Amused, I answered the phone.

"About ten minutes after you left, four people arrived at the mansion—two men and two women. One was your sister."

My heartbeat quickened as my amusement vanished. Finally—a lead. "Are you sure?" And why hadn't we seen Shade?

"Yes—she matches the picture Micah gave me."

"Did you recognize any of the others?" Maybe Rick was with them.

"No, they were all in a car, and she's the only one I got a good look at."

"Did they say anything?" Like how long they were going to be there?

"The only thing I heard didn't make sense." Shade sounded uncertain. "I just caught a snatch of it as they went through the gates."

"What did you hear?"

"Something about performing a . . . blessing at midnight?"

*Oh, crap.* "What did they say?" I demanded. "Did they say who was going to be blessed?"

"No, just something about having delayed it long enough."

Delayed whose? Jen's? Rick's? Fear pounded in my chest, making my voice more abrupt than I intended. "Is that all?"

"I'm sorry," Shade said. "That's all I heard."

It wasn't his fault he didn't know more "Thank you," I said fervently. "If you hear or see anything more, will you call us?"

"Of course."

I hung up and handed the phone back to Dan, turning sideways on the motorcycle to fill him in on what Shade had told me. The more I thought about it, the more angry I became. "Damn it, he played us."

"Alejandro?"

"Yeah. He acted so damned innocent, when all along he must have know what was going on."

Dan's lips tightened, probably restraining himself from saying, "I told you so." Instead, he said, "We don't know for sure that he's involved in this blessing thing . . . and it might not be your sister they're talking about."

I glared at him. "Would you chance it with your family?"

"No—"

"Well, one thing's for sure—she's there. At least I can remove her from danger."

"If her controller will let you," Dan said.

Okay, point taken. "I don't care. I'll make her come with me whether she wants to or not."

I turned back around, but Dan stilled my hand on the throttle. "It's too dangerous."

"I don't care. My sister—"

"It's too dangerous for *her* if we go in, weapons blazing. Especially with only two of us against a houseful of vamps. Backup will increase our chances of getting her out unharmed."

I twisted around to look at him again. "And where are we going to get that?"

"Ramirez."

I thought for a moment, then nodded. "Okay, let's call him."

"This is probably best done in person—it's a hell of a big favor to ask."

"It will take too long—"

"You heard Shade—nothing's going to happen until midnight. We have hours yet."

He was right again, though the energy sizzling through my blood didn't like the delay. "Let's do it fast, then."

I gunned the motor on the Valkyrie and zoomed off toward the West Substation. Fang elected to wait outside as Dan and I went inside. Ramirez was in, though he had someone in his office.

I blurted out, "We need to talk to you. It's urgent."

Ramirez glanced back and forth between us, then dismissed the guy he'd been talking to. "What's up?"

"We need a raid on Alejandro's mansion," I said urgently.

"Why?"

"He's got my sister in there."

Ramirez looked sympathetic, but said, "I can't perform a raid just because her big sister doesn't like who she hangs out with."

"But she's being controlled by a vampire," I protested. "They're going to hurt her." This wasn't some frivolous request—Ramirez knew that.

"Do you have proof of that?"

"No, but—"

Dan cut in. "Alejandro admitted that she's under control."

"By him?"

"No, but—"

"That's not proof," Ramirez said apologetically.

"There's something going down tonight," Dan said. "They may be planning to turn Jennifer into a vampire."

Oh, Lord, it sounded even more real, even more plausible when he said it aloud. "We have to save her," I insisted. "She has no free will. She can't choose this for herself."

Ramirez leaned forward, looking intent. "Do you have proof of this?"

Annoyed by his stupid refrain, I snapped, "One of Micah's people saw her go in to the house, heard them say a blessing had been delayed too long." Quickly, I explained what Lorenzo had told us about the term blessing and what I feared.

Ramirez looked disappointed. "That's it? That's all you have?"

"I know it doesn't sound like much—" Dan began.

"Wait," the lieutenant said. "Let me get this straight. Up until now, you've found nothing to indicate that Alejandro or his movement has done anything wrong, correct?"

I scowled. "Yes, but—"

Ramirez cut me off with a sharp gesture. "You said this Lorenzo didn't recognize the vampires who took your stepfather, that he thought of them as unaffiliated, which means they probably don't belong to the Movement." Overriding my protest, he continued, "And your sister has been working for them for at least a month, unharmed. Do you think your concern might arise from the fact that you're scared for your sister, that you have no other leads, that you want this to be true so badly that you've convinced yourself it is, despite the evidence to the contrary?"

I stared at him for a moment, surprised steam wasn't coming out of my ears. Forcing myself to sound calm and reasonable, I said, "Look, I know it sounds flimsy, but if you give us the people, we'll get the proof."

"Sorry, I can't do it. I can't commit city resources on a tenuous possibility. And without some kind of evidence to back up your claim, I won't be able to get a warrant and I can't justify invading a private citizen's residence without it."

I couldn't believe I was hearing this. "Private citizen? He's a *vampire*. Can the undead own property? Do they have the same rights as the living?"

"The law doesn't recognize the existence of vampires, so as far as it is concerned, if he's walking and talking, he's alive. *And* entitled to the same protection as everyone else."

I appealed mutely to Dan.

He gave me an apologetic look. "He's right. His hands are tied."

"Well, ours aren't," I declared.

Ramirez rose from his desk and jabbed his finger at me. "You two are *not* going in there alone, do you hear me? It's suicide if you do."

And homicide if we didn't. "So you admit it's dangerous?"

"Going into a vampire's den, uninvited, with intent to kidnap or do bodily harm? It's dangerous—and it has nothing to do with whether they're guilty or innocent."

"But—"

"Enough. Promise me that the two of you won't do anything so stupid or I'll toss your butts in jail right now."

"Can he do that?" I asked Dan incredulously.

Dan shrugged. "Probably."

I glared at him. "If we promise, what the hell do you expect us to do?"

"I *expect* you to do your job. Get out there and get me proof. With that, I can help you."

"All right," Dan said. "We'll do that."

Ramirez speared me with a glance, silently demanding my agreement as well.

It went against everything I knew was right, but I had too much respect for the lieutenant to lie to him. Then again, I couldn't do anything to help Jen and Rick if I was in jail. "Okay, okay. But when we get proof, you'd better not slow-roll me."

"I won't," Ramirez confirmed.

I stomped out of the police station, Dan right behind me. As I swung my leg over my motorcycle, I asked, "How can we get proof?"

"Let me think a minute."

Well, I knew what my first thought was—go in anyway and damn the consequences. Those were my second and third thoughts, too. I didn't want to break my promise, but Jen and Rick's lives were in danger. I had to see if Jen was all right, had to find Rick, had to see his fangs for myself.

Mom certainly wouldn't be satisfied with anything less. If I didn't have first-hand knowledge of exactly what had happened to Rick, Mom might do something stupid . . . like go after him herself.

No, that couldn't happen. I couldn't lose another family member to the vampires—even a mother who didn't want me. They might not consider me a part of the family any more, but damn it, they were part of mine.

I had to find out the truth for myself, no matter what the lieutenant said. If only I could rescue them without breaking my promise. I went back over the conversation, looking for a loophole . . . and found it. We'd promised that the two of us wouldn't go in after Jen. Fine—I'd make it just one of us. This was too dangerous for pure humans anyway—Dan's injuries during our previous encounters proved it. Better to let demons battle monsters.

Fang shoved my hand. THAT'S THE TICKET.

But I'd better not share my thoughts with Dan. He'd just try to talk me out of it, or insist on going along. I didn't want to have to worry about him as well.

Dan sat behind me on the bike and got Fang settled. "Let's find out more about the blessing ceremony. If we can prove it's being done, show that the humans who go in to Alejandro's come out as vampires, maybe that'll be enough proof."

"Do you really think that's enough?" I asked.

"Do you have a better idea?"

"No." Besides, I wanted him safely out of the way and this looked like the best way of doing it.

"Okay, then let's check out Micah's database, see what we can find."

Since it was Sunday and the club was closed, Dan called first and Micah agreed to meet us there.

As we drove to Purgatory, I rethought my strategy. When we arrived and parked in the rear, I said, "I've been thinking. You don't need me here, so I'll do some investigation on my own."

"Like what?"

"I'll check out my *Encyclopedia Magicka*, see if there's any mention of the ceremony." Though I knew there was nothing—I would have remembered. "Then I'll visit a psychic friend of mine."

Dan raised an eyebrow. "How will that help?"

"She might be able to tell me what to do, what path to take."

He narrowed his eyes at her, looking suspicious. "You've never mentioned her before."

Because she didn't exist. "Yeah, well, you haven't exactly been open to talk about magic users, have you?"

He shrugged, conceding the point.

"Okay, I'll call you and check in whether I learn anything or not. Then I'll be back to pick you up." If I survive.

"Okay."

Dan went inside the club and I sat for a moment, contemplating Fang. What should I do about him?

WHAT'S TO WONDER? YOU TAKE ME WITH YOU.

I glanced around and saw a reserved parking spot marked "Blackburn." The fancy car in it must be Micah's . . . and it was unlocked. Perfect. Without letting my true intentions show in my conscious mind, I said, "Let's take Micah's car."

But when Fang jumped inside, I shut the door.

Fang stared at me with a mixture of disbelief and fury on his furry face. YOU DID NOT JUST DO THAT.

"I'm afraid I did." He was a very small dog, and no matter how much hellhound he had in him, he was no match for an entire vein of vampires, though he had heart enough to try. I couldn't bear to lose him, either.

LOSE ME? WHO SAYS YOU'LL LOSE ME? He pawed at the window. LET ME OUT.

"I'm sorry, Fang. I have to go to the mansion, and you'll be safer this way." And if I didn't make it back, Micah would take care of him.

NO. NO WAY ARE YOU LEAVING ME HERE. LET ME OUTTA HERE! Fang went nuts, leaping around the car and barking furiously. Ignoring his temper tantrum, I headed home to stock up on weapons. I needed to be ready for anything and everything . . . including the possibility that I might fail, that I might die.

I squared my shoulders. Well if I did, I'd make sure I took the whole freakin' vein of vampires with me.

# CHAPTER SEVENTEEN

I paused at the edge of Alejandro's property, considering my options. This time, I didn't want to announce my presence. Unfortunately, there was a clear line of sight from the front door to the gates. The guards would see me if I used the code to get in.

I scouted the fence. Good—there were some trees alongside. Lousy security, but if you were already dead in a city of mostly humans I guess you didn't worry too much about security.

I hooked a crossbow on my back belt loop and settled a scabbard across my back so I could easily reach the sword's hilt behind my head. Once I was sure they were secure, I shimmied up the trunk then swung up onto a limb. One of the branches conveniently crossed over the dangerous *fleurs de lis* on the top of the wrought iron fence, and I crawled out until I was over the estate grounds.

I paused, assessing the threat. The guards didn't have the advantage of the excellent senses the vamps had, and I hadn't seen any sign of electronic security or dogs—animals wouldn't work for vamps. I was probably safe. I dropped to the ground, relieved when no alarms went off.

The guards remained at the entrance and exit, not patrolling the grounds, so it was easy to make my way silently to the window where I'd seen Alejandro twice before. It seemed to be the happening place.

Sure enough, when I peered in the window, I spotted Jen inside, with Alejandro and three of his lieutenants. Four vamps.

No, make that six. Two more vamps suddenly came into view, dragging Rick between them.

Finally, a break—Jen and Rick were together. Now, if only luck stayed with me and helped me take on six vamps at once. I wasn't sure there was a hope in hell of doing that with everyone coming out alive, but I had to try.

I stared intently at Rick for any signs that he'd been turned, but his mouth was duct-taped and his arms were held securely by the two unknown vamps. He looked pale, but that could be fear, the situation, a lot of things. I still didn't know if he'd been made into a vampire or not, but either way, he needed rescuing.

Unfortunately, I couldn't hear anything they were saying. And if I tried to climb in the closed window, I'd lose the element of surprise. I worked my way around the side of the house until I found a window into an empty room. It opened silently, and I climbed in, then made my way through the dark room.

Cautiously, I peered out into the hallway. No one there. I slipped into the hall, keeping the weapons ready, yet hidden behind my back. Without visible weaponry, I might be able to bluff my way past if I came upon anyone. Luckily, I didn't, and I made it without incident to the room where Jen and Rick were being held.

The doors were too thick for me to hear anything being said inside the room. Shoot—I had to get inside. I unsheathed the sword, got a good grip on it, and took a deep breath. Lola, sensing upcoming action, fizzed to life in my blood. I let her come more fully than I ever had before. In this, we were united with one purpose. As ready as I'd ever be, I burst in through the door, yelling, "Nobody move!"

They all froze for an instant and I took advantage of it to close the door and move aside so my back was against a wall and I was facing all of them.

Alejandro and his three lieutenants were grouped together on the opposite side of the room, with him seated and the three of them behind him. Rick and his captors were to my left, on the other side of the door, and Jen was in the center. Everyone was within range of my sword.

Taking advantage of their initial surprise, I said, "Jen, come here."

Unfortunately, she ignored me, still controlled.

My words seemed to break the spell for the others and they all relaxed a little, probably because I was alone.

"Are you mad?" Luis asked, going all aristocratic and snooty. "What is the meaning of this?"

"Ask Alejandro," I snapped.

Alejandro sighed. "I know this looks bad, but your stepfather is being held because he has become a menace."

"He threw holy water on two of my men," Lily said indignantly.

I suppressed a smile. Go, Rick! "And Jen?" I asked Alejandro.

"I asked your sister to come in so we could discover who is controlling her."

"Have you?"

"Not yet."

I nodded. Just as I'd thought. "Then I'll just have to start killing vampires one by one until she's released."

Alejandro looked hurt. "I thought we had an agreement. Do you not trust me?"

"No." Not where my family was concerned. I aimed the sword at Alejandro to make sure he got the point.

"Don't you dare hurt Alejandro," Jen said.

"So he's your controller," I mused aloud, hoping for confirmation.

Luis just snorted derisively.

"Well, now," Austin drawled. "That would be convenient, wouldn't it? But she's bluffing. Or rather, her controller is, through her."

Lily nodded. "It can't be Alejandro. He's the one trying to change things. He's forbidden this."

I wavered, wondering who it could be. They made sense, but someone had to be lying. The controller could be one of the head honchos—Alejandro, Luis, Austin, or Lily—or even Rosa, who was missing. Then again, I couldn't dismiss the underlings as possibilities either.

But I had to choose one, so I chose Luis. I'd never liked his smarmy attitude anyway. "You first," I said, aiming the point of the sword at him.

I'd hoped for a reaction, but not the one I got.

Jen pulled a pistol from her waistband and pointed it at me with both hands. "I can't let you kill anyone," she said in a steely tone so unlike my sister.

"What idiot gave my sister a gun?"

No one confessed and Jen's gun never wavered.

I had to remember that Jen wasn't in control of her actions, someone else was. "What are you going to do? Shoot me, your own sister?" I hoped there was some small spark of Jen hiding inside, one that would be appalled and be able to break free.

But it didn't work. Jen pointed the gun at her father. "No, I'll shoot him. Or myself." Grinning something more like a grimace, the expression clearly forced onto her face by someone else, she held the gun to her head. "Nobody move or the little girl gets it."

The effect of the controller's words in Jen's mouth was chilling. There was no doubt in anyone's mind now that Jennifer was controlled, obviously by someone in this room. That let Rosa out as a suspect.

"Coward," I accused the controller through Jen. "Reveal yourself and stop hiding behind a young girl."

Jen continued to smirk. "No, I think it's more fun this way." She pulled the hammer back on the pistol, still holding it to her temple.

"You don't want to do that," I said quickly. "If you kill Jen, I'll make sure you and everyone else in this room dies a horrible death."

Jen laughed. "Not before one of us gets you first."

"Us?"

"Oops. Didn't I mention I have allies in the room?"

The vamps all froze, their gazes darting around the small space as if wondering who was on which side. Now no one was certain of anyone else. Well, at least I wasn't the only one in the dark.

Unfortunately, they all did the darting gaze thing. The controller was too clever to let himself be caught that way.

But since he hadn't killed Jen yet, he must have a reason. "What do you want?" And who was I talking to? This was incredibly strange, speaking to Jen as if she were a monster, not knowing who I was really dealing with.

Jen's eyes narrowed as she channeled her master's emotions. "You. I want you to suffer, Slayer. You've caused me nothing but trouble, you and your sister. Made me tip my hand too soon."

I flicked my gaze back and forth among all the vamps. Which one was it? It could be any of them, but I'd bet on Alejandro or one of his lieutenants. But if I chose wrong, killed the wrong vamp, the real evil in the room would pull the trigger and Jen would be dead. *Unacceptable.*

I stalled for more time. "If you didn't want me to come after you, you shouldn't have taken my family."

Rage erupted on Jen's face and she shoved the gun harder against her own head. "Jennifer learned too much too soon. Then you and that sorry excuse for a man came sniffing around and made it even worse."

At first, I thought she meant Dan, until I saw Jen remove the pistol from her forehead and level it at Rick. Rick, whose eyes pleaded with me to save his daughter.

*I'm trying, aren't I?*

Unfortunately, his and Jen's faces were the only ones in the room that showed any expression. How could I figure out which vamp was the controller?

"Maybe I should just kill you," Jen muttered, and the gun swung toward me.

But before I could do anything, Jen swerved to look at the door. Two other vamps came in, dragging two more prisoners— Dan and Fang. Both were completely subdued by their captors, Fang in a cage, and Dan in a headlock with his mouth shut by duct tape. But they hadn't been captured quietly. The vamps looked a bit worse for wear.

You shouldn't have left me, Fang whined, pacing the limits of his tiny cage.

*Sorry, I didn't want you in danger.* Didn't want *this.* My heart sank. I'd hoped someone I cared about would survive tonight, but it was looking less and less likely all the time.

The two newly arrived vamps looked around the room curiously, but settled on Alejandro. "We caught them trying to sneak in."

Jen grinned, her pistol wavering back and forth between Rick and her two new targets. "Excellent. So who's gonna buy it, Slayer? Your partner, your stepfather, your sister, or your little doggie?"

Alejandro shouted, "Shield them."

All of the vamps moved, but halted when Jen yelled, "Stop—

or one of my people will stake you."

Once again, they didn't know who was on which side, and obviously no one wanted to take the chance of getting staked to save a mere human.

"Choose one," Jen barked at me.

"No." *Impossible.*

"Then I will." Using the pistol to point first to herself then the other captives in turn, she said, "Eenie meenie, minie, moe . . . "

No, this couldn't be happening.

Alejandro made an abortive movement, but Austin restrained him, saying, "I won't let you put yourself in danger."

I didn't know where this nursery rhyme would end up, but none of the choices was even thinkable. I had to take action, had to kill the controller. They all appeared to be on the right side, but one was lying. Who was it?

Even if I chose correctly and killed the controller, his minions would probably tear the humans limb from limb.

" . . . if he hollers, let him go . . . "

The demon inside me urged me to do something, *anything*. I couldn't contain this frustration, this lust for revenge much longer.

So . . . why contain it at all? If I enthralled the controller like he was enthralling Jen, *I'd* have all the control.

But if I used my power with so little chance of directing it at only certain men, Dan would be caught by Lola just as surely as the rest.

I had no other choice—Jen was nearing the end of the rhyme and it looked like he would be the first one killed. Better alive and pissed than dead.

For the first time in my life, I *used* my power. Not only did I loose all restraints on Lola, but I put force behind it and *pushed*, willing the men to feel desire and find me irresistible.

Powerful, feeling totally in charge, I commanded, "Freeze."

It succeeded beyond my wildest dreams as every man, totally enthralled, did exactly as I ordered. I could feel the power within me reach out to all of them, compelling their obedience, enjoying their worship of Val Shapiro.

It was as if I had live wires of energy connecting me to each man in the room, whether dead or undead. Where each "wire" entered their bodies, it fanned out in strings of power to touch and penetrate each of the seven chakras, the sacred energy centers of their bodies. Through these invisible lines of power, I felt as though I could pluck a string and feel it vibrate throughout their entire being.

But it was strongest in the second chakra, the one related to sexuality. Experimentally, I strummed the strand that led to that energy center, but I didn't have enough fine control to choose just one. Instead, the power thrummed through every man in the room, freeing their desire, sending their dark, powerful need roiling toward me like an out-of-control tidal wave of lust.

I braced myself for the onslaught, but Lola knew just what to do with it, channeling the powerful slap of desire into the starved power centers of my own body, soaking it up like a sponge.

Somewhere deep inside, I felt sickened by the fact that I could control them like mindless puppets, but I couldn't help but exult in the raw power and energy flowing from them to me, feeding my starved senses.

HOLY CRAP, Fang said in awe. DO YOU KNOW WHAT YOU'RE DOING?

Forcibly, I brought myself back to the here and now. Though it had felt like hours, it couldn't have been more than a few seconds.

Jen turned toward me, eyes narrowed, and pointed the gun at me. "What's going on? What did you do?"

Only a woman controller would ask that question, be *able* to ask that question right now. Without hesitation, I swung my arm back and lopped Lily's head off.

Dan's ex-fiancée's body crumpled to the ground, her head dropping next to it as she bled on Alejandro's pretty rug. Strange, there wasn't as much blood as I expected. But it was one of the grosser things I've ever had to do to get my sister out of a scrape.

Fang sniffed her. THAT'S ONE WAY TO END AN ARGUMENT.

Jen staggered, looking dazed, then stared at the pistol in her hand. She dropped it as if it were a poisonous snake. When it hit the carpet, it went off, hitting one of Dan's captors in the knee. But the vamp was so intent on me, he didn't even notice.

I hoped he wasn't one of the good guys. Either way, he'd heal fast.

"Jen?" I said again, letting the sword point fall.

My sister rushed toward me and threw her arms around me, sobbing and clinging. "Thank you. Oh, thank you for saving me."

Okay, that was the real Jen. Incredibly relieved, I hugged her back, finding it a little easier to control my puppets now.

Lieutenant Ramirez burst into the room, followed by about two dozen men. But they weren't cops. Startled, I recognized some of the bartenders from the club. These were all Micah's friends—part demons. Lola reached out greedily to gather them to her as well, but I stopped her. I could barely handle the ones I already had in thrall.

"What's going on?" Ramirez demanded, looking surprised when no one moved. They all remained intent on me, waiting for my next command.

"Uh, they're under my control," I said sheepishly as I released Jen. "All but Lily who's dead now." I wouldn't apologize for that—Lily deserved what she got.

"So I see," Ramirez said dryly and signaled to his men to stand down.

They milled around, staring curiously at the enthralled men and giving Lily's headless body a wide berth. Surprisingly, I was able to maintain my hold without effort, though it felt odd to be so hyper aware of so many men at once.

"What are you doing here?" I asked Ramirez. "Aren't you the one who said you couldn't help me?"

"I couldn't commit city resources to help you," he corrected me. "But when my wife got a call from Micah, she badgered me to lead the rescue party in an unofficial capacity."

I grinned. "I'd like to meet your wife some day."

Ramirez smiled back. "The feeling is mutual. Besides, we did get proof of a sort. Dan and Micah figured out that Lily was behind all of this. His records kept mentioning a 'Strong Arm' doing the blessings. Or rather Armstrong—Lily Armstrong. Micah contacted me as Dan and Fang headed here."

Oh, no—Dan was still spellbound with the rest of them. I glanced around. "Some of them are Lily's allies, but I don't know which." And I didn't know how to turn this power off selectively any more than I had known how to turn it on selectively—it was all or none.

The lieutenant shrugged. "So ask."

Duh. Of course. "Those of you who were working for Lily, raise your hands."

The two vamps who had held Rick raised their hands, still looking besotted with me.

"Restrain them," Ramirez ordered.

His band of demons jumped to obey, apparently happy to find an outlet for their frustrated adrenaline.

"Hold them tight," I cautioned them, "because I'm going to release them."

And it was easy enough to do, with the demon inside me completely sated for the first time in my life. With only a little regret, I let them all go and drew the succubus's energy back into myself. Now that I was no longer so intimately connected to all of them, I felt relief and a determination to talk to Micah. He was right—I couldn't live my life trying to suppress my demon all the time. I had to learn to live with her.

The first to snap out of the spell were Austin and Alejandro.

Austin rubbed his chin, looking thoughtful. "Interesting power you have there, little lady."

Alejandro stared down at Lily, regret and confusion in his eyes.

I sighed. "Uh, sorry about the rug."

He shrugged. "It is nothing. And I had no idea . . . Why would she do this? She had such potential."

Jen, who had finally released her stranglehold on me, answered. "When I was working at the blood bank, I overheard her talking to someone—that's why she enthralled me. She said she needed you to build the organization with your charisma, but once you had the power base established, she'd take it over and run it her way." Jen shivered. "I don't think you'd like her way."

That was an understatement. But before I could respond, I was suddenly enveloped in a man's arms. Rick, freed of all restraints, had gathered Jen and me into a group hug. "Thank God, both my girls are safe."

Oh, wow. Was I still his girl? Emotion ambushed me, made me want to cling to him like a child. But I'd been hurt so much. Could I trust this?

I stiffened and tried to pull away, but Rick wasn't having it. He squashed us to him and held onto both of us like he'd been terrified he might lose us forever. Not just Jen—me, too.

I gave in. With Lola blissfully satisfied, I realized that for the first time in my life, I could hug him without consequences. As I clutched him and soaked in the wonderful feeling, I also realized that a normal life had been within my grasp all along. Starving Lola didn't work. It made things worse. Made her constantly prowl like a cat in zoo cage. But now, in this moment, I could just be Rick's daughter.

Thank God he was safe, too—he wasn't a vampire. But I couldn't help but say, "I told you not to go after her."

He pulled back to look at me. "I know, I know. And you saved me just in the nick of time, too. They were going to force me to become one of them tonight."

So that's who the "blessing" was for. "I'm just glad I *was* in time."

"Me, too," Rick said fervently. "You were right. You've been right all along, and we've been very wrong." He stroked my face. "I'm so sorry, little one. I'll make it up to you."

Tears stinging in my eyes, I said, "If Mom will let you."

"Don't worry—I'll handle your mother. And if she doesn't like it, she'll answer to me."

"Thanks," I whispered in his ear. I appreciated the sentiment, but knew it wouldn't be as easy as all that. And it would never be like it used to be. "Why don't you take Jen home? She's been through quite an ordeal." And so had he, though he wouldn't appreciate me mentioning it. "One of Ramirez's people will probably take you."

"Good idea. I'll do that."

As he led Jen off to find a ride, a released Fang jumped all over me, incoherent in his joy at seeing me safe.

*Hey, you really love me.*

YES. I MEAN NO—I AM SO TICKED AT YOU.

Dan was right behind Fang, and I wasn't sure I wanted to see his expression, so I bent down to pet Fang.

HOW DARE YOU LEAVE ME BEHIND? He licked my face thoroughly. DON'T YOU EVER DO IT AGAIN.

"Okay, okay. I'm sorry for locking you in the car. But I was afraid you'd get hurt."

"Have you finished talking to everyone else?" Dan asked calmly.

Uh-oh, here it came. The inevitable tongue-lashing. I didn't answer, just straightened to meet his gaze.

His own face was tight and his eyes flashed with anger. "What the hell do you mean by going off without me? You could have been killed!"

I'd expected the anger, but not those words. Funny—he sounded just like Fang. "But I wasn't killed. Instead, I killed Lily. I'm so sorry, Dan." Even if he and his ex had broken up, there still had to be some feeling there.

"Don't apologize for that," Dan said sharply. "She wasn't human anymore. She was a monster."

So what must he think of *me*, who had enthralled everyone indiscriminately?

"Don't look at me like that," Dan said softly. "God, *you're* no monster."

So he was reading my mind now, huh? "Maybe, but I'm not human, either."

"What does that mean? If being human means acting with honor, integrity, and care for others, you're the most human person I know."

Could he mean that? "But . . . I was wrong about my power. I *can* force people—men—to do things."

Shockingly, Dan laughed. "Yeah. When you let loose, you really let loose."

I didn't understand his attitude. "But . . . it's not normal." Not human.

"No, but I doubt it will ever happen again. I know you had no choice, and I could tell you didn't have any idea of your full power before. As Micah said, it's because you've kept it pent up inside all these years. When you let loose, it was bound to be a hell of a ride."

He smiled at me. "And it gave me a whole new perspective on my earlier encounter with Lola. Will you forgive me?"

Stunned, I said, "Of course. So, you're okay with me and Lola now?"

"She's a part of you, one we'll have to learn to deal with together." He grinned. "Besides, every man should have a little Lola in his life. Partners?"

I grinned, allowing a little bit of happiness to sink in. Finally, someone who accepted me as I was—demon and all. This must be what Tessa meant about doing what I hated most to get what I wanted most.

"I'd love that."

Fang nosed me. HEY, WHAT ABOUT ME?

As if he'd heard the hellhound, Dan added, "And Fang, too."

DAMN STRAIGHT. WE ARE SOOOO BAD. MONSTERS OF THE WORLD, WATCH OUT!

Dan put an arm around me. "Between the three of us—well, the four of us, including Lola—we make one hell of a team."

I beamed at him. Yeah—heaven help anyone who stood in our way.

## A Note From Parker Blue

Dear Reader,

When Val Shapiro first popped into my head, I was utterly fascinated by her. Her part-demon nature, her smart mouth, her kickass attitude, and her surprising vulnerability all added up to a character who was a joy to write. Dan Sullivan, with his familial pride and bemused acceptance of Val, was no less so. And Fang . . . let's just say I have the prototype living in my house.

I had so much fun writing the book that when a charity asked for donations from writers to auction on eBay, I offered up the chance to have someone killed in print by a vampire. Lorena Kott won the auction and chose to see herself killed rather than subject anyone else to the ordeal. In appreciation, I gave her a relatively easy death-by-vampire in chapter twelve.

I hope to revisit this world in my next book, for more adventures with Val, Dan, Fang, and the members of the Demon Underground.

To find out more about me, please visit my website at www.parkerblue.net.

> Parker Blue
> Colorado Springs, CO

Lightning Source UK Ltd.
Milton Keynes UK
25 August 2009

143054UK00001B/198/P